Nye Bill

Forty Liars and Other Lies

Nye Bill

Forty Liars and Other Lies

ISBN/EAN: 9783337201654

Printed in Europe, USA, Canada, Australia, Japan

Cover: Foto ©Andreas Hilbeck / pixelio.de

More available books at **www.hansebooks.com**

ORTY LIARS

AND

OTHER LIES.

BY BILL NYE,

AUTHOR OF "BILL NYE AND BOOMERANG," ETC.

ILLUSTRATED BY HOPKINS:

" Praised be all liars and all lies!"—BYRON.

CHICAGO

W. B. CONKEY COMPANY

CONTENTS.

4 *Contents.*

Contents. 5

4

OVERTURE.

This volume, the second of a household series, by the same author, comes in response to a clamoring appeal on the part of the American people. The former work, though hastily prepared and hurled into space without warning, was far more successful and contagious than I had dared to hope.

In adopting the title affixed to this book, I have given the impression that many of the abstruse statements contained herein are not true. I hope that this will not injure the sale of the work or mitigate its horrors.

I desire, in this connection, to thank those who purchased the former library of song concocted my me, thus enabling the publishers and myself to live in our present style of oriental pomp and princely magnificence. From the royalty received on the first volume of the series, I have gathered a rich harvest. I have moved into a larger residence, where I pay the rent, instead of changing my location each month as formerly. As another evidence of my emancipation from abject poverty, I will state that I have reduced my collection of dogs to one cream-colored pet, in whose veins flows the blood of every known variety of dog of which history informs us.

This book marks an era in the history of classical literature. The spelling may be eccentric in places; and the etymology, syntax and prosody may be erroneous and abnormally picturesque, but the emaciated statements contained in its pages will shine on through the coming years, long after the statistics compiled with so much care by my comrade in the great field of literature, the United States Entomologist, shall have disappeared in a shoreless sea of oblivion.

It is also the initial step in the world's great march toward universal frankness. Instead of waiting for the beautiful and accomplished reader to search out and nail the prevarications with documentary evidence, there is a tacit admission on the start by the author that some little trifling falsehoods may have crept into the work, owing to the hurry and rush of preparation, and the unavoidably superficial criticism prior to its publication.

I will state in closing, that I hope there will be no ill-feeling on the part of those who are mentioned personally in the following pages, and who are still alive, and comparatively vigorous. Several of these articles which have appeared in newspaper form, have been settled for by the persons referred to, and thus a disagreeable delay incurred in issuing this volume. It is to be hoped that no further retribution will be meted out, or if the vengeance of disaffected parties be not sufficiently and fully glutted, they are requested to call at the publishing house in Chicago and glut their demoniac vengeance on the artist who illustrated the former book.

BILL NYE.

Laramie City, Wyo.,
February 15, 1882.

FORTY LIARS, AND OTHER LIES.

THE FORTY LIARS.

AT a regular round-up of the Rocky Mountain division of the Independent Order of Forty Liars, on Saturday evening, the most noble prevaricator having directed the breath tester to examine all present to see that they were in possession of the annual password, explanations and signals, and to report to the most noble promoter of twenty-seven karat falsehoods whether all were so qualified to re- main, and the report having been satisfactory, the most noble prevaricator announced that after the report of the custodian of campaign lies for the past year and the annual statements of the division bar- tender and most noble beer yanker had been handed in and passed upon, the next business to come be- fore the division would be the nominations and the election of most noble prevaricator to serve during the year 1881.

"Under the rules of our order," said the M. N. P., "ten minutes will be given each aspirant for the of- fice named in which to address the meeting. It is understood that the time shall be devoted to short anecdotes, personal reminiscences, etc., and the brethren will be given ample scope to enlarge upon

any details which the subject may suggest. Our
usual custom is to devote at least one hour to this
highly entertaining exercise, and I call to mind
now some of the most enjoyable moments of my
life spent in listening to others or in constructing
for the amusement of others a few of the most entertaining and instructive falsehoods that the history of our most noble order has known.

"We have several prominent visiting members
here from other parts of the country, among whom
I am gratified to name Brother Eli Perkins, Brother
O'Keefe, of Pike's Peak, and Brothers Morey and
Barnum, from the east, who will address the meeting, perhaps, for a few moments after other business has been disposed of."

After singing the opening ode, accompanied by
the lyre, the usual order of business having been attended to, the addresses of aspirants for the office of
M. N. P. of the Rocky Mountain division were called
for.

The last speaker was Brother Jedediah Holcomb,
who thus addressed the assemblage:

"Most noble prevaricator of the Rocky Mountain
division of Forty Liars, and brethren of the order:
Many years ago, when I was a mere stripling, as it
were, and just upon the verge of manhood, so to
speak, I was sitting on the green grass south of
Chicago, near where Drexel boulevard comes into
South Park, thinking of my hard luck and wishing
that my future might be more prosperous than my
past.

"That locality was then a howling wilderness
compared with what it is now, and where to-day
the beautiful drives and walks are so inviting there

was nothing then but prairie and swamp, with here and there a scrub oak tree.

"Chicago was a stirring western city then, but she was young and small. She had not then accumulated the fabulous wealth of new and peculiar metropolitan odors which she now enjoys, and in place of the rich, fructifying fragrance of the stock yards, there was nothing but the wild honeysuckle and the dead horse.

"Out where some of the most beautiful residences now stand there was nothing then but the dank thistle nodding in the wind, or the timid pic-nic bumble bee, hanging on the autumn bough and yearning to be gathered in by the small boy.

"As I sat there long ago, and, shrouded in the September haze, was dreaming of a fortunate future for myself, I heard the muffled tread of innumerable feet drawing nearer and nearer. The sound was like the footfall of a regiment of infantry approaching, and I arose to see what it was.

"I had not long to wait, for soon there hove in sight a very singular spectacle. First came a large Illinois hog at the head of a long column of Illinois hogs, all marching in Indian fashion, and grunting with that placid, gentle grunt which the hog carries with him. On closer examination into this singular phenomenon, I saw that all the hogs, except the leader, were blind, each animal having his predecessor's tail in his mouth throughout the long line, • consisting of 13,521 unfortunate, sightless hogs, cheerfully following their leader toward water.

"I was never so struck with the wonderful instinct of the brute creation in my life, and my eyes filled with tears when I saw the child-like faith and confidence of each blind animal following with im plicit trust the more fortunate guide.

"Soon, however, a great dazzling three-cornered idea worked its *way into my intellect. Dashing away my idle tears, I drew my revolver and shot off the leader's tail, leaving the long line of disconcerted and aimless hogs in the middle of a broad prairie, with no guide but the dephlogisticated tail of a hog who was then three-quarters of a mile away.

"Then I stole up, and taking the gory tail in my hand, I led the trusting phalanx down to the stock yards and sold the outfit at eight cents, live weight.

"This was the start of my dazzling career as a capitalist, a career to which I now point with pride. Thus from a poor boy with one suspender and a sore toe, I have risen to be one of our leading business men, known and respected by all, and by industry and economy, and borrowing my chewing tobacco, I have come to be one of our solid men."

When Brother Holcomb ceased to speak, there was a painful silence of perhaps five moments, and then Brother Woodtick Williams moved that the rules be suspended, and Brother Holcomb declared the unanimous choice of the order for the Most Noble Prevaricator, to serve till 1882.

Passed.

Then the quartette sang the closing ode, and each member, after hanging up his regalia in the anteroom, walked thoughtfully home in the crisp winter starlight.

"I LED THE TRUSTY PHALANX DOWN TO THE STOCK YARDS."

SITTING BULL.

HIS SPEECH BEFORE THE SIOUX COMMON COUNCIL.

The following speech 'of Sitting Bull has been specially translated and reported by our Indian editor, who is also wholesale and retail dealer in deceased languages, and general agent for home-made Sioux rhetoric and smoke-tanned Indian elo-quence. New laid Indian laments with bead trim-mings. , Compiler of novel and desirable styles of war dances. Indian eloquence furnished to debat-ing clubs and publishers of school readers:

"Warriors and war-scarred veterans of the fron-tier: Once more the warpath is overgrown with bunch grass, and the tomahawk slumbers in the wigwam of the red man. Grim-visaged war has given place to the piping times of peace. The cold and cruel winter is upon us. It has been upon us for some time.

"The wail of departed spirits is on the night wind, and the wail of the man with the chilblain answers back from the warrior's wigwam.

"Children of the forest we are few. Where once the shrill war-whoop of the chieftain collected our tribe like the leaves of the forest, I might now yell till the cows come home without bringing out a quorum.

"We are fading away before the march of the paleface, and sinking into oblivion like the snow-flake on the bosom of the Stinking Water.

"Warriors, I am the last of a mighty race. We were a race of Chieftains. Alas! we will soon be gone. The Bull family will soon pass from the face

of the earth. Ole is gone, and John is failing, and
I don't feel very well myself. We are the victims
of the paleface, and our lands are taken away.

"A few more suns and the civilization, and valley
tan, and hand made sour mash, and horse liniment
of the paleface will have done their deadly work.

"Our squaws and pappooses are scattered to the
four winds of heaven, and we are left desolate.

"Where is The-Daughter-of-the-Tempest? Where
is The-Wall-Eyed-Maiden-With-the-Peeled-Nose?

"Where is Victoria Regina Dei Gracia Sitting
Bull? Where is Knock-Kneed Chemiloon? Where
are Sway-Back Sue and Meek-Eyed Government
Socks?

"They have sunk beneath the fire-waters of the
goggle-eyed Caucasian. They have succumbed to
the delirium triangles, and when I call them they
come not. They do not hear my voice. Their moans
are heard upon the still night air, and they cry for
revenge. Look at the sad remnant of the family of
Sitting Bull, your chief. One sore-eyed squaw is
left alone. Her face is furrowed o'er with the famine
of many winters, and her nose is only the ruin of its
former greatness. Her moccasins are worn out, and
the soldier pants she wears are too long for her.
She also is drunk. She is not as drunk as she can
get, but she is hopeful and persevering. She has
also learned to lie like the white man. She is now
an easy, extemporaneous liar. When we gather
about the camp fire and enact our untutored lies in
the gloaming, Lucretia Borgia Skowhegan Sitting
Bull, with the inspiration of six fingers of agency
coffin varnish, proceeds to tell the prize prevarication, and then the house adjourns, and nothing can

be heard but the muffled tread of the agency corn
beef, going out to get some fresh air. Lucretia
Borgia is also becoming slovenly. It is evening,
and yet she has not donned her evening dress. Her
back hair is unkempt, and her front hair is unbung.
Pretty soon I will take a tomahawk and bang it for
her. She seems despondent and hopeless. As she
leans against the trunk of a mighty oak and
scratches her back, you can see that her thoughts
are far away. Her other suspender is gone, but she
don't care a cold smooth clam. She is thinking of
her childhood days by the banks of Minnehaha.

"Warriors, we stand in the moccasins of a mighty
nation. We represent the starving remnant of the
once powerful Sioux. Our pirogue stands idly on
the shore. I don't know what a pirogue is, but it
stands idly on the shore.

"When the spring flowers bloom again, and the
grass is green upon the plains, we will once more go
upon the warpath. We will avenge the wrongs of
our nation. I have not fully glutted my vengeance.
I have seven or eight more gluts on hand, and we
will shout our war-cry once more, and mutilate some
more Anglo-Saxons. We will silence the avenging
cries of our people. We will spatter the green
grass and grey greasewood with the gore of the
paleface, and feed the white-livered emigrant to the
coyote. We will spread death and desolation everywhere, and fill the air with gum overshoes and remains. Let us yield up our lives dearly while we
mash the paleface beyond recognition, and shoot his
hired man so full of holes that he will look like a
suspension bridge.

"Warriors, there is our hunting ground. The buffalo, the antelope, the sagehen and the jackass rabbit are ours. Ours to enjoy, ours to perpetuate, ours to transmit. The Great Spirit created these animals for the red man, and not for the bilious tourists, between whose legs the chestnut sunlight penetrates clear up to his collar bone.

●　●　●　●　●　●　●　●　●　●　●

"Then we will ride down on the regular army, when he is thinking of something else, and we will scare him into convulsions, and our medicine men will attend to the convulsions while we sample the supplies.

" Then we will take some cold sliced Indian agent, and some bay rum, and go on a pic-nic.

"Warriors, farewell. Be virtuous and you will be happy; but you will be lonesome, sometimes. Think of what I have said to you about the council fire, and govern yourselves accordingly. We will not murmur at the celluloid cracker and cast iron codfish ball, but in the spring we will have veal cutlets for breakfast, and peace commissioner on toast for dinner. The squaw of Sitting Bull shall have a new plug hat, and if the weather is severe, she shall have two of them.

"Warriors, farewell. I am done. I have spoken. I have nothing more to say. Sic semper domino. Plumbago erysipelas, in hock eureka, sciataca. usufruct, limburger, gobraugh."

SOME SUPERSTITIONS.

When you come to make a list of all the singular superstitions of those you know, it is wonderful how many intelligent people are the victims of the most unreasonable whims.

For instance, we are acquainted with a lady who is well educated, and far above the average class of those who constitute the great army of the superstitious, and yet she never allows a breakfast to be prepared in her house on washday of anything but giblets of codfish and tit-bits of superanuated grub left over during the preceding week. Her husband has struggled to convince her of the utter absurdity of this practice, and tried to show her that there is nothing to it, but all his efforts have been worse than useless.

A friend of ours, too, who is a college graduate, and who hoots most of the follies of the day, is still so superstitious on one point that he is a slave to his singular whim. He will not pass up the same side of the street on which a creditor of his is coming down. He says he never has good luck if he sees a creditor over his left shoulder, or meets one face to face. Some are superstitious about white horses, owls, and so forth, but this man says he never met a creditor but right away after that he heard of some one being dunned.

Another acquaintance of ours is so completely under the control of an old woman's notion that he calls down upon himself time and again the scorn of his friends. He seems to think that there is something fatal about seeing a contribution box on Sunday. He, therefore, gets up and rushes out of church just before the collection is taken up, rather than bring disaster down upon himself and family.

Still another friend of ours, and who comes into *The Boomerang* office every few days, has a superstition that if he were to spit in the cuspidore he wouldn't live to get home. Some day he will find that he had better reverse the theory, or he will meet with the most horrible death that has ever occurred in this region.

The most matter-of-fact man we know, and one who would be considered the very last to be affected by these old traditions, says he don't care for new moons over his left shoulder, howling dogs at midnight, or any thing of the kind; but when he sees a woman with a big stone chasing a mooley cow, he is always sure to hear of a new-made grave.

It is said that even President Garfield has his little peculiarities in this line. When we were boys together in Ohio, he would never get into a watermelon patch at night where there was a bulldog. He said that wherever there was a bulldog every thing was sacred. So superstitious was he about this style of bird, Garfield said to us once that he would just as soon rob his mother's grave as to enter the hallowed precincts where the bulldog reigns.

Then he showed us a pair of overalls with a seat to them that looked as though it had sat down on a buzz saw.

James G. Blaine has a superstition about kicking an old felt hat on the 1st of April.

Carl Schurz has a mortal dread of holding a post mortem examination on a live hornet.

Attorney General MacVeagh, who is bald, will never brush his head with the brush that the hired girl has borrowed from his dressing case. He says that the long hair tickles his scalp, and the girl is almost sure to lose her situation. It is a bad sign.

Roscoe Conkling never chews his own tobacco. He thinks that if he were to do so he would come to want, and he would rather, if anyone suffers, that it should be his friends.

General Hancock is so superstitions about seeing a dark horse over his right shoulder that it throws him into convulsions.

Henry Ward Beecher says that if, in walking out in the yard, he sees a clothes line and saws it across his windpipe, it is a sure sign that some one will get licked.

General Sherman says that he cares nothing for the usual warnings and bad signs, but he would go around seven blocks to avoid a woman with a garden hose and a limber sun-bonnet.

An old journalist we once knew was so suspicious about railroads and different lines of transit that he wouldn't take a journey over any railway until he had a note from the superintendent that could be shown to the conductors on the way. He said he tried to make a trip once without this precaution, and met with a terrible accident. Nobody else was hurt, but he was thrown off the train and over an embankment twenty-seven feet high into a frog pond eleven feet deep. He thinks the conducto had something to do with it.

DECORATION DAY AMONG THE UTES.

The Decoration Day celebrated among the Utes falls about one week earlier than with us, and was duly celebrated this season by that tribe. We can only give the oration delivered on that occasion by Colorow, and as reported expressly for *The Boomerang*:

Warriors of My People: To-day we meet beneath the budding cottonwood and the blue sky, to scatter mountain flowers and dandelion greens above the graves of those who have fought for our land. We gather to-day to vow once more that the paleface shall never plow our homes in peace, or decorate the tombs of our forefathers with his lardy da style of agriculture.

To-day our people are not all here. We are but a minority report. Our warriors are more and more seldom as the years roll on. Some of us can remember when the united war cry of our host struck terror to our enemies. Now we are only a base ball club. We only wait till the Great Spirit shall call us home, when we shall join the ransomed throng.

Disastrous war and liquid delirium tremens have thinned our ranks, until we are about as plenty as the greenback party.

We stand to-day above our city of the dead, and strew forget-me-nots and empty, desolate peach cans o'er the graves of our noble slain.

They died that we might live. They laid down their lives that the Ute nation might drag out a miserable existence among the powers of the earth.

Colorow calls to mind the day when our people were as the stars above us at night for multitude.

To-day we are nothing but a bobtail funeral procession, and when we hold a mass meeting I get so lonesome that I wish I was dead.

Our warriors once thirsted for the conflict. Now they thirst to fill their red hides full of liquid damnation.

When we were a great nation, our chieftains were tall as the mountain pine, and had some style about them. They hungered for war, and ached for a grand knock-down-and-drag-out every two weeks. When they got bilious, they would go out and kill the members of a congregational church, and then all would be well. Now they hunt up a one-legged man, or an invalid who has come to Colorado for his health, and kill him with a double-barrel shotgun.

This is not noble. It shows a lack of culture. It is poor taste.

The dead who lie buried here, died in battle. They didn't die of indigestion. They died in the heat of battle, with the war cry of our people ringing in their ears.

Most of you who hear my voice to-day will die of softening of the brain. Some will die of gout, and others of smallpox, unless you are too indolent to catch it. If some one will bring a fatal disease to you that is contagious and don't cost anything, you will all be planted this fall before huckleberries are ripe.

When you gather in the spring to go upon the war path, it makes me tired. Your serried columns look like a turkey gobbler in a gale of wind.

You are about as effective in a campaign as a stump-tail bull in fly time. If you would all agree to die and let me decorate your graves every spring

with cauliflowers and dead cats, I would consider it
the greatest effort of your lives.

Warriors, adieu. I call you warriors from force
of habit. Remember our noble dead. Although you
cannot die nobly yourselves, you can come and scatter warm tears and bacon rinds about the graves of
those who did die nobly.

Let us cherish the memory of those who fought
for us, and when another spring shall come with its
blue-eyed daisies and soft south wind, try to see
how many of you will occupy reserved seats in the
mysterious realms of shade.

WAKING UP THE WRONG MAN.

WOODTICK WILLIAMS AND THE FEVERISH HORNET.

" Yes, that's so," said Woodtick Williams thoughtfully, as he squirted a half a gill of tobacco juice
through his teeth at a bumble-bee's ear, and then
looked out across the divide, and beyond the foot-
hills, toward the top of the range where the eternal
snow was glittering in the summer sun.

"You are eminently correct. The gentleman
from Buckskin has stated the exact opinion of the
subscriber, sure as death and semi-annual assess-
ments.

"Every profession has its style of lead and its
peculiar dip toward the horizon. From the towering
Congressman down to the neglected advance-agent
of the everlasting Gospel, every profession, I allow,
has its peculiar lingo. Every pork-and-beans pilgrim from the States that's been in my camp for
twenty-seven years has said that the miner slings

more unnecessary professional racket than anybody
else; but that ain't so. Take folks as they assay,
from blossom-rock to lower level, there ain't much
difference.

"Nine years ago, I and Timberline Monroe and
Katooter Lemons, from Zion, struck the Feverish
Hornet up on Slippery Ellum. First we knew the
prospecting season had closed up on us, and, as the
layout for surface had pinched out, we decided to
sink on the Hornet, just for luck.

"So Timberline, Katooter and me went over to
Huckleberry Oleson's store at the lower camp and
soaked our physiognomy for chuck, and valley-tan,
and a blastin' outfit for the job.

"Down five foot she showed 150 colors to a hunk
of rock no bigger'n a plug of tobacker, with wall
rocks well defined both sides and foot wall slick as
a confidence game in 'Frisco.

"The quartz, with a light coat of gouge, looked
as if she'd been jammed through the formation like
a Sabbath school scholar's elbow through a custard
pie, and it had crushed the prehistoric stuffin' and
preadamite sawdust out of the geological crust in
good shape.

"'Katooter,' says I, 'if she shows up this way all
the way down, I be teetotally dodbuttered if I don't
think we've cornered the sugar at last. We'll run
her down to ten foot and see how she looks to the
naked eye.'

"Ten foot down she'd widen to three foot between
walls, with solid gray quartz as pretty as a bank
book. Then we made a mill run of five pounds in a
half-gallon mortar and cleared up a dollar's worth
of dust on the blade of a long-handled shovel.

"The prospectus of the Feverish Hornet was very cheering indeed.

"I sat down on a candle-box and sang something. I always twitter a few notes when I feel tickled about anything.

"Katooter listened to my singing a little while, and then he went down the gulch murmuring something about my music and intimating that prosperity always had its little drawbacks after all.

"He slid down to the Frescoed Hell and jammed his old freckled hide so full of horse liniment of the vintage of '49 that he got entirely off the lead, and drifted so far into poverty rock that he didn't know Timberline nor me from a stomach-pump.

"That's generally the way with men that turn up their noses at vocal music.

"Well, he got no better so rapidly that next day he was occupying a front seat at the biggest delirium triangle matinee you ever heard of, and was the sole proprietor of the biggest aggregation of seal-brown tarantulas and variegated caterpillars and imported centipedes that ever exhibited in Columbia's fair domain.

"Every little while he'd nail some diabolical insect crawling up his sleeve or gently walking through his hair, and then he'd yell like a maniac and pray and swear like a hired man.

"The atmosphere seemed to be level-full of bumble bees as big as a cookstove, and every time they'd cuddle up to him or sink on him with their sultry little gimlets, Katooter would jump up and whoop like a Piute medicine-man trying to assuage a wide waste of turbulent cucumber.

"At these times Katooter would lay aside his
wardrobe, and, throwing me into the fire-place and
Timberline under the bed, he would wander forth
into the starlight, with the thermometer down to 37
degrees, and wrapped in nothing but his surging
thoughts.

"By the time Timberline and me would get up
and swab the cobwebs and cinders out of our eyes,
Katooter would be half way up the gulch and lighting out like a freckled Greek slave hunting for a
clothing store.

"First along we used to run after him and try to
tire him out and corral him, but he was most too
skipful, and apparently so allfired anxious to put all
the intervening distance he could between himself
and the fuzzy tarantulas and fall style of centipede,
that he made some pretty tall time, considering the
poor trail and the light mountain air.

"Then another thing; when we got to him he was .
so pesky mean to hang on to.

"You've probably tried before now, when you was
small, to catch the boy who tied your shirt to the
top limb of a dead tree, and you have thrown all
your energy into the effort, but you decided after a
while to wait till he got his clothes on before you
punished him.

"That's the way it was with Katooter. He was
the smartest man I ever tried to gather into the
fold. We'd think we had him, and all at once he'd
glide between our legs like a yaller dog and laugh a
wild kind of laugh that would run the thermometer
down 13 degrees, and away he'd glimmer up the
trail like a red-headed right of way.

"So I got mad at last, and used to chase him with a lariat and Yellow Fever.

"Yellow Fever was a sorrel mule that belonged to the firm. We called him Yellow Fever because he was so fatal.

"Well, when Yellow Fever and me got after Katooter with the lariat, we most always gathered him in.—[Bless my soul, how I'm stringing this yarn out.]

"Well, to make a long story short, Katooter rallied after a while, and during the spell his chilblains was convalescing, and some more new skin growing on his system where he had barked it off running through the sage-brush, and falling into old deserted prospect holes. I had an offer of $50,000 for my third in the Feverish Hornet, and sold.

"Then I went down to Truckee and bought a little house of an old railroad man down there, and grub-staked myself for the winter, and allowed I'd lay off till the snow left the range in the spring.

"One night, about half after 12, I judge, I heard somebody step along to the window of my boudoir. Hearing it at that time of night, I reckoned that something crooked was going on, so I slid out of bed and got my Great Blood Searcher and Liver Purifier, with the new style of centre fire and cartridge ejector, and slid up to the window, calculating to shove a tonic into whoever it might be that was picnicing around my claim.

"I looked out so as to get a good idea of where I wanted to sink on him, and then I thought before I mangled him I'd ask him if he had any choice about which part of his vitals he wanted to preserve, so I sang out to him:

AFTER KATOOTER ON YELLOW FEVER.

"Look out below there, pard, for I'm going to call the meeting to order in a minute! Just throw up your hands, if you please, and make the grand hailing sign of distress, or I'll have to mutilate you! Just show me about where you'd have the fatal wound, and be spry about it, too, because I've got my brief costume on, and the evening air is chill!"

"He didn't understand me, apparently, for a gurgling laugh welled up from below, and the party sings back:

"'Hullo, Fatty, is that you? Just lookin' to see if you'd fired up yet. You know I was to come round and flag you if second seven was out. Well, I've been down to to the old man's to see what's on the board. Three is two hours late and four is on time. There's two sevens out and two sections of nine. Skinney'll take out first seven and Shorty'll pull her with 102. It's you and me for second seven, with Limber Jim on front end and Frenchy to hold down the caboose. First fire is wrong side up in a washout this side of Ogallalla, and old Whatshisname that runs 258 got his crown sheet caved in and telescoped his headlight into the middle of the New Jerusalem. You know the little Swede that used to run extra for Old Hotbox on the emigrant awhile? Well, he was firing on 258 and he's under three flats and a coaloil tank, with a brake beam across his coupler, and his system more or less relaxed. He's gone to the sweet subsequently, too. Rest of the boys are more or less demoralized, and side-tracked for repairs. Now you don't want to monkey around much, for if you don't loom up like six bits and go out on the tick, the old man'll give you a time

check and the Oriental Grand Bounce. You hear
the mellow trill of my bazoo?'

"Then I slowly uncorked the Great Blood Purifier,
and moving to the footlights where the silvery
moonbeams could touch up my dazzling outlines, I
said: 'Partner, I am pleased and gratified to have
met you. I don't know the first ding busted thing
you have said to me, but that is my misfortune. I
am a plain miner, and my home is in the digestive
apparatus of the earth, but for professional melody
of the chin, you certainly take the cake. You also
take the cake basket and what cold pie there is on
the dump. My name is Woodtick Williams. I discovered the Feverish Hornet up on Slippery Elm. I
am proud you know. Keep right on getting more
and more familiar with your profession, and by and
by, when nobody can understand you, you will be
promoted and respected, and you will at last be a
sleeping-car conductor, and revel in the biggest mental calm, and wide shoreless sea-of intellectual stag-
nation that the world ever saw. You will———.'

"But he was gone.

"Then I took a pillow sham and wiped some pulverized crackers off the soles of my feet, and went
to bed, enveloped in a large gob of gloom."

SKOWHEGAN ONDERDONK ON THE PLAN OF SALVATION.

"As regards impromptu speeches," said Woodtick
Williams, as he breathed softly on a piece of blossom rock and looked at it earnestly through his
pocket-glass, "I was never what you might call a

natural, easy, graceful, extemporaneous speaker in public.

"I can sit down on a boulder or an old powder-keg and reel anything off to the boys in a tolerably loquacious and instructive style, but when I get up before a big mob and begin to scatter a few preg-nant gems of thought around among the audience I get wild and skittish, and want to go home.

"Then when I take my seat, the big ideas that adjourned when I was on the rostrum come throng-ing back to me, and fill me so full of inspiration, and dumb yearning, and warm, earnest swearful-ness that it seems as if I'd bust.

"Once, I remember, I was called on by the Gen-eral Passenger Agent and Acting Manager of a nar-row gauge Sabbath-school at Salt Lake in an early day to address the kids of Zion. The floor manager had me down for a thirty minutes' dissertation on 'The Uncertainty of Terrestrial Things,' or some such racket as that, and I thought I'd have to work it mighty fine to say all that was surging and throb-bing in my teeming brain, but when I sat down, and mopped the dew off my marble brow, and looked at my watch, I found that I'd only been a fraction over seven minutes.

"All that I can remember of the dad blistered speech is about this:

"'Dear children of Zion, I'm afraid I'll encroach on your time—but—I want to say a word—that is, a few words—I won't detain you long—or, at least, not very long—a few words about salvation and—firearms.

"'Never fool with firearms that have not been loaded. Don't do it.

" 'I once knew a boy who looked down into the silent depths of an old double-barrel shotgun that had not been loaded since Columbus discovered America, and all at once he went crashing through the Zodiac, and he is up there somewhere now. All we ever found of him was a stone-bruise and the place where he had been. O, it's awful!

" 'I also knew a little lad with soft, curling hair and deep violet eyes. Everybody loved little Ephraim. But one day he turned his attention to the mystery that clung to an old smooth-bore that Daniel Boone used to have, and that had never been loaded since. This gun had stood around in the corner for about a century, and been kicked and battered by every one, just taking it all pleasantly so as to throw people off their guard, and when the hired girl swept up little Ephraim there wasn't a dry eye in the house.'

" Then I apologized for not saying anything on salvation, because I had taken up so much time, and sat down.

" But it took old Jim Onderdonk to speak without any preparation. We called him Skowhegan Onderdonk, because he came from Skowhegan, and he was tall enough to whitewash the sky, if he had a step-ladder. He never had to stop and cough and take a drink of water while he thought of a hard word. O, no. Just give him a grown person's dose of Cemetery Promoter, and he'd address a caucus or a funeral, he didn't care which.

" One day I heard him speak to the children on the subject of 'The Efficiency of Prayer.'

" He always announced his subject beforehand, not because he ever alluded to it afterwards in any

way, but because he had noticed that most public
speakers had a subject to speak on.

"As near as I can call to mind now, Skowhegan
Onderdonk spoke about as follows:

"'Dear children, did you ever stop to think that
what we are to-day and what we will be to-morrow
and the next day and the day following and next
week and next month and next year and all through
our eventful lives is not so much what we in vain
anticipation regard ourselves retrospectively as
what we ultimately were or some day might previously be?

"'Did you ever stop to consider how much we
may find out by ascertaining?

"'Journeying adown life's rugged pathway, did
you ever stop to ponder, dear children, upon the
cold, hard fact that the longer you live the older
you become, and as you acquire knowledge you
gradually get to knowing more?

"'Ah, let us learn a valuable lesson from this
eternal truth and flee from the wrath to come.

"'Let us promise ourselves to-day — right now,
without a moment's delay — that, as we continue to
ram facts into our systems and glean intelligence,
we will at the same time become better informed.

"'Try to impress this never dying truth upon
your minds: that whatever we do not do at once or
at some time in the future, unless some one else
does it, will in all human probability remain undone.

"'We should learn from this the importance of
these things that are most essential.

"'I might talk to you for hours with pleasure of

these things, but I cannot take up the time, On-
more suggestion, and I will close.

"'You are all young now. The future is before
you. This will seem singular to you at first, but
when I explain it to you you will see at once that if
it were anywhere else it would seem out of place
and unhappy.

"'You will readily see that Providence has so
wisely ordered things that not only in the economy
of Nature does the uncertain subsequently follow
closely upon the already forgotten previously, but
the hazy and obscure past was at one time the un-
born germ of the dim and incandescent directly, em-
bosomed in the great unknown finally, and shrouded
in the prismatic colors of the boundless ultimately.

"'I am afraid, however, that you do not quite
get at the never-dying truth that I am trying to elu-
cidate to you. As I said before, the future is before
you. If you understood this thoroughly you would
rejoice over the Omnipotent wisdom which placed it
in that position, but you are now young and you
think you can see little places where the Creator has
missed it.

"'In the fluff and bloom and exuberance of youth
you naturally feel as though the general management of the universe is open to criticism. You see
here and there little irregularities in the Divine
economy where you could have improved upon it if
you had been consulted as to the policy of the administration. This has taken up a great deal of
your time and worn you out. When you get older
you will throw off a good deal of this responsibility
and it will be a great relief to you.

"'Looking back upon my own childhood I can see here and there in the light of a chastened experience, where if I had not done just as I did perhaps I should have done differently.

"Instead of wearing myself out with anxiety and fretting over the fear that my parents would come to some bad end, if I had taken more relaxation and rest I would have been better off to-day. Instead of worrying over a change in the plan of salvation or improving the time-card of the heavenly bodies, if I had rubbed glycerine on the backs of my feet where they were cracked open, I would have been happier then and I would have entered upon a useful manhood instead of being the physical wreck that I am now, worn out sitting up nights for fear that the heavenly bodies would crash into each other.

"'This is not only true of all things but of everything else.

"'There is a great field of thought open to you here, and I simply call your attention to it. I haven't the time nor ability to enlarge upon it, but I leave it for your consideration. As you grow older and learn more of the way creation is managed, you will gradually endorse it and approve of it until you are old and gray-headed, and then you will admit that the whole system is arranged and governed as well as you could have done it yourself.

"'Go where information is turned loose at reduced rates and absorb all you can. Let it soak into you. It won't hurt you after you get accustomed to the novel sensation a little.

"'Then in after years you can write a large encyclopedia of what you don't know, and you will look

back to this time in your history and thank me for
calling your attention to these little matters that
pertain to your soul's eternal welfare.'"

THOUGHTS

It seems that quince seeds are now largely used
by the girls in convincing their bangs to stay bung.
That is, the quince seed is manufactured into a
mucilage that holds a little flat curl in place a week.
In consequence of this quince seeds have increased
in price and decreased in quantity till the girls pay
seven prices for them or go without.

If they would adopt our style of bang, much
trouble and expense would be avoided. We bang
our hair with a damp towel, and it don't bother us
again for two weeks. Being the proprietor, in the
first place, of a style of hair of the delicate color
peculiar to a streak of moonlight, it didn't at any
time make much difference whether we did it up in
tin foil every night or not, and now that cares like
a wild deluge have come upon us thick and fast, we
have enlarged our intellectual skating rink and we
find, with unalloyed pleasure, that the time we once
devoted to parting our pale, consumptive tresses can
be entirely devoted to excessive mental effort, and
pleasant memories of a well spent life.

FIFTY CENTS' WORTH OF GUSH.

How gently comes back to us the memory of the
years that are sped, and how tenderly do little incidents of our half-forgotten past hover down upon
upon us as we come unexpectedly upon little articles

which bring back the tender memories of what is half reluc antly drifting into the hungry maw of the long ago.

It is thus that the golden woof in the bright fabric of your last summer pants, stained with a telltale touch on the rear breadths, brings back to your soft eye the misty light of forgotten days, with their wealth of picnic and custard pie, and the glad thrill of voluptuous calm that settled upon you when you sat down in the lunch basket last year.

THE SPRING STYLE OF PHENOMENA.

As it is now time to introduce the spring style of sensational, heavenly symptoms by telegraph, we publish the following dispatches in order to be ahead of other journals and also for the purpose of getting it off our mind.

SHOWER OF HARDWARE.

OSHKOSH, Wisconsin, April 15.—A heavy shower of ten-penny nails and door-hinges fell here this morning. There were no clouds in the sky at the time, but thunder, lightning and Roman candles were among the celestial symptoms.

A man named Drew, who was playing croquet near the Baptist church, was struck on the head by a falling door-hinge and knocked down.

He is yet insensible, but he never was very sensible.

It is hoped that more croquet players were killed by the torrent of hinges.

FALL OF COLD GRUB.

KALAMAZOO, April 15.—At about 1 o'clock this morning a tremendous shower of pickled tripe and codfish balls fell here, literally covering the ground to a depth of six inches.

Afterwards a slight shower of black pepper and Halford sauce fell, and the free lunch counters have gone into bankruptcy.

It is supposed by scientists that a railroad lunchroom on the planet Saturn has busted, and busted so hard that the fragments struck the earth. This theory, however, is scoffed at by many of our leading men.

POLYGAMOUS PHENOMENA.

SALT LAKE, April 16.—At about 9 o'clock this morning the clear sky became suddenly clouded, and at a quarter of 10, a terrific shower of fine combs, Mormon toe nails, New Orleans molasses, blanc mange, railroad spikes and buckwheat batter fell here, accompanied by a perfect tornado and a strong smell like the spring bonfire in a back yard.

There are many theories afloat relative to it, one being that President Garfield's Anti Polygamous policy has busted a large wad of Mormon relics that has been drifting through space, and it has fallen to the earth in this form.

HASHED NIHILIST.

ST. PETERSBURG, April 15.—A shower of flesh fell here this afternoon from a clear sky. Later investigations seem to point, however, to the supposition that it is mostly scrambled Nilhilist.

One of the peasantry here this morning recognized a fragment with a strawberry mark on it, and says the late lamented was a pronounced nihilist.

It is presumed that a large party of nihilists were out on a picnic in an adjoining town, and that one of the party, to test a new bomb which he had recently constructed, playfully threw it at a fat woman who cannot be found.

STUCK ON A BIG WORD.

CHICAGO, April 16.—At a very early hour this morning people were aroused from sleep by the falling of what sounded like hail upon the roof. The sound continued for perhaps fifteen minutes, accompanied by a slight trembling of the earth, but no other symptoms.

This morning after daylight, it was found, instead of hail, there had been a heavy fall of false teeth and big Prussian words.

All that is known of the strange phenomenon is, that an old man undertook to lecture in Peoria on the night of the 15th, on the subject of the Franco-Prussian war. He got stuck on a big word, and busted in the middle of his lecture.

An inquest will be held as soon as sufficient teeth are collected to enable the coroner to proceed with any degree of certainty.

A SHOWER OF FLESH AT COLLINS.

FORT COLLINS, April 16.—This forenoon our people were amazed at the appearance of a slight cloud in the sky, followed by a short shower of flesh and pants buttons.

The following dispatch received here from Denver, is supposed to have something to do with it:

DENVER, April 16.—Last evening a fat man from Ohio arrived here, and undertook to break a bronco mule. The mule is well known here as the most vigorous bucker in the Rocky Mountains. He was called Asiatic Cholera, because he was so fatal, and had already killed three Ohio men.

The deceased wore, when last seen, a Centennial watch with buckskin guard, and brass buttons riveted in his pantaloons. Anyone finding buttons or watch of this description, or any other portion of the deceased, by forwarding the same in registered letters to his family at Columbus, Ohio, will be suitably rewarded.

HE IS MAD.

A fine-haired, pink cambric cuss, with the rich Castilian name of McCafferty, has been over the Union Pacific railroad recently, and he didn't find things so nice as he had been accustomed to. He pours out his woes in the Omaha *Bee*, and says that the employes of the road are not gentlemen, and eat with their hats on, and he is very mad, indeed.

Probably Mr. McCafferty was never away from home before. No doubt his mother don't know he is out.

He says that "none but gentlemen should have charge of passenger trains." That is true in some cases. If the traveling public averaged up as well

as we do when we travel, then none but gentlemen
should have charge of passenger trains; but when
the company kindly offer to ship a car-load of hogs
in a Pullman car, there ought to be a Texas drover
with a prod-pole to take charge of it.

The Count D'McCafferty don't want to sit at the
table with a conductor who eats with his hat on.
Well, ding bust it, the conductors didn't used to eat
with their hats on, anyway, until the tourists got to
stealing the hats of train men, and the latter had to
protect themselves some way.

A conductor isn't able to buy a plug hat every
trip, and then have it stolen by a snoozer from New
Jersey. Of course not. Their salaries are not large
enough.

We are acquainted with many of the employes of
this road, and they are gentlemen. If there is an
employe on the road who isn't a gentleman, and
the Duke D'McCafferty will let us know who he is,
we will discharge him, we don't care if it's the
president of the road.

There are lots of men who travel, and who are
like Mr. McCafferty. They don't have much at
home, and when they travel they want to make up
for the starvation they will have to endure when
they get back.

As a rule, when a man wants the porter to come
and tuck him into bed every night, and fan him,
and lull him to sleep with some plaintive melody,
you can bet that that man, when he is at home,
sleeps in a hay-mow with a cellar door over him.

If he complains about the food and swears at the
waiters, it is safe to say that when he is clustered
around his own festive board, he fills himself up

with baled hay and bran mash, and wipes his nose on the table cloth.

You ought to see us when we travel.

We are wreathed in smiles all the time, no matter what happens. We buy everything that the news agent has to sell, green apples, worms, and everything, and we never repine as some do. We break forth into melodious song sometimes, and then the people go forward into the smoking car, or madly throw themselves from the moving train.

It is always best to be chipper and gay when you travel. If a fellow-passenger snores loudly and disturbs you, go and bang him across the snoot with a valise, laughing merrily all the time. Don't murmur and complain and make everybody wretched and unhappy, nor rush madly into print, but go and soak your head and reduce the swelling, and have some little degree of style.

That's the safe way to do. Don't give yourself uead away, as Stewart's body did, but keep still and see how other people behave, and try to learn all you can, so that some day you will have the requisite ability to whack a bull team at $30 per month.

MORE HIGH ART

Yesterday a man came into *The Boomerang* office with the wild, hunted look of a married man whose wife has two majority in the house and full control of the senate.

After he had heaved a sigh as large as a box car, and scratched his back on the oriental hat rack, he asked if he might have a word with the high art editor.

A pensive blonde, with his feet in the waste paper
basket, was pointed out to him, and the domestic
minority poured out his woes:

"I s'pose you manage the fresco business for this
periodical, and you want to bring art, and frill, and
home decorations up to a high standard.

"Well, my wife is some on home decorations herself, and what I wanted was a suggestion once in a
while from your paper that would seem to tone her
up and elevate her tastes, as it were. She is away
behind. I want to try and discourage her from
plastering the shanty with Michael Angelo paint-
ings that come off from peach cans and tobacco
pails.

"It clashes a little to have a plaster cast of
Shakespeare in one corner of the room, and a picture peeled off a baked bean can in the other. It
brings poetry and grub too close together. My idea
is that æsthetics and cold chuck should not be
brought into immediate contact in art. They don't
harmonize.

"That's why I told Amanda not to hang 'Moses
in the Bulrushes' contiguous to her painting of a
Magnolia ham.

"Last week she got hornswoggled into buying
some Japanese tidies of a leading bric-a-bracker.
He told her they were the latest thing in tidies, and
she bought seven for twenty-one cents.

"We have only three chairs that are able to be
out, anyway, and one of them is foundered pretty
bad, so four of the tidies had to be nailed up on the
wall.

"The perspective in these tidies is very bad.
Another thing, the red flannel dado on the sky don't

suit me. Then the sand-hill crane is bigger than the pagoda, or the corral, or whatever it is, and the firecracker funny business is bad for sore eyes.

"I have brought one of the tidies along. It speaks for itself.

"Imagine a man coming home tired and hungry and sitting down on a tidy that has the scarlet fever. Think of a home made desolate with a howling wilderness of stump tail storks standing on one foot and trying to think of a big word.

"Put yourself in my place, and try to imagine a home filled with a nightmare of red wash bills with picturesque Japanese congressmen in their shirttails, as it were, drinking tea out of majolica washbowls.

"I am not a hard man to please, but I feel as though something ought to be done. Of course it wouldn't do for me to suggest a change to my wife directly, because she would put a symphony in navy blue and sage green on my brow with a gothic potato masher, but if the leading paper of the country should come out, you understand, and say that there had been a change, and that blue tailed snipes and bow-legged Chinamen had gone out of style, and warm meals and porterhouse steak were growing in favor, with a leaning toward ham and egg as home decorations, I think that perhaps the old woman might tumble to the racket."

That is why we have published the above interview. We want to do all the good we can.

THE FORTY LIARS.

THE APRIL MEETING.

Last evening, at the pavilion on Second street, the Rocky Mountain division of the Forty Liars held its regular monthly meeting.

After singing the opening ode beginning,

> Brethren of our joyous choir,
> Twang, O twang the sounding lyre,

the report of committees was called for. The Most Noble Breath Tester, as chairman of the committee .for the investigation of crooked breaths, reported that the total number of members of the Independent Order of Forty Liars for the past year, who had been investigated for retailing their breath without a license, was twenty-seven. Of that number, twenty had been discharged for lack of testimony.

Fines and costs collected from this source, $49.00.

Expenses of investigating committee:

Mileage, $1.00.

Drinks, $48.00.

The report of the committee was accepted and the committee discharged.

A committee of five was then appointed by the Most Noble Prevaricator, to ascertain and report at the next regular round-up, some practicable method, if possible, for copyrighting the prevarications of the order, and also to make estimates on the probable cost of publication for the use of the members.

After the regular order of business, the Most Noble Prevaricator announced that the next thing in order would be the Communications and Good of the Order.

Under this head, the Custodian of Campaign Lies read the following letter from a brother on Alder Gulch:

ALDER GULCH, April 2nd, 1881.
DEAR BRETHREN OF THE ORDER:

In view of the severity of the past winter, and consequent suffering, the following occurrence has been brought forcibly back to my mind:

In '49 there was, on the dividing line between the Territory of Montana and the English Possessions, a small tribe of Indians known as the Poposhinkick-ers, or Hump Back Centipedes.

These Indians lived mainly on mountain beetles, crippled coyotes, and the delightful climate.

There were five of our party camped on the river east of the range where this tribe wintered, in '68, but we didn't steal any of their provisions or rob their bug orchards.

Our party consisted of Charles Francis Adams Muzzy, *alias* Short and Dirty, Christopher Colum-bus Bangs, *alias* Wappyjawed Chris, Bjornstjerne Bjornson Erickson, *alias* Polyglot Pete, Josephus Henry Clay Miles, the cook and myself.

We had a pretty good time of it during the fall and early winter, but in December it began to show signs of a very long and severe winter, and the game left us, so we were put on short allowance be-fore Christmas. By the 5th of January, '69, we be-gan to be alarmed, for our own supply had nearly given out, and the biggest game in the country about us was the frozen beetle, the food of the Po-poshinkickers, and these lay deep under the snow.

Starvation was upon us, and death, hundreds of
miles from any white man's house or settlement,
seemed certain.

Short and Dirty went out and wallowed through
the snow all day, in the hope that he might kill an
antelope or a jack rabbit, but he came home worn
out and empty handed.

Then Wappyjawed Chris tried it with no better
.success, and so did Polyglot Pete and myself.

Then Josephus Henry Clay Miles, the cook, went
out with his Henry rifle and brought in some antelope steaks, the snow being so deep he couldn't
bring in the whole animal. This raised the spirits
of the party, for it showed that game had not entirely deserted the country. After the cook had used
all the venison, going each day for it where he had
killed and left it, we all by turns made the effort to
get a shot at game, but with no better success.

Then Josephus Henry Clay Miles went out again,
and before 3 o'clock in the afternoon came home
with some choice antelope, already to put in the
frying pan.

Thus it went on through the long, dreary months
that followed. Though we traveled for leagues
through the snow, none of us could get a shot at
anything, but Josephus Henry Clay Miles, the cook,
saved our lives by his shrewdness and good luck.

One day in early spring, Polyglot Pete stumbled
on to the ham bone of a Poposhinkicker, with a part
of the flesh still on it. He couldn't understand it.
He went over to their camp to see if they had
missed any one of their number; but the camp was.
deserted.

4

He came back to our camp, bringing the bone. He seemed thoughtful, and didn't eat any dinner. After dinner he called all the boys out to look at the bone he had found.

Josephus Henry Clay Miles allowed that one of the Poposhinkickers had gone out to catch a coyote by the hind leg for breakfast, and after he had caught him, the coyote had got the advantage some way and taken the Poposhinkicker for breakfast, but the rest of the boys said that a theory like that was untenable. It was too vague and unsatisfactory. Then we took Josephus Henry Clay Miles, the cook, with us, and went out in search of more Indian remains, so that we could hold our inquest on them, but we could find no more anywhere.

The tribe had entirely disappeared, too, and no one could hear where they had gone until one day the following summer Josephus Henry Clay Miles, the cook, was shot by "Coupon John," over in Helena, and the doctor told him if he had any remarks to make before he crossed the range, he'd got to talk fast.

Then Josephus Henry Clay Miles called me to his bedside, and while death was glazing his eye and his breath came labored and thick, he said:

"Judge, I'm going to die, and I might as well tell you a secret. I saved your life last winter. Yours and all the rest. I'm cornered now, and I admit that I saved you all from starvation."

"Yes, yes, I know it," said I. "You are a noble, generous man, and we'll never forget you."

"That's all right, pard, that's all right, but it was tough on the Indian department, you bet. If winter had lingered in the lap of spring another week,

it would have been all day with us. We ate the last
Poposhinkicker the day that prairie dogs began to
get ripe."

He smiled a little sickly smile, gurgled a low gurgle or two, curled up into a cold hard lump and died.

I went away because I felt lonely in the presence
of death, and besides, I didn't feel well.

Starvation is a very serious thing, but it is a far
more serious thing to eat up a whole Indian tribe in
one winter and not know it. ·Then, too, the feeling
of remorse that comes over a man when he finds it
out! Ah! it is terrible.

It seems that Josephus Henry Clay Miles, the
cook, had picked off, one by one, the entire tribe,
by watching his chance when one would be alone
gathering moss agates and potato bugs for his breakfast.

I don't eat wild meat of any kind now. My child-
like faith and confidence have been tampered with,
and I am a vegetarian now.

If other people would do as much toward settling
the Indian question as we did, the interior department could take a picnic this summer.

But adoo.

I enclose my dues for this quarter.

SALUBRIOUS J. SMITH,
Past Worthy Prevaricator.

After the reading of the communication, the Most
Noble Prevaricator announced that the meeting
would close with the ode:

> Hark, from the tombs a doleful sound,
> Mine ears attend the cry.
> Brethren, come view the cheerful spot
> Where ye shall shortly lie.

After which the various members filed slowly out, and left Brother Holcomb, the Most Noble Prevari-cator, to turn off the gas and lock up.

A WORD ABOUT WILD SHEEP.

Scribner's Monthly has the following little frag-ment of information relative to western zoology, which we cheerfully reprint. Not so much on ac-count of its novelty, but for the breezy style in which it is narrated:

" At the base of Sheep Rock, one of the winter strongholds of the Shasta flocks, there lives a stock-raiser who has the advantage of observing the movements of wild sheep every winter; and in the course of a conversation with him on the subject of their diving habits, he pointed to the front of a lava headland about a hundred and fifty feet high, which is only eight or ten degrees out of the perpendicular. 'There,' said he, 'I followed a band of them fellows to the back of that rock yonder, and expected to capture them all, for I thought I had a dead thing on them. I got behind them on a narrow bench that runs along the face of the wall near the top, and comes to an end where they couldn't get away with-out falling and being killed; but they jumped off and landed all right as if that were the regular thing with them."

We don't wish to rub off the flush and bloom of this story, because we hate to have any one sit down on a favorite lie of ours, but there are little weak places in the above statement. For instance, a mountain sheep has bowels. He uses them in de-ducting the nutritious properties of the bunch grass and moss agates which he puts into his system. Examination by well known anatomists has shown, that the bowels of the mountain sheep are constructed on the old plan instead of being made of Bessemer steel, with copper rivets and dust-proof brass cap, as is generally supposed.

A fall of 150 feet perpendicularly would mix up the works of a mountain sheep so that he wouldn't know whether he had diphtheria or inflammation of the bowels.

Again, the mountain sheep, like all vertebrates, has a spinal column, something like the editorial column of this paper. The general impression that the backbone of a mountain sheep is made of vulcanized rubber and spiral springs is incorrect. If he were to jump 150 feet, therefore, toward the center of the earth, something would have to flummix.

The chances are that he would find his lumbar vertebrae in his vest pocket and his gambrel joint jammed through his liver. We do not deny that the mountain sheep has a forehead that is harder to drill a fact through than that of the average spring poet, but his forehead only protects his intellect. It don't prevent his hind legs jamming through his diaphragm when he jumps 150 feet, and strikes on a chunk of prehistoric granite.

We don't want to say anything disrespectful of *Scribner's Monthly*, because it is older than we are, and we want to be respectful to old age; but whenever you find a place where a flock of mountain sheep have jumped down a precipice 150 feet deep, you can go and gather up more giblets of wild mutton than you will use all summer

AN EVIDENCE OF SPRING.

The imperial czar of all the tramps was in town to-day. He is traveling *in cog.*, and don't want us to say anything about his presence in the city, for fear the nihilists would get after him.

He is making his sixteenth grand semi-annual farewell bridal tour of the United States. He is a bachelor.

This tramp has the spring style of trousseau, consisting of a costume which, by pulling a tenpenny nail out of the bias folds in front, the entire costume will fall to pieces.

He is looking over the town with a view to investment. If the saloon keepers will leave enough beer in the kegs they stand out on the sidewalks to make a bonus sufficient to warrant him in remaining here, he will do so. He is highly pleased with the town, and says that people have been very kind to him so far, leaving their washings out on the line till after the gloaming, and in other ways showing their free, open, generous western natures.

He says Laramie seems to be a good summer resort for health and pleasure seekers, and that the chickens do not roost so high as he feared they would.

The imperial czar of all tramps says that the ovation tendered him by the police yesterday was very gratifying.

He says he would have made some remarks to that effect, but before he could recover his composure and get his spinal column back into plumb, the police had retired and were kicking a tramp over the top of the opera house by request.

THE FIRST BLOSSOM OF THE SPRING.

The imperial czar wears his hair cut curly, with axle grease and hay in it. He is not very fastidious in his personal appearance, but dresses like a spring poet. He will, this afternoon, once more appear in his favorite flying leap through space, followed by the box-toed boot of the marshal.

WOMAN'S TEARS.

He must be a brute, indeed, who can bring tears to a woman's eyes. His heart must be of stone to enjoy the spectacle of a woman bathed in a flood of wild emotion, with the convulsive sobs shaking her lithe form, while grief, like a tornado, tosses her about like a paper collar box on the bosom of the boiling torrent.

Few men have the hardihood to look a grief-stricken woman in the face while her nose swells up, angry and irritated, in the distance. Few men are so lost to all the better feelings of our nature as to do an act which will thaw out the frizzes and flood the features of the woman he loves.

This is one reason why many men are kind to their wives, who would otherwise be cruel and heartless. They do not want to see the wife of their bosom looking as though she had erysipelas in her nose.

It isn't the grief of the wives that is killing off our husbands. It is the terrible shock to their æsthetic taste. No husband can bear to view the howling waste after the washout has subsided and the bridge is repaired.

Then, fellow men, on our journey to the tomb, let us resolve that we will not do or say anything

that will bring the hectic flush to the nose of her to
whom we have vowed lifelong fidelity. Let us, so
far as possible, stave off the storm, and if tears
must be shed, let us shed them ourselves. Most of
us are so ding busted homely that it don't make any
difference whether we color our nose cherry red or
sage green.

Then again, if we weep pretty promisciously, and
keep our noses middling red, perhaps we can fool
the temperance people, and thus regain some of the
respect we have lost.

HOW A MINE IS WORKED

"I wish you would tell me all about the way men
get gold and silver out of a mine, my dear," said a
lady in East Laramie the other evening to her husband, as he peeled off his coat and sat down in three
chairs for the evening. "I hear you talk with your
friends so much about mining, and I am not able to
understand it, or converse with people intelligibly
about it."

"Well, what kind of mining do you want to hear
about; gold or silver, quartz or placer, deposit or defined lead?"

"Well, all of them briefly. I want to know
whether they scrape off the gold from the under side
of the ground, and wash the dirt off in the creek, or
how is it?"

"Well, they don't scrape it off the under side of
the ground, exactly. There you are in error. In
placer mining, they have to collect the dust and pan
it out with a gold pan,"

"Oh! they have to use a gold pan, do they? That must be what makes mining so expensive. Does the pan have to be solid gold?"

"No. It isn't made of gold. It is simply to pan gold; hence the name. In quartz mining, the prospector first finds the float, and tracing it to the lead, he begins to dig for the purpose of ascertaining how extensive it is, and what it will assay."

"Oh, that is it. I thought they first bored into the ground with a paystreak until they found the shaft, and then they drifted for the assessment, and when they found that, they just put a blast in the indications and salted the dump. Now it seems that you don't do that way. You follow up the micacious slate till you strike the bias fold. Then you see if you can find a color that matches with the copper-stained trilobites, that you prospect and you——"

"No, I must stop you there. You are getting a little off the vein. You probably have the right idea, but you are using terms that are not correct. After they get the wall rock on the dump and pinch out the night shift, they salt the contact and blast the vertical chilblain. Then they drift for the blossom rock, baled hay and poverty till they strike the varicose vein. After that it is a short job to put on the bias folds and sample the stockholders. When the bituminous duplex bisects the brocaded porphyry and scallops the gouge with cross-eyed shirrings and bi-carbonate of bilious colic interlaced with moire antique wads of gray copper and free milling erysipelas. This is not always the case, however, for indirectly or inversely, perhaps more, or sometimes less, as the case may be, and still we might or might not, according to whether we did or not, but also besides, if not always, as already described, perhaps, yet I wouldn't be positive of anything which might be doubtful."

Then he laughed a cold, hard laugh, and went to bed. If husbands would always explain these things to their wives, how much pleasanter our homes would be,

THE AVERAGE MAN.

Careful research shows that there are only two men out of a possible 500 who know how to do the marketing. The other 498 don't hit it very accurately.

This article is devoted to the hopeless majority of those who either don't buy anything or who buy the wrong thing. The man who is told in a delightfully vague and indefinite way in the morning to "get something for dinner," goes down town, and, while on his way to the market, his attention is called to a chunk of ore that goes away up in the thousands, and which a new arrival has brought down from the mountains. While looking it over, a man comes along who wants to see the aforesaid man of family at his office. Then they adjourn to the office, and, wrapped in business, he don't ever think of the matter of food again.

He goes home humming a low tune to himself, and thinking what a good, true, noble wife he has, and what a staving Delmonico layout for a dinner she can get up.

When he gets in the house, she looks at him more in sorrow than in anger, and they sit down to boiled rice and the shattered remains of a mackerel.

The methodical man, after breakfast, writes down the order in his note book for

3 dozen eggs,
3 porterhouse steaks,
¼ yard silicia,
3 boxes strawberries,
2 dozen pearl buttons,
1 loaf bread,
3 bars soap.

These he writes as his wife gives them to him. A woman prefers to mix her order for grub with an order for dry goods.

The methodical man does not look in his note book again until the following autumn.

Then he reads it as a curiosity, and smiles and congratulates himself because he has saved $5 in provisions that he has forgotten.

Then there is the man who buys in bad taste. He buys a good deal some days, and very little other days, but he is always arranging to have a dinner of lobster salad and pie, or a banquet of baked beans with strawberries and cream. He don't know what articles match, and if he arranges to have a custard pie and sausage, he thinks that he has secured a triumph.

What does he know about taste and pleasing artistic effect? What does he know of the dreamy harmony of scalloped oysters and celery, or the outrage upon cultured taste when a dinner is concocted in which olive green is matched with navy blue?

This is the style of man who loves to go into the pantry at 9 o'clock p. m., when stillness and the protecting shadows of night shut down on him, and put the most delightful medley of crabapple jelly and sardines, and rhubarb pie and cheese, and Charlotte russe and dried beef, and jam and nightmare, and cucumbers and vinegar and ice cream into his vitals that ever delighted the heart of an ambitious coroner.

Indeed, this is becoming an age of artists in every line and department, and the man who don't have any soul or eye for the beautiful in the grub line, and who don't understand a symphony in hash, might as well curl up in the corner of a fence and die.

A HEADLIGHT IN VIEW.

THE CONDUCTOR'S STORY OF A NIGHT TRAIN ON THE UNION PACIFIC.

"Yes," said the conductor, biting off the tip of a cigar and slowly scratching a match on his leg, "I've seen a good deal of railroad life that's interesting and exciting in the twenty years that I've been twisting brakes and slamming doors for a living.

"I've seen all kinds of sorrow and all kinds of joy —seen the happy bridal couple starting out on their wedding tour with the bright and hopeful future before them, and the black-robed mourner on her way to a new-made grave wherein she must bury the idol of her lonely old heart.

Wealth and pinching poverty ride on the same train, and the merry laugh of the joyous, healthy child is mingled with the despairing sigh of the aged. The great antipodes of life are familiar to the conductor for every day the extremes of the world are meeting beneath his eye.

"I've mutilated the ticket of many a black-leg and handled the passes of all our most eminent dead-heads. I don't know what walk of life is more crowded with thrilling incidents than mine."

"Ever have any smash-ups?"

"Smash-ups? Oh, yes, several of them. None, however, that couldn't have been a good deal worse.

"There is one incident of my railroad life," continued the conductor, running his tongue carefully over a broken place in the wrapper of his cigar, "that I never spoke of before to any one. It has caused me more misery and wretchedness than any one thing that ever happened to me in my official career.

"Sometimes even now, after the lapse of many years, I awake in the night with the cold drops of agony standing on my face and the horrible nightmare upon me with its terrible surroundings, as plain as on the memorable night it occurred.

"I was running extra on the Union Pacific for a conductor who was an old friend of mine, and who had gone South on a vacation for his health.

"At about 7:30, as near as I can remember, we were sailing along all comfortable one evening with a straight stretch of track ahead for ten or fifteen miles, running on time and everybody feeling tip-top, as overland travelers do who get acquainted with each other and feel congenial. All at once the

train suddenly slowed down, ran in on an old siding
and stopped.

" Of course, I got out and ran ahead of the engine
to see what the matter was.   Old Antifat, the engineer, had got down and was on the main track looking ahead to where, twinkling along about six or
seven miles down the road, apparently, was the
headlight of an approaching train.   It was evidently ' wild ' for nothing was due that we knew of at
that hour.

"However, we had been almost miraculously
saved from a frightful wreck by the engineer's
watchfulness, and everybody went forward and
shook old Antifat by the hand and cried and thank-
ed him till it was the most affecting scene for a
while that I ever witnessed.   It was as though we
had stopped upon the very verge of a bottomless
chasm, and everybody was laughing and crying at
once, till it was a kind of a cross between a revival
and a picnic.

"After we had waited about half an hour, I should
say, for the blasted train to come up and pass us,
and apparently she was no nearer, a cold, clammy
suspicion began to bore itself into the adamantine
shell of my intellect.   The more I thought of it, the
more unhappy I felt.   I almost wished that I was
dead.   Cold streaks ran up my back followed by hot
ones.   I wanted to go home.   I wanted to be where
the hungry, prying eyes of the great, throbbing
work-day world could not see me.

" I called Antifat one side and said something to
him.   He swore softly to himself and kicked the
ground, and looked at the headlight still glimmering
in the distance.   Then he got on his engine and I

yelled 'All aboard.' In a few moments we were
moving again, and the general impression was that
the train ahead was side tracked and waiting for us,
although there wasn't a side track within twenty
miles, except the one we had just left.

"It was never exactly clear to the passengers
where we passed that wild train, but I didn't explain it to them. I was too much engrossed with my
surging thoughts.

"I never felt my own inferiority so much as I did
that night. I never so fully realized what a mere
speck man is upon the bosom of the universe.

"When I surveyed the starry vault of heaven and
considered its illimitable space, where, beyond and
stretching on and on forever, countless suns. are
placed as centers, around which solar systems are
revolving in their regular orbits, each little world
peopled perhaps with its teeming millions of struggling humanity, and then other and mightier systems of worlds revolving about these systems till
the mind is dazed and giddy with the mighty
thought; and then when I compared all this universal magnificence, this brilliant aggregation of
worlds and systems of worlds, with one poor, grov-
elling worm of the dust, only a little insignificant
atom, only a poor, weak, erring, worthless, fallible,
blind, groping railroad conductor, with my train
peacefully sidetracked in the gathering gloom and
and patiently waiting for the planet Venus to pass
on the main track, there was something about the
whole somber picture that has overshadowed my
whole life and made me unhappy, and wretched,
while others were gay.

5 .

"Sometimes Antifat and myself meet at some liquid restaurant and silently take something in memory of our great sorrow, but never mention it. We never tear open the old rankling wound or laugh over the night we politely gave the main track to Venus while we stood patiently on the siding.

SLIDING DOWN LEAD MOUNTAIN.

Lead Mountain in North Park is a very steep mountain. It is so steep that if a vein of quartz has much dip, it runs through the mountain and out into the delightful climate on the other side, and sticks into space like a sore thumb.

Well, when the weather warms up in the spring, and the balmy breath of April begins to start the asparagus and the perspiration a little, the south side of Lead Mountain is a pretty smooth place, and a man has to stick his toenails into the face of nature clear up to his elbows, or he won't be there after awhile.

The clay thaws out and puts the polish on the mountain, so that in climbing the hill, a man's recoil is more than his propulsive velocity.

The other day a miner went up there, before the side of the mountain got warmed up in the morning. and after he had prospected around a few hours, he decided to return.

He returned a good deal quicker than he aimed to. He came in ahead of time about two weeks.

Most every one at the foot of the hill, of course. was glad to see him, but they were so surprised at his rash and hasty return that they didn't have any band out, and the speaker hadn't fixed up his impromptu speech of welcome already.

The miner himself seemed to regret this hasty move on his part. If he hadn't been in such a hurry to come in, two weeks ahead of schedule time, he wouldn't have worn out his wardrobe so much.

As it was, he only had on his shirt collar and his boot heels, and he wasn't at all certain about them.

He backed off about ten yards and crawled into a gunny sack, and then he told them how it was.

He said he knew he wasn't due there at that time, but in turning around, both feet struck out toward the milky way, and then he sat down, and as he shed his clothes, he gathered velocity till, when he got to the foot of the hill, the velocity that he had accumulated was about all that he had on, and he felt as though he had sat down on a conflagration.

The side of the hill looks now as though a gents' furnishing house had busted up in business there.

In twenty years from now some old goggle-eyed relic hunter will find the fragment of a tobacco box or a suspender buckle, and he will present it to some scientific warehouse of prehistoric pitch-forks and pre-Adamite shotguns, and he will write a long article showing how the civilized nations of his day have not excelled, or even equaled, the mighty achievements of the people who inhabited this country in the second and third centuries.

Some people will be fooled by it; but there is one man now living, and whose system is frescoed with court-plaster all over, pretty near, and he won't take it in. He will have the documents to show that it is an error.

A FATAL THIRST.

From the London *Lancet* we learn that "many years ago a case was recorded by Dr. Otto, of Copenhagen, in which 495 needles passed through the skin of a hysterical girl, who had probably swallowed them during a hysterical paroxysm, but these all emerged from the regions below the diaphragm, and were collected in groups, which gave rise to inflammatory swellings of some size. One of these contained 100 needles. Quite recently Dr. Bigger described, before the Society Surgery, of Dublin, a case in which more than 300 needles were removed from the body of a woman. It is very remarkable in how few cases the needles were the cause of death, and how slight an interference with function their presence and movement cause."

It would seem from the cases on record that needles in the system rather assist in the digestion and promote longevity.

For instance, we will suppose that the hysterical girl above alluded to, with 495 needles in her stomach, should absorb the midsummer cucumber. Think how interesting those needles would make it for the great colic promoter.

We can imagine the cheerful smile of the cucumber as it enters the stomach, and bowing cheerfully to the follicles standing around, hangs its hat upon the walls of the stomach, stands its umbrella in a corner, and proceeds to get in its work.

All at once the cucumber looks surprised and grieved about something. It stops in its heaven-born colic generation and pulls a rusty needle out of its person. Maddened by the pain, it once more attacks the digestive apparatus, and once more accumulates a choice job lot of needles.

Again and again it enters into the unequal contest, each time losing ground and gaining ground, till the poor cucumber, with assorted hardware sticking out in all directions like the hair on a cat's tail, at last curls up like a caterpillar, and yields up the victory.

Still, this needle business will be expensive to husbands if wives once acquire the habit and allow it to obtain the mastery over them.

If a wife once permits this demon appetite for cambric needles to get control of the house, it will soon secure a majority in the senate, and then there will be trouble.

The woman who once begins to tamper with cambric needles is not safe. She may think that she has power to control her appetite, but it is only a step to the maddening thirst for the soul-destroying darning needle, and perhaps to the button-hook and carpet stretcher.

It is safer and better to crush the first desire for needles than when it is too late to undertake reformation from the abject slavery to this hellish thirst.

We once knew a sweet young creature with dewy eye and breath like timothy hay. Her merry laugh rippled out upon the summer air like the joyful music of baldheaded bobolinks.

Everybody loved her, and she loved everybody, too. But in a thoughtless moment she swallowed a cambric needle. This did not satisfy her. The cruel thraldom had begun. Whenever she felt depressed and gloomy there was nothing that would kill her ennui and melancholy but the fatal needle cushion.

From this she rapidly became more reckless, till there was hardly an hour that she was not under the influence of needles.

If she couldn't get needles to assauge her mad thirst, she would take hair-pins or door keys. She gradually pined away to a mere skeleton. She could no longer sit on one foot and be happy.

Life for her was filled with opaque gloom and sadness. At last she took an overdose of sheep shears and monkey wrenches one day, and on the following morning her soul had lit out for the land of eternal summer.

We should learn from this to shun the maddening needle cushion as we would a viper, and never tell a lie.

ORATION.

DELIVERED JULY 4TH, BY POP-EYED CATERPILLAR, OF THE UTE NATION.

WARRIORS OF MY PEOPLE:

You come together to-day beneath the forest shade, to celebrate the white man's anniversary.

It is a proud day for the paleface. It marks the crowding years since he got the bulge on his oppressors. It is the tally by which he reckons the flight of time since he banged the snoot of tyranny.

This glorious day is not for the red man. He feels the thrill of conscious pride and greatness, it is true, but he awakes on the following day to find nothing but vain regret. The joy of the red man is fleeting. It is a hollow mockery, a snare and a delusion. I see the flush mantle in your dark cheeks to-day, but to-morrow it will be but a bob-tail flush.

A FEW PRELIMINARY REMARKS.

The patriotism you feel to-day will only give place to depression and gloom. You are proud now, and complacent, and drunk. You are brave and high-strung, and heap bad man from away back; but when another sun shall rise upon White river my people will be subdued.

Look at Bran Mash Susan. She comes here to-day clothed as the Goddess of Liberty. She is the fair daughter of the full moon. That is why she is full.

Look at Peeled Nose Blizzard, the daughter of the whirlwind. She represents the state called by the paleface the Empire state. She is clothed in a flour sack, as the emblem of purity. Across her back, in red letters, is the inscription:

SNOWFLAKE

F L O U R.

X X X X

That is because she is the flower of our tribe.

And yet she, too, is as drunk as a biled owl. As her tawny features are turned toward mine I see that she does not know whether there are two ora-tors or nine addressing this audience.

Look at Vinegar Bitters Pocahontas. Clothed in a coffee sack and gloom, she is in the land of slum-ber. On this great day she sleeps the hours away, while the blue-tail fly frolics over her copper colored nose.

We were once a nation of orators. Our people once listened to the silvery tones of those who told them of their wrongs and bade them brace up.

Now the shattered fragment of a great nation gath-ers in the hot canyon, wrapped in nothing but a brown study, and snores through the tardy hours.

A few more summers, and your tale will be told.
The red man never weeps. He may suffer, but he
scorns to cry like a woman. Pop Eyed Caterpillar's
heart is filled with sorrow for his people, but he will
not squeal. His soul is full of agony, but he will
not give way to scalding weep.

Each year we go upon the warpath, but we do no
damage. We kill a few consumptives, it is true,
but it is not a glittering success. Our warriors are
too prone to relent when there is danger near.
They spare the paleface who happens to be armed
and show mercy to the able-bodied Caucasian with
the double-barreled shotgun. He always spares the
paleface who is loaded.

Once we went upon the warpath to protect our devoted squaws. Then they were fair to look upon,
and brave and true. We gladly faced death to
show our devotion to the bronze beauties of our nation.

Now it is not so. Times have changed. The
maidens and matrons of our tribe are not beautiful.
They have ruined their complexion with fat pork
and whisky. You can purchase a whole herd of
them at 5 cents a bunch.

Most of them would stop a clock with their wild
peculiar beauty. Look at Coyote Kate, who walked
away with the clam-shell bracelets voted to the
most beautiful belle of the White River Agency.

Her nose is three-quarters of an inch out of plumb,
and she has a wart over her eye like a moss agate.

Warriors! must we lay down our lives in order to
leave a widow who wears cavalry pants, and whose
cooing voice sounds like the sad refrain of a planing
mill?

I trow not.

When we die and are laid to rest beneath the cot-tonwood in the valley, we want to be mourned over by brown-eyed gazelles, whose general appearance will not kill the vegetation.

We cannot give up our heart's blood for sweet-hearts and wives with feet like a sugar cured ham, and hair like the soft tresses of a bald-headed shoe brush.

The only hope for our tribe is for each warrior to plight his troth to one of these club-footed damsels, and then rush madly into battle, that they may climb the golden stair, and thus evade their horrid fate.

If there be aught that would nerve our flagging warriors to brave death and destruction, it is this.

PATRICK OLESON.

OR, THE NEW STYLE OF SPRING ANECDOTE.

Many years ago, on the banks of the Pulgarlic River, lived a poor boy named Patrick Oleson. When Patrick was only a year old, his father and mother got into a little difficulty, in which the mother was killed. The father, as soon as he re-gained his composure, saw that he had gone too far, and when the sheriff came and marched him off to jail, he frankly confessed that he had been perhaps too hasty.

Still, public opinion seemed turned against him; and in the following spring Patrick's father was unanimously chosen by a convention of six property-

holders of the county to jump from a new pine platform into the sweet subsequently.

The affair was a success, and Patrick was left an
orphan at the tender age of one and one-half years
to wrestle for himself. His first impulse was to write
humorous letters to the press, and thus become afflu-
ent; but the papers that were solvent returned his
letters, and the papers that accepted them busted
the subsequent autumn. So Patrick decided that as
soon as he could complete a college course that
would fit him for the position, he would either enter
the ministry or become a railroad man.

While at college he read the story of an engineer
who had saved the life of a little child by grabbing
it from the cow-catcher while the train was going at
lightning speed, and, as a result, was promoted to
general passenger agent of the road.

So Patrick decided to be a railroad man and save
some children from being squashed by the train, so
that he could be promoted and get a big salary. He
therefore studied to fit himself for the position to
which he aspired, and after five years' hard study
he graduated with high honors and a torpid liver.

He then sought out a good paying road that he
thought he would eventually like to be president of,
and applied for a position on it.

By waiting till the following spring he got a job
braking extra, averaging $13 per month, till one day
he screwed up a brake too tight and wore out a
wheel on the caboose. After that he was called into
the office of the superintendent, as Patrick supposed,
to take the superintendent's place, perhaps; but the
superintendent swore at him and called him Flat-

wheel Oleson, and told him he had better hoe corn and smash potato-bugs for a livelihood.

Patrick felt hurt and grieved, and, more in sorrow than in anger, he got the oriental grand bounce, and had to rustle for another job. This time he tried to secure the position of master mechanic; but when the road to which he applied found out that he didn't know the difference between the cow-catcher and the automatic air brake, Patrick was appointed as assistant polisher and wiper extraordinary at the roundhouse.

All this time he never drank a drop or uttered a profane word. No matter how much he was imposed upon, he never got mad or quarreled with the other men. He sometimes felt sorely tried, but he saw that other railroad men did not swear, so he did not.

After nine years of mental strain in the roundhouse, he was put on the road as a fireman on 259. he was now, after sixteen years' hard study and perseverance, on the road to promotion.

Just as soon as he could find a child on the track, some day, and snatch the innocent little thing from the jaws of death, he felt that he would be solid. Sometimes he would allow his mind to dwell on this subject so long that his fire would go out and the engineer would report him, and the old man would lay him off to give him a chance to think it over.

Three years Patrick fired on 259, and there wasn't a child that got within 1,300 feet of the track when his engine came by. They seemed to know that Patrick was perishing to save a child from being flattened out by the train.

He began to get discouraged. He said he would
try it another year, and if he failed he would have
to give up railroading and go to congress.

One day he had just fired up the 259 in good shape
and looked out of the window ahead, when he saw
a little child toddling along towards them and only
a few yards away, while the engine shrieked like a
demon, and the little chubby baby came on toward
the rushing monster, whose hot breath, with short,
sharp hisses, rushed through the June morning.

Patrick felt that the joy or sorrow of a whole lifetime was in store for him. It was not only life or
death to the joyous parents, but it was the culmina-
tion of the hopes and fears, the agony, the self-denial and the disappointments of his whole life, and
the opening up of a new future to him, or it was another lost opportunity and the continuation of a
long, dreary, uneventful journey to the grave.

He was out on the pilot in an instant. He did not
breathe. The rushing engine trembled beneath him,
and like a flash the still laughing child was in his
strong arms.

He had triumphed. The goal was reached. The
great struggle was over, and in a few days he would
be president of the road. He got home, and a man
came toward him with a document of some kind.
His breath came short and hard. It was probably
his credentials as president of the road. He took it
and read it over in a sort of dream. It was only a
notice that his board bill had been garnisheed, and
the superintendent told him that he must pay it or
the company would have to squeeze along without
his services.

In the morning the papers had a short account of Patrick's bravery, but it was spoken of simply as "an almost fatal accident," and Patrick's name appeared as Ole Fitzpatrick. He began to feel that he wasn't getting a fair shake. His promotion to the presidency of the road seemed to lag. There was a hitch in the senate probably about his confirmation or something of that kind. The acting president of the corporation selfishly retained his position, and looked so healthy, and seemed so pleased with himself that Patrick lost all patience.

One day a man with a wart on his nose met Patrick on the street and asked him if he was the gallant fireman of 259 who saved a little child a week or two ago.

Patrick said he was.

The man grasped his hand and said:

"That was my child. It was almost the only child I had. I only had nine others, and would have been almost childless if little James Abraham Garfield had been busted. You have done a brave, noble act, and the Lord will reward you. I am a poor man, as you would readily guess by my clothing and the fact that we have ten children. I cannot reward you with wealth or position, but I don't want to seem ungrateful or close or contiguous. Come with me, my benefactor, and I will shake you for the drinks."

Then Patrick Oleson went away where he could be alone with his surging thoughts. He is now running a hurdy gurdy in the San Juan country.

This story is only partially true. The main fact, however, viz.: that a child wasn't run over by a train, is true. It is different from most stories about

saving children; but the spring style of story is a little different from that of former seasons, anyway.

In the spring style of prevarication, the engineer
will either fail to grab the child in time and there
will be nothing left on the track but a gingham
apron and a grease spot, or, if he succeeds in saving the child, he will not get the position of ser-
geant-at-arms and a gold-headed cane, as was formerly the style.

THE EDITORIAL DESK.

People have heard for centuries of the museum
which is contained in a boy's pockets, and the wild
and dazzling array of curiosities from the four quarters of the globe which are concealed in the recesses
of a young lady's portmonaie, but it has remained
for the heaven-born genius who pens these lines to
write up the editor's desk.

For the sake of convenience, we will take our own
desk and dissect it.

The desk on which we are writing is a flat black
walnut arrangement, with drawers on the left down
to the floor, and pigeon holes on the right, leaving a
square aperture between, through which we run our
legs, allowing them to protrude about a yard beyond
the desk, and to dally with the letter press on the
other side. While writing a deep and particularly
choice and all-wool editorial, we scratch one foot
against the other and dig our toes into the carpet.

We state this simply to enlighten the average
reader on one of the peculiar phases of genius.

On the top of the desk are the *Free Press, Hawk-
eye, Oil City Derrick,* and some other exchanges,

with their vitals cut out. Near by are the iron
scissors, with wabbly blades, that have done the
damage.

There is also a glass inkstand, with some coagu-
lated ink and dead flies in it, a match box with no
matches in it, four crippled and disabled pens, a
pile of neglected and moss-covered bills with the
editor's name at the head, and apparently sent by
anonymous parties, as there is no signature at the
bottom.

Then there is a cob pipe, with the end of the stem
chewed up, and showing what an inspired grip the
editor holds it by when he writes a poem on " The
Cold, Dead Memories of the Busted Past."

On top of all these, some blank paper and manuscript are corded about nine feet high.

In the first drawer are some envelopes, an un-
answered letter from Queen Victoria, and a package
of Old Judge smoking tobacco.

In the next drawer there are a lot of letter heads,
some bill heads, a poem on " Towser's Excursion up
the Flume," and a pair of kids once white as the
beautiful snow, but now considerably damaged.

Then there is a faded spray of mignonette, or cat-
nip, or something of that character, a bit of pale
blue ribbon that fell from her hair in the cherished
long ago, and near it a forgotten $20 gold piece, an
annual pass over the Panama canal, a defunct meal
ticket and a clove.

In the third drawer is a letter from Roscoe Conkling acknowledging the receipt of the last speech
we wrote for him, and promising us that he would
quit chewing tobacco next fall. Then there are

lot of expired passes over various eastern roads, an
old deck of cards that we secured at great cost intending to write a caustic article on the vice of High
Low Jack and the Game.

In the pigeon holes are letters from Eli Perkins
and Mr. Childs, and a poem on "The Sore-Eyed
Pollywog's Sorrowful End," by Henry Ward
Beecher, but having been written on both sides it
was laid aside.

Then there are also an assortment of fly hooks,
some silk line, and a leather-covered Etruscan jar,
with the almost forgotten fragrance inside of rattlesnake antidote and cramp discourager. Then there
is a leather book with another assortment of hooks,
one still baited with the dried mummy of a grass-
hopper.

Besides these there are two stubs of lead pencils,
a cigar holder, a well worn Bible, and a confidential
postal card from George Washington, asking if it
would be advisable to cross the Delaware on the ice
in August.

In a little box, snugly imbedded in jeweler's cotton, is a bent and disfigured suspender button, rust-
ed with innumerable tear drops and grimy with
time and disuse. It is all that is mortal of the man
who asked: "Is this hot enough for you?"

Then there are tearful and misspelled letters from
R. B. Hayes, asking us about what policy he had
better pursue relative to civil service reform, and
requesting suggestions about making root beer and
going without a hired girl. There are, too, letters
from Professor Proctor and other sky prospectors,
asking us to go with them and gather some fresh
laid comets as soon as we could leave our work.

There are also earnest, noble, letters of tearful regret and grief-stricken promises to do better, written
by ex-Secretary Evarts, in which God is spelled with
a little g, and cabbage is spelled with a k.

And yet there are people who think an editor's
desk is not rich in memories of the dead and busted
long ago.

THE ORIENTAL STRING BEAN PROMOTER.

Tu Long, the Chinese Le Duc of South Laramie,
hasn't been very successful with his farm this year.
The spring was early enough to warrant a good crop,
but somehow things didn't work right. Tu Long's
farm, which is about the size of a door mat, lies five
feet higher than the creek from which he is supposed
to get his irrigation, and the labor necessary in order to coax the water up this side hill has occupied
a good deal of his time, and been the cause of a good
deal of cross-eyed, fire-cracker profanity on the part
of the meek and lowly heathen.

When disaster and affliction get after a Chinaman
it is as good as a scientific lecture to watch the
course of the proceedings.

Just as the rutabaga conservatory got to looking
pretty plenty, the latter part of June, there was a
frost in South Laramie that gathered in the crop and
made it look sick. This made Tu Long gloomy. He
began to lose faith in the club-footed bass-wood god
that he kept behind the door.

He said hard, mean things about Buddha or
Gehenna, or some other great Chinese deity, and
made remarks, in his broken way, that reflected on

the general management of the universe, and the Rocky mountain region in particular.

But he planted some more China cabbage, and water-proof lettuce, and patent chilled radishes and other tropical plants, and patiently carried water to them in an old oyster can. He did everything that a solicitous Chinaman with no other visible means of support could do to make that garden blossom like the rose, but it wouldn't blossom. It just seemed to hang fire, somehow, and fool along till the Fourth of July, and then a Texas cow that had just completed her fortieth day without food walked into the plaza where the consumptive lettuce and convalescent cabbage stood, waiting for a merciful death to put them out of their misery, and she ate up the products of the entire ranch. Then she ate the ghastly relics of the frostbitten crop, and wiped her feet on the onion beds.

When the glad morning dawned in all the beauty of a mountain daybreak, with the glorious orb of day slowly climbing the Black Hills, and the summer landscape of green bunch grass on the western divide slowly melting into the deep green of the mountain pines, and then all at once changing to the eternal whiteness and snow-capped glory of the eternal hills, Tu Long slowly awoke and stretched his limbs.

Then he said something that sounded like the squeak of an old-fashioned bedstead.

Then he arose. He dressed himself by putting on a hat and sticking his unnatural feet into a couple of wall pockets with cork soles that stood near by.

Then he went to the door to see how the laminated

steel turnips and galvanized carrots were looking.
They were not there.

They had melted into the great unknown. Where
they once stood there was a boundless waste of ruin
and desolation and a bronco cow, whose breath
smelled strong of onions.

Tu Long picked up the stave of an old kerosene
barrel and went after that cow in a blind, impulsive
way, that took up the morning session and filled the
summer sky full of wild-eyed Chinaman and chao-
tic cow.

Tu Long now buys his vegetables in Ogden, and
has them expressed to him. He desires also to rent
his farm to a baseball club for one year, with the
privilege of extending the lease from July 4th on
through the revolving years of eternity.

Our exchanges are saying a good deal about the
longevity of those who jump the rope. Big-Nose
George, formerly a highway robber of our acquaintance, died from over-exerting himself in that way.
He tried to jump clear over the place where the rope
was tied, but the boys pulled the barrel out from
under him, and he took a hop, skip and jump over
the battlements into the wide stretch of mystery.

STRIVE TO EXCEL.

Many years ago, when the State of New York was
in a wild and unsettled condition, and infested by
the wolf, the bear, and the army worm, there lived
on the banks of the Hudson a little boy with soft
blue eyes and a sore toe.

He early learned that what was worth doing at all
was worth doing well, and so whatever he did, he

did the best he knew how. No matter whether he was called upon to hoe the waving corn or to put a split stick on a dog's tail, little William always did his level best.

Thus he grew to manhood, always striving toward perfection in everything. When he was sent out into the world he cast about in his mind to know what he should do for a livelihood.

It soon occurred to him that robbing the mountain stage coaches of Wyoming and Colorado would be a middling remunerative calling, and, as it required no special outlay of capital, he adopted it as his profession.

Though at times unfortunate, he was always cheerful. When he robbed a stage coach containing only one passenger, and he an editor, with nothing in his pocket but a buckskin string and a pass, he never murmured or complained. He would ask the editor in that merry, frolicksome way of his to give him a puff, and then he would let him go.

Years went slowly by, the summer succeeding the balmy spring, and autumn following on the heels of summer, according to a time-honored custom, when one day William stopped a down coach from the mines, and in the mellow moonlight jabbed his revolver into the window, coupled with a request for scads.

There seemed to be a reluctance on the part of the passengers to contribute any wealth, but they lavished about a bushel of buckshot on William and his gang. It seemed that they didn't have any money, but such as they had they cheerfully turned over to the outlaws.

When the smoke had cleared away, William was found with some buckshot under his shoulder-blade and his nose shot off. All his men were extremely deceased.

Then they took William to a hospital and tenderly watched over him till he got well. After that these good Samaritans clubbed together and hung him. But it was a grand success. William was hung with more eclat than anyone else had ever been. People who witnessed the exercises said that they never new a man to straighten out a rope with more unstudied grace and earnest zeal than William did.

He seemed to throw the whole vim and concentrated energy of a lifetime into this emphatic gesture.

As he hung there limp and exhausted at the end of the rope, the chairman of the vigilance committee said, while he took a cigar from William's vest pocket and lit it, that he had never known a man to jump into the bosom of the great uncertain with more chic or more sprightly grace and precision than William had.

This should teach us the importance of doing everything thoroughly and well. Whatever we undertake, aim to do it better than anyone else. It is better to be hung and know that we have brought out all there was in the part, and to know that we expiated our crimes in a way calculated to win the respect of all, than even to run for the senate and get scooped.

PARABLE OF THE WEDDING GARMENT.

The kingdom of heaven is like a certain railroad king who made a marriage for his son.

And sent forth his servants to call them that were bidden to the wedding, and they would not come.

Again he sent forth other servants, saying, tell them which are bidden; behold, I have killed the old hen, and prepared the wedding dinner, and opened a keg of nails, and all things are ready for the blow-out.

But they made light of it, and went their ways, one to his farm, another to his drug store, and another to his grist mill, and the remainder took the servants and entreated them spitefully, and put a tin ear on them, and frescoed them with Michael Angelo eggs.

But when the railroad king heard of it, he bounced the entire outfit, and shut off on their passes and raised their freight tariff, and busted them up in their business, and smote them sore on the gable end of their intellects, and made it red-hot for them.

Then said he unto his servants, the wedding is ready, but they which were bidden were not worthy.

Go ye, therefore, down to the side-tracks and into the roundhouse, and the water-tank and cabooses, and gravel trains, and gather together as many as ye shall find, and tell them to come over to the wedding feast and fill themselves up.

And the servants went forth and rounded up as many as they could find, both bad and good, and bade them to the feast.

And when the king went into the reception room he found there a man who had not on a spike-tail coat, and low-neck shoes, and clocked socks.

And he saith unto him, "Pardner, how cometh it that thou art here without any store clothes on, and wearing instead, a linen duster and jim-crow raiment generally?"

And the man was speechless at first, but he answered yet again:

"O, railroad king! live forever. I know that I am here without a wedding garment; but, behold, I am a conductor on thy line, and I have reformed and have ceased to 'knock down,' and, behold, thy servant is poor, for he is trying to live on his salary."

And the king was very wroth, and he told the usher to gather him in and to take him by the slack of his raiment and cast him over the outer wall, and there was weeping and gnashing of teeth.

And while the wedding guests made merry and whooped it up, the man who was cast out did steal around to the back door and become solid with the cook, and filled himself up with the wedding feast on the side.

And it came to pass that when he had eaten of the fatted calf and the wedding cake, and absorbed all the champagne that he could carry away, he crawled into the hay-mow and slept till the cock crew.

And when the morning was come he journeyed over the railroad track toward Salt Lake, for behold, he was a tramp.

THE FUN OF BEING PRESIDENT.

It is not an enjoyable treat sometimes to be the editor of a paper, and mould public opinion at so much per mould and complimentary tickets to the sleight-of-hand performances, but with its care and worry, its heartache and apprehensions, it is more comforting on the whole than being president.

When we were a boy, and sat in the front row among the pale haired boys with checked gingham shirts at the Sabbath School, and the teacher told us to live uprightly and learn a hundred verses of the Scriptures each week so that we could be president, we thought that unruffled calm and universal approbation waited upon the man who successfully rose to be the executive of a great nation.

With years and accumulated wisdom, however, we have changed our mind.

Now we sit at our desk and write burning words for the press that will live and keep warm long after we are turned to dust and ashes. We write heavy editorials on the pork outlook, and sadly compose exhaustive treatises on the chinch bug, while men in other walks of life go out into the health-promoting mountains, and catch trout and woodticks. Our lot is not perhaps a joyous one. We swelter through the long July days with our suspenders hanging in limp festoons down over our chair, while we wield the death-dealing pen, but we do not want to be president

Our salary is smaller, it is true, but when we get through our work in the middle of the night, and put on our plug hat and spike-tail coat and steal home through the all-pervading darkness, we thank our stars, as we split the kindling and bed down the family mule, that on the morrow, although we may be licked by the man we wrote up to-day, our official record cannot be attacked.

There is a nameless joy settles down upon us as we retire to our simple couch on the floor and pull the cellar door over us to keep us warm, which the world can neither give nor take away.

We plod along from day to day, slicing great wads of mental pabulum from our bulging intellect, never murmuring nor complaining when lawyers and physicians put on their broad-brim chip hats and go out to the breezy canyons and the shady glens to regain their health.

We just plug along from day to day, eating a hard boiled egg from one hand while we write a scathing criticism on the sic transit gloria cucumber with the other.

No, we do not crave the proud position of president, nor do we hanker to climb to an altitude where forty or fifty millions of civilized people can distinctly see whether we eat custard pie with a knife or not.

Once in awhile, however, in the stillness of the night, we kick the covers off and moan in our dreams as we imagine that we are president, and we wake with a cold damp sweat (or perspiration as the case may be,) standing out of every pore, only to find that we are not president after all, by an overwhelming majority, and we get up and steal away to the rain-water barrel and take a drink, and go back to a dreamless, snoreless sleep.

THE ANTELOPE AS A PET.

United States Marshal Schnitger is a very kind hearted man, and he loves to have all kinds of pets about his home. Among the animal favorites that hang around the marshal's house on the banks of the Laramie is a pet buck antelope.

This little animal is just growing a nice pair of horns, and he is as proud of them as a young man is who has the bulge on a moustache, and has called it out far enough so he can get hold of it.

Yesterday morning the marshal had been romping with the antelope, and the two had become pretty sociable, and were having a good deal of fun, when the marshal all at once lost his hat off and stooped down to pick it up. He is pretty fat, and he didn't hurry about it, but stooped over leisurely, and in such a way that his back was turned toward the antelope.

A buck antelope has a good deal of dry humor in his nature, and when he saw the marshal in that shape he ran back a few yards, so as to accumulate momentum, and aimed a lick at him that struck him near the pistol pocket.

This surprised the executive branch of the United States courts of Wyoming so that it didn't rally for a minute, and the facetious antelope repeated the joke.

The last time he got his horn hooked into the marshal's pantaloons, and when the bystanders rushed in and separated Major Schnitger from his pet, the latter had some fragments of clothing that he did not need, and the marshal apologized as he backed into the house and changed his pants.

The buck antelope, although timid and apprehensive in his wild state, is frolicsome and full of mirth-provoking antics after he has been domesticated and acclimated.

THE MORMONS.

The first installment of imported Mormons passed through here yesterday on its way to Zion. To all appearances, the stock of nihilists and foreign vagabonds is considerably reduced, and this year the prevailing style of imported Mormon will be the trichina impregnated variety left over from last year's round-up. Those who passed through yesterday were in a damaged condition, and nothing but the pure bracing air of the Jordan and a liberal dose of saltpetre can get them through the summer.

When they got here their trainer took the hose and turned it on the cages to purify the air a little, and then he let some of the more docile ones out for exercise, but there were some women in the rear car that the railroad authorities would not allow at large for fear they would scare the engines off the track.

One type of the proselyte Mormon is a man with three overcoats, and a pair of wooden shoes on, and a woolen lap-robe tied in a jaunty style around his neck. Most of them are afraid they will take cold. Their fears about taking a bath seem to be equally noticeable.

Bigamy, trigamy or polygamy can have no repulsive features for such people. Judging from their appearance, no horror could shock them unless it be a chunk of Castile soap and fresh air.

It is said that Mormonism is an abnormal growth upon our free institutions. This is true. It is a fungus growth like the toadstool above the ruin of an old hen ranch. It rises into the sunlight of freedom and towers toward the clear blue sky like a sore toe in a gale of wind.

It attaches itself to the life-giving institutions of America and hangs upon it like a freckle on the brow of beauty or an egg dado on a white vest.

We boast of the rights of free-born American citizens, and yet we allow the old dead horse of Mormonism to lie around among our young and growing territories till the pioneers of civilization have to wear patent clothes pins on their noses all summer while they make the desert bloom like the roses.

We don't want to seem at all officious or dictatorial just because we wield the mighty civilizing ball club of the press, but we would like to suggest that so long as polygamy and other forms of legalized prostitution are given the cushioned seats on the frontier, and impecunious white men with only one wife have to stand around and enjoy the show from the peanut gallery, the drawbacks of opening up a new country are too noticeable, and too contiguous.

OUR COMPLIMENTS.

We have nothing more to say of the editor of the Sweetwater *Gazette*. Aside from the fact that he is a squint-eyed, consumptive liar, with a breath like a buzzard and a record like a convict, we don't know anything against him. He means well enough, and if he can evade the penitentiary and the vigilance committee for a few more years, there

is a chance for him to end his life in a natural way.
If he don't tell the truth a little more plentifully,
however, the Green River people will rise as one man
and churn him up till there wont be anything left of
him but a pair of suspenders and a wart.

THE WOES OF A ONE-LEGGED MAN.

Yesterday morning, while the main guy of *The
Boomerang* sanctum was putting some carbolic acid
in the paste pot, nnd unlimbering his genius, and
tuning his lyre preparatory to yanking loose a few
stanzas on the midsummer cucumber, a man with a
cork leg, and the chastened air of one who is second
lieutenant in the home circle under the able and effi-
cient command of his wife, came softly in and sat
down on a volume containing the complete poems of
Noah Webster.

He waited patiently till he could catch the eye of
the speaker, humming softly to himself—

"Green grows the grave by the wild, dashing river,
    Where sleeps the brave with his arrow and quiver."

When the time had arrived for the lodge to open
up unfinished business, communications and new
business, he ran his wooden leg through the rounds
of a chair and said:

"I desire to make a few remarks on the subject of
home government, and the rights a husband may
have which his wife is bound to respect."

"Yes; but we don't enter the family circle with
our all-prevading influence. We simply attack
evils of a public or general nature. You should
pour your tale of woe into the ears of an attorney.

He will dish out the required balm to you at so much per balm."

"I know, but this is not strictly a case for the courts. It's a case which raises the question of the husband's priority, and agitates the whole social fabric.

"Last week I celebrated my 43d birthday, or I started to celebrate it, and circumstances over which I had no control arose and busted the programme, as mapped out by the committee of arrangements.

"It was the intention of the party, consisting of myself and several others of our most eminent men, to go over to Sabille canyon with a mountain wagon and a pair of pinto plugs for a little wholesome recreation. We had some weapons for slaying the frolicsome jack rabbit and the timid sage hen, and had provided ourselves against every possible rattlesnake contingency also. We had taken more precautions in this direction, perhaps, than in any other, and were in shape to enjoy the wild grandeur of the eternal hills without fear from the poisonous reptile of the rugged gulches and alkali bottoms of this picturesque western country.

"We were all loaded up in good shape for the trip and drove around to my house to get a camp kettle and some lemons. I went into the pantry to get a couple of pounds of sugar and a nutmeg.

"My wife met me in the pantry and roughly and brutally smelled of my breath.

"This was not the prerogative of a true wife, but she weighs 200 and is middling resolute, so I allowed her to do so, although every man's breath is his own property, and if he allows his wife to take advantage of her marital vows to smell his breath

UNSCREWED HIS LIMB.

on the most unlooked for occasions, what is to become of our boasted freedom?

"I then went up stairs into a closet after a lap robe and a pillow to use in case any of us got sunstruck.

"My wife came in just then, and as I started away with the pillow, she tripped me up so I fell inside the closet, and before I could recover from my surprise, she sat down on me in such a solemn and impressive manner that my eyes hung out on my cheeks like the bronze door knobs on a Pullman car.

"There I was in the impenetrable gloom of a closet, with the trusting companion of my home life flattening out my stomach till I could feel my watch chain against my spinal column. She then unscrewed my cork leg in a mechanical kind of a way and locked it up in the bureau drawer, putting the key in her pocket.

"After that she fastened the closet door on the outside, and told the party that I would be unable, owing to the inclemency of the weather, to take part in the exercises at Sabille canyon.

"All through that long, long weary day, I stood around on one leg and looked out of the window, thinking what a potent spell is exerted over the wooden-legged man by an able-bodied wife.

"It is a question, sir, which is of vital interest to us all. Must the one-legged minority continue thus to subserve the interests of the two-legged majority? I ask you, as the representative of the all civilizing, all leveling, all powerful and all jewhillikin press, how long the cork-limbed, taxation-without-representation masses must limp around the house and sew carpet rags, writhing in the death-like grip of a two-legged oligarchy?"

He did not wait for an answer. He simply gathered up a few of our freshest exchanges and stole softly down the stairs.

We decline to make any comment one way or the other, because we do not know that the country is ripe for the discussion of this question, but it deserves cold, calm, candid thought on the part of all thinking men, to say the least.

DOLLARS AND SENSE.

Sometimes an advertising agency in the east sends us a proposition which shows a style of wild, rash liberty which cannot be conducive to thrift and prosperity.

One of these concerns the other day made a proposition to us to run a quarter-column ad. of a preparation which would make whiskers grow on a meerschaum pipe. The ad. was to run in the daily and weekly one year, and copies of both papers were to be sent to the agent. During that time $250 worth of local notices were to be inserted also.

The whole thing, at our rates, would have figured up about $400, and the princely sum of $30, less thirty-three and a third per cent., the charges of the agency, was lavishly offered.

Of course we want to encourage the healthy growth of new and attractive styles of whiskers in Wyoming. We want to see a whisker industry spring up here on the frontier that will rival the crops of older and more civilized countries, but we cannot herald the glad tidings of whisker balm all over the United States and southern New Jersey just for the pure and innocent pleasure of seeing a picture in our paper day after day of a man with a beard on him like a buffalo overcoat.

Whatever will forward the interests of our young territory in any way we hope to assist so long as we can do so, and still obtain enough to pay freight on sight drafts and lead pencils. But we cannot wear out our young life trying to inaugurate a tropical growth of whiskers, just for the satisfaction of being called a philanthropist, with our toes sticking out through our boots.

We want to see the Liver-pad, the Vinegar Bitters and Moustache Promoter industry in this country reach a degree of prosperity which will be the envy and admiration of older States, but we desire also to obtain a handsome competence and to acquire that amount of arrogance and grub which wealth and position yield.

We hope we will be forgiven for this selfish and mercenary spirit, but it has obtained the mastery over us, and we are the willing slave of a wild, uncontrollable desire to revel in one shirt while the other is in the wash.

SITTING BULL'S RETURN.

HIS SPEECH ON THAT OCCASION

Warriors of My People: I have just completed my last grand farewell surrender to the paleface. It was the greatest effort of my life. With my people I have made several bridal tours into the British possessions, and now I have returned to the domain

of our Great Father, completing the most dazzling
and effulgent semi-annual constellation of surrenders that the world has ever known.

I wish to thank the people of my tribe for their
uniform obedience and perfect faith in me, without
which the grand round of surrenders would have
been a failure.

I desire also to thank the members of the press
throughout the country for the aid and encouragement extended by them all. Whenever I sent a
special to any paper, stating that I had once more
surrendered, it was always greedily paid for and
published. By this means I have inaugurated a
system of co-operation and attractive surrenders
that has been the envy and admiration of the civilized world.

The military posts, too, of both America and the
possessions of Great Britain, have been increased
until the fatigue and suffering necessary in order to
surrender to remote military camps have been
largely done away with. There has been no time
in the history of the northwest when the comfort
and convenience of surrendering hostiles have been
so carefully considered as now.

It is so arranged that Indians on the warpath,
if overtaken by stress of weather, or unfrequency of
grub, may, by a few days' journey, reach a military
post or cantonment, to which they may surrender
and be clothed and fed.

The Sioux pic-nic has thus been brought to a state
of perfection which guarantees to the much-abused
and put upon hostile a fair share of mental relaxation and pastoral peace, without the impending

starvation which has been heretofore a serious
drawback to the massacre industry.

I hope by another season to so plan our summer
vacation that we may establish a continuous line of
picturesque suburban cemeteries along the boundary
between the United States and the provinces. I
shall so arrange that at suitable outposts we will ac-
complish the customary abject surrender, and secure
the repose and government chuck which we require.

Our style of humility and broken-hearted contrite
spirit for next season will be much the same as
heretofore, with such additions and changes as the
circumstances may seem to require.

THE ENGLISH JOKE.

The average English joke has its peculiarities. A
sort of mellow distance. A kind of chastened reluctance. A coy and timid, yet trusting, though
evanescent intangibility which softly lingers in the
untroubled air, and lulls the tired senses to dreamy
rest, like the subdued murmur of a hoarse jackass
about nine miles up the gulch.

He must be a hardened wretch, indeed, who has
not felt his bosom heave and the scalding tear steal
down his furrowed cheek after he has read an English joke. There can be no hope for the man who
has not been touched by the gentle, pleading, yet all
potent sadness embodied in the humorous paragraph
of the true Englishman.

One may fritter away his existence in chasing the
follies of our day and generation, and have naught
to look back upon but a choice assortment of robust
regrets, but if he will stop in his mad career to read

an English pun, his attention will be called to the solemn thought that life is after all but a tearful journey to the tomb.

Death and disaster on every hand may fail to turn the minds of a thoughtless world to serious matters, but when the London funny man grapples with a particularly skittish and evasive joke, with its weeping willow attachment, and hurls it at a giddy and reckless humanity, a prolonged wail of anguish goes up from broken hearts, and a sombre pall hangs in the gladsome sky like a pair of soldier pants with only one suspender.

If the lost and undone victim to the great catalogue of damning vice and enervating dissipation will for a moment turn his mind to the solemn consideration of the London Punch, and wrestle with it alone where the prying eyes of the world cannot penetrate, though unused to tears, the fountains of the great deep in his nature will be opened up, and he will see the blackness of intense darkness which surrounds him, and be led to penitence and abject humility.

The mission of the English humorist is, to darken the horizon and shut out the false and treacherous joy of existence—to shut out the beauty of the landscape and scatter a $2 gloom over the glad green earth.

English humor is like a sore toe. It makes you glad when you get over it. It is like having the small-pox, because if you live through it you are not likely to have it again.

When we pass from earth and our place is filled by another sad-eyed genius whose pants are too short and who manifests other signs of greatness,

let no storied urn or animated bust be placed over
our lowly resting place, but stuff an English conundrum so that it will look as it did in life, and let it
stand above our silent dust to shed its damp and bilious influence through the cemetery as a monument
of desolation and a fountain of unshed tears, and
the grave robber will shun our final resting place as
he would the melon patch where lurks the spring
gun and the alert and irritable bulldog.

THE PISTOL.

The righteous war against the carrying of pistols
is still going bravely on all over the country and the
mayors of the larger cities are making it red hot for
everyone who violates the law.

This is right. No man ever carried one that he did
not intend to kill some one with it. If he does not
intend to kill some one, why does he carry a deadly
weapon? The result is that very often a man who
if he had gone unarmed as he ought to, would have
been a respected citizen, becomes a caged murderer
with a weeping, widowed wife and worse than or-
phaned children at home.

We used to feel at times as though here in this
western country we were having a pretty lonesome
time of it, never having killed anybody, and we began to think that in order to command respect we
would have to start a private cemetery, so one time
when we had a good opportunity we drew our pop
on a man and shot at him.

He often writes to us now and tells us how healthy
he is. Before we shot at him he used to have trouble with his digestion, and every spring he was so

bilious that he didn't care whether he lived or not. Now he weighs 200 and looks forward to a long and useful life.

Still the revolver is not always a health-promoter. It is more deadly as a general rule for the owner than anyone else. Half at least of the distressing accidents that occur as a result of carrying a pistol, are distressing mainly to the man who carries the weapon.

We sometimes think that if editors would set the example, and instead of going around armed to the teeth, would rely on the strength of their noble manhood and a white oak club, others would follow and discard the pistol. For a year we have been using a club, with the best results, and although the exercise has been pretty severe at times, the death rate has been considerably reduced, and many of our citizens have been spared to bless the community with their presence.

Let the press of the country take hold of this thing, and the day will come when a man may enter the editorial office as fearlessly as now he goes into the postoffice.

Nothing unnerves a man like going into a sanctum and finding fragments of an old acquaintance scattered over the velvet carpet, or ruthlessly jammed into a porcelain cuspidore.

SOLILOQUY OF THE WATERMELON.

I am a lonely watermelon, the first one of the season. As I sit here in the market, people come in and thump me, to see if I am ripe, and then go away.

It is very sad to be the first watermelon of the summer. Customers look at me with a scared expression of countenance, and then buy two cucumbers and an onion.

Once a bonanza man took out his check book and asked the market man how much he wanted for me and when he was told he burst into tears and said he would have to deny himself the pleasure of a watermelon or put off going to Europe till next year.

One man who owned 40,000 head of beef, got the news that the stock market had gone up a cent and a half in Chicago, and he got so reckless that he came in and asked what I was worth, intending to have me put in a setting as a shirt stud, but the price frightened him, and he went out sadly and bought a line of ocean steamers.

I would rather be less valuable and have more love and affection. Now people look upon me coldly, and pass by on the other side. It is making me gloomy and melancholy.

I once had a pleasant home among those who were kind and good to me. Boys used to come in the silent night and steal my relatives, and carry them away and devour them. But even that was better than to be put in a glass case and to pine away the lonely hours. People who couldn't buy a fractional interest in me come and criticise me and call me queer. Men who haven't seen ten cents since last election, roll me around and ask the price, and make me mad.

I've an all-fired good notion to slide off the shelf and smash my brains out, I'm so unhappy.

THE BOOMERANG DOG.

We received day before yesterday at this office, by express from Rock Springs, a gloomy and peculiar dog as a testimonial of regard.

He is evidently a cross between a coyote and the measles, possessing at the same time the untaught grace of the former, and the general debility of the latter.

His advent into Laramie has been the crowning success of his life. He has attracted a great deal of attention since the first moment of his arrival, and still exhibits to crowded houses.

He has a quiet, modest, unassuming way of eating everything in town, which wins every one.

Nobody can look into his patient, sorrowful eyes unmoved. He has a look of utter woe and desolation which commands the respect of the most thoughtless.

He has lost nearly all his hair from grief, apparently, and that which remains is very lonely.

His legs are long and limber, and his ears have a dejected and wilted appearance.

Those who are acquainted with his inner life wish that he would die and be forever at rest.

He evidently cannot live long. This is partly owing to his physical condition, and partly to the fact that at the rate he is eating now, the food supply will gradually peter out, as we might say.

The altitude seems too high for him, and he will probably yield to the inclemency of the weather before long.

There is a look in his eye that is not of this earth,

and the gradual droop of his tail shows that death is lurking near him.

He may fade gradually away, like a wood violet in the dissolving heat of summer, or he may be knocked galley west by an old pick handle. No one knows how he will meet his end, but he will be wiped out sooner or later, and his bald-headed tail will cease to wag. In whatever form death may come he will be ready. He is ripe now, and ready to be snuffed out. His vitality is very meagre, and before the pumpkin pie hangs ripe and luscious on · its bough, he will have wung his way into the great unknown and unascertainable.

If this poor, little wanderer didn't have the leprosy, and the same musical voice that Peas has, we would take more comfort in him. As it is, we can't look at him without pity, and a great, consuming sympathy.

A WORD ABOUT CARVING.

It is not alone the fact that the amateur carver misses the joints and tries to cut through the largest bones, that fills him with regret and his lap full of sage and onions. It is the horrible thought that the entire company is looking at him.

No matter how the perspiration may trickle down between his shoulder blades, or how the hot flashes may chase the chills up and down his spinal column, or how much his eyes may be dimmed by unshed tears, the rest of the company never allows his interest to flag a moment.

We remember one time we were called to assume the management of a free-for-all carving tournament at the home of a dove-eyed dumpling whose kind regard we desired to catch on to as far as possible.

How clearly come back to us now the smiling faces of the guests, the rippling laugh, the bald-headed joke, the thanksgiving conundrum, ahd all as merry as a marriage bell.

We call to mind the girlish laughter of that one whose very existence, as she sat on our left that day, seemed cemented and glued to our own.

As we sharpened the glittering blade on the ringing steel, we felt buoyant and proud. Proud to think how we would slice the white, calm bosom of that deceased hen. Proud to think how in our mind we had laid out the different pregnable points about that old cackler, and in the anticipation of applause glad and free, when we had accomplished the warfare and victory and stuffing had perched upon our banner.

We softly jabbed the shimmering fork a-straddle of the breast bone, tore off a few goose pimples from under the wings of the late lamented, gouged out a few shattered fragments from the neck and tried to cut a sirloin steak off the back.

An oppressive gloom seemed to pervade the air. The old hen didn't have her joints where we had them laid out in our mind. She was deformed. She seemed to be a freak of nature.

It rattled us and unnerved us.

We gouged wildly at the remains, squirting the gravy right and left, and filling the air with fragments of bread crumbs and sage.

By some kind of omission or miscalculation, we made a wild stab at the back of the late lamented hen, and with a frenzy born of repeated defeats and depressing failures, the knife struck the platter with a loud crash, and ceasing not in its untamed fury, glanced aside, and in an instant buried itself with a sickening thud in the corset of the hired girl.

With difficulty we drew out the glittering blade, now ensanguined with the gore of a fellow creature, wiped it on the table cloth and fled. Out into the cold unsympathetic world, out into the crash and confusion of struggling humanity, to battle on through life under an assumed name.

This is why we tremble and turn pale when our past life is inquired into by biographers. That is why a baked fowl makes us quail.

This is why we always sign our nom de plume to a promissory note. That, too, is why we travel *incog.* and without baggage.

THE SAMPLE COPY FIEND.

Recently it seems to us as though a large number of people throughout this country have nothing to do but write postal cards to newspaper publishers, asking for a sample copy of their paper.

This is a new and growing industry. It costs only one cent to get a sample copy, and at that rate the average bore of this denomination expects to get a $3 weekly one year for fifty-two cents.

Of course the sample copy free lunch fiend has to write every week and sign a different name, but that don't injure his feelings any. He has nothing else to do, and it drives away ennui.

Perhaps these people think we are publishing a paper just to wear out our young life, but that is where they fall into a common error.

We are trying to acquire a competence, so that we can carry a summer cane, and have a special mug at the barber shop, with our monogram on it, and that is why we ask pay for things sometimes when it seems unlady-like and eccentric.

The man who gets his literature by smouging sample copies is generally a man who obtains a precarious livelihood by posing as an artist's model of a wild-eyed snide.

People who enclose stamps will be waited upon just as soon as the mailing brigade can catch up a little, but those who enclose a chunk of taffy in a postal card and look for this priceless repository of electrotyped brain, will anxionsly watch through the gloaming till a late hour, but they will wait in vain.

HOW THEY SALT A CLAIM.

"I wish you would explain to me all about this salting of claims that I hear so much about," said a meek-eyed tenderfoot to a grizzly old miner who was panning about six ounces of pulverized quartz. "I don't see what they want to salt a claim for, and I don't understand how they do it."

"Well, you see, a hot season like this they have to salt the claim lots of times to keep it. A fresh claim is good enough for a fresh tenderfoot, but the old timers won't look at anything but a pickled claim.

"You know what quartz is, probably?"

"No."

"Well, every claim has quartz. Some more and some less. You find out how many quartz there are, and then put in so many pounds of salt to the quart. Wild cat claims require more salt, because the wild cat spoils quicker than anything else.

"Sometimes you catch a sucker too, and you have to put him in brine or you lose him. That's one reason why they salt a claim.

"Then again, you often grub stake a man "——

"But what is a grub stake?"

"Well, a grub stake is a stake that the boys hang their grub on so they can carry it. Lots of mining men have been knocked cold by a blow from a grub stake.

"What I wanted to say, though, was this: you will, probably, at first, strike free milling poverty, with indications of something else. Then you will, no doubt, sink till you strike bedrock, or a true fissure gopher hole, with traces of disappointment.

"That's the time to put in your salt. You can shoot it into the shaft with a double-barreled shotgun, or wet it and apply it with a whitewash brush. If people turn up their noses at your claim then, and say it is a snide, and that they think there is something rotten in Denmark, you can tell them that they are clear off, and that you have salted your claim, and that you know it is all right."

The last seen of the tenderfoot, he was buying a double-barreled shotgun and ten pounds of rock salt.

There's no doubt but a mining camp is the place to send a young man who wants to acquire knowledge and fill his system full of information that will be useful to him as long as he lives.

THE WOMAN WITH THE HOSE.

We have spoken of the garden hose before, but in the former article we were unable to produce the steel engraving that should have gone with it. One of the staff, it seems, had loaned the steel plate to Scribner, of New York, to work into an article on medieval art.

The garden hose has risen within the past few years from comparative obscurity to where it commands the respect and attention of a civilized world. In the hands of a woman who is talking to some one in the house, it becomes an instrument of great potency and uncertainty.

By being on your guard at all times, you may dodge the primeval cow, or the deadly wheelbarrow, but the garden squirt is inevitable and unavoidable.

Death itself may be delayed sometimes by surgical skill and constant care, but the wild, weird moisture of the garden hose is ever lurking near and looking for its victim. It follows a man like the transcript of an old judgment in the district court.

We once knew a man who was successful in business, and surrounded by everything that goes to make life desirable.

He didn't owe anybody and nobody owed him. He owned a handsome residence with velvet lawns, and cast-iron bulldogs on each side of his front steps. He had horses and carriages, with his monogram on the harness, and a large chattel mortgage on the whole thing, and there was nothing that money would buy that he did not have.

But there was a Nemesis camped on his trail. It was in the form of a sad-eyed bilious woman, who lived next door, and who was armed with a garden hose.

She had one glass eye that she couldn't most always rely on, and she wore a large sun bonnet, that had a droop to it like the Chicago cattle market.

This man would catch the direction of the glass eye, and make calculations accordingly, but he generally got bathed in cold water and astonishment. When he wasn't misled by the glass eye, he got fooled by the limber sun-bonnet, till finally he got desperate. He gradually became despondent and cynical. When his wife made humorous remarks to him he would not laugh, as he was wont to do. At first she thought he had a boil or something of that kind gnawing at his vitals, but he would not tell her the cause of his woe.

He bore it in silence till the close of the summer, and when the maples were crimsoned with the dying splendor of the autumn, one day they brought him home on a cellar door, and laid him out in the off bed-room with his store clothes on.

Toward the close of a sunny day in autumn the sombre funeral line slowly filed away from the elegant mansion, and as it moved past, there was a loud hiss through the silent air, and a torrent of cold water that drenched the entire procession.

It was the garden hose with its last sad squirt.

THE FEMALE BARBER.

Women are now tackling every profession and style of business. There is hardly a path of life

adown whose shaded paths we do not find the young
lady sauntering in her charmingly careless manner.

Many of them are becoming barbers, and successful ones, too.   There is a gentle touch required by a
barber which is very grateful to the victim, and
which is easily picked up by the lady apprentice.

There is a nameless joy steals into a man's soul
when a musical voice tickles a man's ears as he lies
in the chair with his eyes closed, while the tips of
rosy fingers take him by the nose and pry open his
mouth and a dainty twist of the wrist fills his back
teeth full of soap and rain water.

O, woman!   Little do you know what a power for
good do you possess.   When you jab a man's head
back against the gable end of the barber chair, and
hang it over behind so that his Adam's apple sticks
up into the scented air like the breast bone of an old
gobbler that has died of starvation, you have the
great, manly lord of creation where he is as weak
and tractable as a child.

Then you can wear him out with an old razor that
you have shaved the whole broad universe with.
Then you can peel off one feature after another and
throw it into an old nail keg, and while you slice
him up into sausage meat you can talk to him and
make him think he is having a chunk of luxury
ladled out to him such as no other living man ever
got.

If a female barber is handsome, she can shave her
customers with a bed-slat and powder their faces
with Cayenne pepper and giant powder, and it will
be all right.

A homely female barber, however, would havı
nothing to do but to hone up old razors and think
about the sombre past.

JOINT POWDER.

"It don't do to fool with joint powder," said an
old-timer, yesterday, in *The Boomerang* office. "It's
powerful stuff. I had a $10,000 mine over in the
Queen of Shelby district in '54, called the Goshallhemlock claim. I was offered $10,000 for it, with
$5,000 in sagebrush placer stock besides, if she
opened up as well ten foot further down.

"We put in a blast of joint powder, and when we
went to make an examination, we couldn't find the
Goshallhemlock with an assessor and a search warrant. The hole was there, but there wasn't quartz
enough to throw at a yaller dog.

"My idea is to sell a mine just before you put in
the joint powder, and then if the buyer wants to
blow the property into the middle of next Christmas
let him do it."

A FRONTIER INCIDENT.

Calamity is the name of a man who lives in the
gold camp of Cummins City. He has another name,
but nobody seems to know what it is. It has been
torn off the wrapper someway, and so the boys call
him Calamity.

He is a man of singular mind and construction.
The most noticeable feature about Calamity is his
superstitious dread of muscular activity. Some peo-

ple will not tackle any kind of business enterprise
on Friday. Calamity is even more the victim of
this vague superstition, and has a dread of beginning work on any day of the week, for fear that
some disaster may befall him.

Last spring he had a little domestic trouble, and
his wife made complaints that Calamity had worn
out an old long-handled shovel on her, trying to
convince her about some abstruse theory of his.

The testimony seemed rather against Calamity,
and the miners told him that as soon as they got
over the rush a little and had the leisure they would
have to hang him.

They hoped he would take advantage of the hurry
of business and go away, because they didn't want
to hang him so early in the season. But Calamity
didn't go away. He stayed because it was easier to
stay than it was to go. He did not, of course, pine
for the notoriety of being the first man hung in the
young camp, but rather than pull up stakes and
move away from a place where there were so many
pleasant associations, he concluded to stay and meet
death calmly in whatever form he might come.

One evening, after the work of the day was done,
and the boys had eaten their suppers, one of them
suggested that it would be a good time to hang Calamity. So they got things in shape and went down
to the Big Laramie bridge.

Calamity was with them. They got things ready
for the exercise to begin, and then asked the victim
if he had anything to say. He loosened the rope
around his neck a little with one hand, so that he
could speak with more freedom, and holding his
pantaloons on with the other, he said:

"Gentlemen of the convention, I call you to witness that this public demonstration toward me is entirely unsought on my part. I have never courted notoriety.

"Plugging along in comparative obscurity is good enough for me. This is the first time I have ever addressed an audience. That-is why I am embarrassed and ill at ease.

"You have brought me here to hang me because I seem harsh and severe with my wife. You have entered the hallowed presence of my home life and assumed the prerogative of subverting my household discipline.

"It is well. I do not care to live so.long as my authority is questioned. You have already changed my submissive wife to an arrogant and self-reliant woman.

"Yesterday I told her to go out and grease the wagon, and she straightened up to her full height and told me to grease it myself.

"I have always been kind and thoughtful to her. When she had to go up in the gulch in the winter after firewood, my coat shielded her from the storm while I sat in the cabin through the long hours. I could name other instances of unselfishness on my part, but I will not take up your time.

"She uses my smoking tobacco, and kicks my vertebræ into my hat on the most unlooked for occasions. She does not love me any more, and life to me is only a hollow mockery.

"Death, with its wide waste of eternal calm, and its shoreless sea of rest, is a glad relief to me. I go, but I leave in your midst a skittish and able-bodied widow who will make Rome howl. I bequeath her to this camp.   She is yours, gentlemen.   She is all I have to give, but in giving her to you, I feel that my untimely death will always be looked upon in this gulch as a dire calamity.

"The day will come when you will look back upon this awful night and wish that I was alive again; but it will be too late.   I will be far away.   My soul will be in the land where domestic infecility and cold feet can never enter.

"Bury me at the foot of Vinegar Hill, where the sage hen and the fuzzy bumble bee may gambol o'er my lowly grave.

· "When Calamity had finished, an impromptu cau-cus was called, and when it was adjourned, Calam-ity went home to his cabin to surprise his wife.   She hasn't fully recovered from the surprise as we go to press.

ANSWERS TO CORRESPONDENTS.

Emeline. — No, child, an enemata is not a new style of blanc mange.   We cannot, therefore, give you the receipt for making it.

Henry Clay Oleson.—Your poem entitled "An Ode to a Seed Cucumber," is accepted.   We will work it off on the public in the form of newspaper wrap-pers, or sell it to lay under a carpet.

J. Oolong Smythe.—No, we would not advise you to use concentrated lye in committing suicide.   It is not a painless death.   If you still yearn for a bright immediately, you can sit down on a curve of the Union Pacific railway and let a cattle train glide across you a couple of times.   You may not be a very handsome corpse, but that style of death chases away all doubts that might cloud the minds of a coroner's jury.

Caroline Van Amburgh. — Your poem, which you call, "The Lonely Life of the Cross-Eyed Clam," will be returned to you on receipt of fifty cents back freight charges. You shouldn't try to make the word "bilious" rhyme with "epiglottis," as it breaks the harmony, and you ought to change the wording a little in these lines:

> Oh, sunny sea, oh, placid sea,
> Dearer than all the world to me,
> Nurse on your bosom, so warm and calm,
> The cold and cross-eyed orphan clam.

Carl Schurz. — You are evidently in error about the Ute Indians. They are not farming much this summer, so your proposition to sell them 1,000 Pitts thrashing machines at a discount is of no practical utility. The chances are that if they had 1,000 Pitts thrashing machines they would trade the entire lot before fall for a plug hat and a pair of red suspenders. The Utes run more to red suspenders and physical calm than they do to agriculture and Pitts thrashing machines. They started an onion patch on White river two years ago, and it looked at one time as though they would at least raise one onion to each five adults on the reservation, but one morning they got into a discussion about some agricultural point while weeding the fruit, and when they got through the onion bed looked as though there had been a premature explosion there, and the onions were so mixed up with copper-colored ears and other Indian fragments that the whole thing was abandoned.

THE HEN V. SCIENCE.

Dear reader, did you ever wrestle with a hen that had a wild, uncontrollable desire to incubate? Did you ever struggle on, day after day, trying to convince her that her mission was to furnish eggs for your table instead of hovering all day on a door knob, trying to hatch out a litter of front doors?

William H. Root, of this place, who has made the hen a study, both in her home life and while lying in the embrace of death, has struck upon an argument which the average hen will pay more attention to than any other he has discovered in his researches.

He says the modern hen ignores almost everything when she once gets the notion that she has received a call to incubate. You can deluge her with the garden hose, or throw old umbrellas at her, or change her nest, but that don't count with the firm and stubborn hen. You can take the eggs out of the nest and put a blooded bull-dog or a nest of new-laid bumble bees in place of them, and she will hover over them as assiduously as she did before.

William H. Root's hen had shown some signs of this mania, so he took out the eggs and let her try her incubator on a horse rake awhile, just so she could kind of taper off gradual and not have her mind shattered. Then he tried her at hatching out four-tined forks, and at last her taste got so vitiated that she took the contract to furnish the country with bustles by hatching out an old hoopskirt that had gone to seed.

Mr. Root then made an experiment. We were one of a board of scientists who assisted in the consultation. The owner of the hen got a strip of red flannel and tied it around her tail.

The hen seemed annoyed as soon as she discovered it. No hen cares to have a sash hung on her system that doesn't match her complexion. A seal brown hen with a red flannel polonaise don't seem to harmonize, and she is aware of it just as much as anybody is.

That hen seemed to have thought of something all at once that had escaped her mind before, and so she went away.

She stepped about nine feet at a lick on the start, and gained time as she proceeded. When she bumped her nose against the corner of the stable she changed her mind about her direction. She altered her course a little, but continued her rapid style of movement.

Her eyes began to look wild. She seemed to be losing her reason. She got so pretty soon that she didn't recognize the faces of friends. She passed Mr. Root without being able to distinguish him from a total stranger.

These peculiar movements were kept up during the entire afternoon, till the hen got so fatigued that she crawled into a length of old stovepipe, and the committee retired to prepare a report. It is the opinion of the press that this is a triumph of genius in the line of hen culture. It is not severe, though firm, in its treatment, and while it of course annoys and unmans the hen temporarily, it is salutary in its results, and at the same time it furnishes a pleasant little matinee for the spectators. We say to those upon whose hands time hangs heavily these long days, that there is nothing that soothes the

ruffled mind and fills the soul with a glad thrill of
pleasure like the erratic movements of a decorated
hen. It may not be a high order of enjoyment, but
it affords a great deal of laugh to the superficial foot
to those who are not very accomplished, and who
laugh at things and then consider its propriety afterward.

A SUGGESTION.

It is clear to our mind as we write this that there
ought to be a vigilance committee organized in
Washington, District of Columbia. When crime
gets too common and life isn't valued very much in
the west, there is generally a committee of property
holders organized whose object it is to discourage
murder and throw out inducements for robbers and
cut-throats to go away.

We do not claim that the people of the west are
always right. They haven't the advantages, some
of them at least, that eastern people have. Out here
we are generally at least six weeks behind on the
latest hitch in poodle dogs and colic but we aim to
do about the correct thing before we get through re-
gardless of cost.

Colleges are not very thick here and a man can
ride a hundred miles sometimes and not see the codfish ball that is so common to more advanced civilization. Still our people are high strung and proud.
They have rough crude notions about hanging a red
handed murderer that might shock the sensitive nature of a Washington politician, but when our leading men decide on a lynching bee it is generally
crowned with success.

The accused may be compelled to stand on a rough kerosene barrel and go through the exercises without his notes but when the barrel is kicked one side and quiet is restored it generally turns out that life is more secure to those who remain.

It is now suggested by jealous outside physicians and surgeons in the east who were not called on in the president's case, that Guiteau didn't kill Mr. Garfield, but that he has been killed by the medical treatment he has received. This offers a fine loophole for the assassin to creep out of and makes a point upon which shyster lawyers, and medical experts who have filled the New Jerusalem with their patients, may show themselves off through the press of the country.

We have only this to say: Let Guiteau be sent to Carbon station, Wyoming, from which point Dutch Charlie and Big Nose George were able to look over into the mysterious realm of the bright beyond, or let him come to Laramie City, where the time honored telegraph pole still waits to deal out substantial justice to those who are hankering for the kind that works instantaneously.

Then if some of these bald-headed pill makers who are willing to shield the assassin in order to pat their own inordinate vanity on the back, desire two or three dollars' worth of new-laid Wyoming justice, we will give them what is left after Guiteau is attended to.

We have no idea that this suggestion will be accepted because it is uncouth and lacks the softened and chastened repose of manner and elegant diction which are the results of an older and more refined civilization, but we lay it on the altar of our common country with that open, generous style of ours which is so characteristic.

Still there is one weak point in the suggestion, and we admit it. If lynching should once get a start in Washington, or if those who have been in public life at the Capitol were to become the victims of a fearless vigilance committee, the census of 1890 would look as though the Asiatic cholera had swept over the land.

Or it may be that, in the halcyon days agone, when o'er these grass envelveted slopes and sage environed plains, the festive Ute, clothed in nothing but a little brief authority, fled from hillock to hillock, and from mountain peak to mountain peak, this was the point where the brave chieftains, with the gory scalps of the busted pilgrims, and around this ring they waltzed and swaggered through the livelong night.

Not having bathed since they went on the warpath, they naturally pranced around till they knocked the soil of the valley off their feet, and killed the growing grass.

This is made more plausible from the fact that a petrified Indian chilblain was found there in the spring.

All of these theories may be incorrect, but we give them to show that when it comes down to historical research, we are no slouch.

AN AWKWARD POSITION.

Those who are familiar with the geographical history, so to speak, of Wyoming, are aware that this territory was formed from western Dakota, but

few realize that the giant legislative brain of those
days in defining the boundaries of Wyoming forgot
a chunk of Dakota and left it west of Wyoming,
and entirely unprovided for, with this territory intervening between it and Montana.

This would be all right if a fragment of a country
wanted to wander off by itself and commune with
nature, but this at last becomes monotonous.

A political division may enjoy a picnic for a few
weeks, free from the ties of civilization, but when it
comes time to pay taxes, the inhabitants sigh for
the good old days when they had something to
swear at.

Of course, Dakota has made no provision for this
isolated huckleberry patch, and as it has never
been legally awarded to any other state or territory,
there she stands, obedient to no law free as the
mountain breezes that fan her cheek.

She knows no crime and no punishment. If a
man walks up to another, and blows the top of his
head off, the only way to measure out substantial
justice to the offender, is to gather a surprise party
and a funeral bee together, and hang him up to a
slippery elm tree. When a man gets drunk there,
he gets no $10 and trimmings. The court there is
taking an eternal vacation.

You don't have to pay a dog tax there every
spring, nor bow to the annual assessment of the central committee.

Life is one unceasing round of pleasure. Lawyers
don't live there, because there is no law. Justices
of the peace do not flourish there, because there is a
wide shoreless sea of stagnant rest in the common
drunk business. No taxation, no representation, no

crime and no punishment. If you can kill a man, and do it so the popular feeling will not be aroused, you are O. K., and if you can steal a man's watermelons and not get full of buckshot, or leave the slack of your overalls in the teeth of a big mournful bulldog, you can sail down the stream of life about as serene as a mud-turtle on the calm bosom of a frog-pond.

RING MOUNTAIN.

Speaking about mountains, there is a mountain on the left of the Cummins City road near the Sunrise mine which, for singularity and eccentricity, takes the cake.

It is called Ring mountain, partly because that is its name, and partly because on the face of the mountain near its top, and plainly visible from the road, there is a large black ring, which shows up plainly in contrast with brown and gray of the mountain itself.

It is acknowledged by every one who has seen it to be the strangest freaks of nature that this region, so prolific in such things, can boast.

The soil of this ring is quite dark, and that is all there is to it. It is a perfect circle, or nearly so, and no wear and tare of the elements makes any difference in its singular individuality.

Many theories are advanced as to the cause of this natural freak, but none are very thick or durable.

Perhaps there was a big circus in that locality a thousand years ago, and the great men of this region were inside the big tent looking at the animals, and all at once the earth began to swell up at that point and hump itself like a hired man, and there was nothing left there except a paralized circus ring, and two or three old jokes, and the unpaid bill for advertising.

Then again, perhaps it is a fairy ring, and at night, when the moon is high in the midsummer sky, and the bullfrog is softly cooing to its mate, and the violet-eyed pole cat steals forth in the silver moonlight, and the tomcat on Vinegar Hill is trilling a few bars of something low and soft, the fairies gather on Ring mountain and have a huge old time.

HOW A NEW CZAR IS INAUGURATED.

In order to answer a great many inquiries at once, we take this method of reaching our friends who have personally expressed their curiosity in relation to the above all-absorbing subject:

When it is properly brought to the notice of the royal obituary observer, by the undertaker extraordinary, that a vacancy has occurred in the czar department, notices are posted in the most public places asking for sealed bids which are to be opened at the end of thirty days, the party bidding to state fully what he will do the czar business for per annum, and board himself.

At the end of thirty days, a committee of five men, to be selected by the chair, meets and opens the bids. The situation is awarded to the lowest and best bidder, the fortunate party whose bid is accepted being entitled to all the torchlight processions, bombardments and shooting matches usually dealt out to royalty, free of charge.

9

The chairman of the committee, upon awarding the contract to the fortunate bidder, then issues a schweitzerkase, requiring the high muck-a-muck and imperial pie-biters of the realm to congregate on a special date and put the kibosh on the new czar. The procession moves in about the following order to the winter palace, where the ceremony takes place:

1.
Drum major, with gold-headed cane and short-tailed coat.

2.
Orlando Whoopenkoff's royal brass band, playing "Twinkle Star."

8.
One hundred dragoons, with drawn swords.

4.
Five hundred civil officials, with drawn salaries.

5.
The new Czar, with Bessemer steel overcoat on.

6.
The royal embalmer and imperial taxidermist, marching arm in arm.

7.
The Czar's own private stretcher, borne by the members of his household, and to be used in case of accident.

8.
The royal physician, bearing arnica and court plaster

9.
The imperial undertaker and coroner extraordinary, marching arm in arm.

10.
Peasantry, carrying bombs.

11.
Serfs, carrying the spring style of hand grenade.

12.
Rough Skuff, Ragtag and Bobtail of the realm, carrying nitroglycerine cans, torpedoes, concentrated lye, double-barrel shotguns, etc., etc.

The procession, after reaching the three-cornered tower, crosses the donjon keep, passes through the culverin, and enters the parquette, where the oath to support the constitution and faithfully perform the duties of the office, turning over such funds as may come into his hands as czar, and which he does not need in his business, is administered.

The life insurance companies then revoke their policies on the life of the new czar, and the ceremonies close with a triumphal march in G.

This constitutes the regular order only, and glad surprises may be contributed at any time by the Nihilists.

These surprises, which are fixed up for the czar, break up the dreary monotony of all solemn ceremonies peculiar to his people, and add very materially to the general success of the occasion.

It is only proper to add, in this connection, that, with the feeling now existing toward the czar on the part of the Nihilists, the salary has been raised, as it should be, and now the czar receives sufficient to place him above want for three weeks, and then bury him in good shape.

FRENCH IDEA OF THE UTE WAR.

The following we clip and translate from one of our Paris exchanges. There are enemies of ours who will say we do not exchange with the Paris papers, and that we do not know a word of French; but we consign such vituperative foes to oblivion and obloquy, and some more places of that kind:

THE UTE WAR.

We have already in America the rebellion called of the journalism of that country, the Ute war. This Ute, he make disturbance, occasioned by reason of anti-treating law enacted by Kansas parliament, which is Ute mental reservation. Viscount de Colorow, he been what we shall call the readjuster. He readjusted the scalp of one Meeker, who is now in what we shall call the Celestial City. He have vamose up the stair of gold already.

The Ute also make of himself a great party in the Republique. This shall elect the president, unless the deadlock be fractured.

The Ute, which is the bloodthirsty warrior, has his home in which we shall call the wigwam of New Jersey, which is over against Oshkosh, and tributary to that sovereign which we shall call Kalamazoo.

LETTER FROM CHICAGO.

CHICAGO, September 23, 1880.—I arrived here from the north on Tuesday evening. The demonstration was on a larger scale than I had even looked for. It was gratifying, indeed, to one who loves the spontaneous approval of his fellow-citizens. I do. The procession was very fine, consisting of 'busses, hacks, carriages, express wagons and the police, followed up by promiscuous citizens. There was a little misunderstanding about who should deliver the address of welcome. So about two hundred healthy orators, of the Denis Kearney decoction, all started in at one and the same time to give me the freedom of the city, at twenty-five cents per free-

doin. There is a good deal of this class of freedom now on the Chicago market.

Chicago is a thriving, enterprising town on the Lake Michigan coast. It is the county seat of Cook county, so that all the county officers live here.

If a young man with the requisite degree of pluck and determination were to start a paper here, and could get the county printing and go without a hired girl, he could do first-rate.

Chicago is a rival of Laramie as the most desirable outfitting point for North Park. It also does some outfitting for South Park and several other parks.

Yesterday I went to South Park to drive along the boulevards and see the fountains squirt. The boulevards are now in good shape. They are about the bouliest boulevards I have seen for five years.

When I sell the Boomerang mine I am going to buy me a park. Some days when I feel frolicsome, it seems to me as though if I couldn't have a nice large park of my own, with velvet lawns and cool retreats in it, where I could be alone and roll around over the green sward, and kick up my heels in the chastened sunlight, I would certainly bust.

South Park has an antelope, a bison, an elk and several other ferocious animals. They seem lonely, and time hangs heavy on their hands, so to speak.

Going out to the park we met a funeral procession headed by a remains. When we were coming out of the driveway on our return, we met the same procession. It had trasplanted the deceased in good shape, and was racing horses on its way home through the park. The minister belonged to the same family with the United Grand Junction Ebeneezer Temperance association, and although he was ostensibly holding on to his horse with all the reserve forces on hand, he seemed to keep the rest of the procession at a respectful distance all the way.

It was about the most cheerful funeral I ever saw, with the officiating minister leading down the home-stretch and the hearse at a Maud S. gait rattling along at his heels, followed by the bereaved family coming down the quarter stretch in 45. It reconciled me a great deal to death to see this. If I could be positively certain that my friends and acquaintances would take it that easy I could die happy, but I know they won't. I have seemed to work my way into the affections of those who come in contact with me from day to day, so that when I die I know just how it will be. There will be one of the wildest panics ever known in the history of civilized nations. Groceries and all kinds of provisions will depreciate in value fifty per cent., and watermelons will be almost a drug on the market.

Allow me to digress for a moment. Watermelons are very high at Laramie, and there is the standing joke that for three years I haven't had sufficient decision of character and spinal column to make up my mind whether I would build or buy a watermelon. Here watermelons are more plentiful. They grow low down on the branches of the melon trees so that on a still evening one can easily knock them off with a club. So easy in fact is that feat that I could hardly restrain myself from taking a little stroll one pleasant evening to pick one or two luscious specimens from the heavy laden boughs. So strong was this feeling at least that I could not overcome it without an unusual strain, and my physicians tell

me not to do anything that will overtax my moral
nature. They are afraid that something would
break and tear the whole vast fabric of integrity
from its foundation.

So I went out with a brother of mine who could
be depended upon. I took along my old pocket
knife that I have had for fifteen years, and which
has received the silver medal, sweepstakes prize
and handicap silver service in a score of go-as-you-
please melon-plugging matches for the champion-
ship of the known world. But we were not very
fortunate. The world is growing cynical and fast
losing faith in mankind, I fear. People have quit
putting their money into savings banks and are beginning to plant their watermelons in new and obscure places. Just as the casual observer learns the
position of an eligible melon patch the proprietor
changes the combination on him.

I found multitudinous changes among old friends
and associates when I got home, and was struck
with the ceaseless work of time's effacing fingers,
but nowhere did I find such cause for sorrow and
regret as in the falling off and change of base which
I found in the matter of melon cultivation.

We were exposed to the night air until past 1
o'clock, coming home tired and disappointed with
three small ones apiece, which we hid in the hay-
mow, according to a time-honored custom in the
family, and retired.

The next day we both made a noble resolution to
discard this unfortunate habit which we had con-
tracted, partly because we were old enough to know
better, and partly because we had in the hurry and
precipitation of the evening previous, stolen and

carried four miles a half dozen melons of the citron
variety, that tasted like a premature pumpkin and
smelled like cod liver oil and convalescent glue.

I had also lost my revolver. When I go out
nights I always go armed, and for that reason I
have gained the unenviable reputation of being a
bold, bad man. Many people think that I am thirst-
ing for the lives of my fellow men and feel low-
spirited and wretched unless I am shooting large,
irregular holes through the human family, but this
is not true.

I never killed any one in my life, unless death was
richly merited. I have never taken a human life
that society was not made better and safer by the
act.

This revolver was the same one that I used four
years ago when I shot at a burglar in Laramie. He
as endeavoring, at the dead hour of midnight, to
get into the window, and I feared that his intentions
were not honorable. He knew that I was alone in
the house, my wife having gone away on a visit,
and so taking advantage of her absence and my
timidity, he was endeavoring to force an entrance
into the house. I don't know what ever nerved me
to such an act of lofty heroism, but I marched softly
out of the front door with noiseless tread and shot
him.

Then I went back to bed and wondered what action the authorities would take with me. Whether
it would be considered justifiable homicide and I ex-
onerated, or whether I would be held without bail to
answer at the next term of court for murder. Then
I wondered what I had better do with the corpse.
At first I thought I would run down and notify the

coroner; then I concluded to go and see the victim, and see if life were extinct. Finally I compromised the matter by falling into a troubled sleep, from which I awoke on the following morning. I went out to the place where the burglar had been shot, but he was not there. With a superhuman will power he had dragged himself away somewhere to die. He had also destroyed all traces of blood before getting away

This was the last of the matter till the following September, when I received this letter:

OMAHA, September 3, 1876.

Dear Sir:

You doubtless think that I harbor ill-will and bitterness toward you because you shot me last summer, but such is not the case. I write to express my gratitude and everlasting friendship.

For years I had been an invalid, and last summer owing to my weak and helpless condition and consequent loss of employment, I became deranged. That accounts for my wild and insane idea that your residence was the abode of wealth and affluence.

It was the delirium that precedes death. Ah, my benefactor, my noble deliverer from death, how shall l tell you of my never-ending gratitude?

How like an angel of mercy you stood up before me that night in your *robe de nuit* and shot me!

How like a blessed seraph you looked at me, with your polished joints glittering in the flash and dazzle of your peerless beauty!

I have been rapidly gaining ever since, in weight and strength. I am now married and happy, and I cheerfully point you out to my friends as the one who, by your health-promoting markmanship and

vitality-restoring revolver, brought me back from
death to hope, health and happiness.

Yours truly,   THE-MAN-YOU-SHOT.

Since that I have called that revolver my Great
Health Invigorator and Blood Purifier.

THEY GAVE HIM AWAY.

ABSALOM WORTHLESS SPATES, late Secretary of
Wyoming, was not the proprietor of a very robust
intellect. It is rumored that he got mixed up with
some other man in some way, and by mistake was
sent out west to poultice Wyoming. A prominent
Maryland man was asked to get up the necessary
papers for sending Spates to a preparatory institute
for lop-eared idiots, and the papers got mixed with
those of a young man who was figuring for an ap-
pointment as Secretary of this territory. That's why
Spates came here.

Well, Spates got it into his head that, when he
got out here he was a sort of Grand Caliph of the
Solar System, and General Western Agent for the
whole planetary world.

He entered into the Garfield campaign, and traveled through the east, last fall, making speeches, till
the people wished they had died of cholera infantum.

He came back to Omaha flushed and triumphant.
He was positive that the Republican ticket would be
victorious, and a glorious majority march to the polls
in November.

He went to a meeting at Omaha, and paid the
chairman $5 to introduce him as a political speaker.
Then he addressed the meeting till the wildly en-

thusiastic audience was so carried away that nobody was left but an old fat man from Council Bluffs, who was sound asleep.

The *Herald* man could not attend the meeting, so about 10 o'clock he asked Sorenson, of the *Republican*, what Spates had said, etc.

Sorenson was too busy and life was too short, so he told the, *Herald* man that the best thing would be to attach himself to Mr. So-and-so at the Withnell, who could tell him all about it. Then Sorenson fixed it with the central office so that the *Herald* man was given the *Republican* office again instead of the Withnell, and Kent, of the *Bee*, was stationed at the instrument for fear that Sorenson's voice would be recognized, the latter dictating to Kent what to say.

The next morning about the following appeared in the *Herald:*

"The meeting last evening at the Academy of Music was quite well attended, though not very enthusiastic. A. Worth Spates, of Vinegar Hill, Wyoming, addressed the assemblage. The speaker is not prepossessing, as his legs are too limber and his intellect a little too hollow chested. Mr. Spates said:

"I am very much worn out, having addressed a great many large assemblages within the past few weeks, upon the momentous question: 'Whither are we drifting, and if so, to what extent?'

"I am grieved to say that, although I have used all my wonderful mental powers in behalf of the republican party, we are in danger of getting left.

"At one place I was greeted with some old condemned eggs, that smelled like Stewart's body, and, as my speech was a triumph of oratorical power, I am led to believe that the republican principles that I advocate were not in good odor with the people. The eggs certainly put me in bad odor with those who were present.

"I'm afraid we are busted.

"I addressed one meeting at Oil City, Pennsylvania, and the audience arose and bombarded me with decayed vegetables and other anonymous communications.

"I am afraid that the nation is to become the victim of an armed neutrality, or the horrible ravages of *vice versa.*"

When Mr. Spates saw the speech as reported by the *Herald,* he felt grieved and hurt, and sought to drown his sorrows in the flowing bowl.

The police put him on board the western bound train, and when he got lucid again he was up near Ogalally, Nebraska, with a large pain in his head.

The most horrible part of this tale is that it is true.

OUR FIRST CIRCUS "AD."

Yesterday a young man with the good clothes of a bunko steerer and the glad, effulgent look of a great man who is comfortably full, came into *The Boomerang* office, and after some mental labor at the desk of the society editor who had gone over across the street for a bologna sausage, produced the following advertisement which he desired inserted for two weeks on the fourth page of the *The Boomerang:*

SEASON OF 1882.

Grand farewell bridal tour of the only double-and-twisted, all-wool aggregation, the world's congress of wonders and torchlight procession of arenic talent, headed by a living phalanx of gold-bespattered chariots and winged monsters of the briny deep, followed by the most jewhillikin gosh-all-hemlock e xposition of camels wish twisted tails, wappy-jawed giraffs and speckled hyenas from Father India, squeaking babboons with purple snoots, Early Rose dromedaries from Europe, slim tailed birds of paradise, and big snakes from everywhere.

Bear in mind the day and date.

The Royal, Imported, Perihilion Stunner of the known world, will be in Laramie on its way to visit the crowned heads of Europe, July 4th, for one day only.

Don't fail to see the bearded lady on the flying trapez, or the wild-eyed lunatic from Skowhegan, Maine, in his scrumptuous swoop from the top of a flour barrel to the middle of the arena.

Voluptuous reserved seats made of two by four scantling set on edge.

Come early, and secure your seats.

This is the only whoopemuplizajane show on earth.

The gentlemanly agent then gave us ten bread tickets for reserved seats, and went away.

The last we saw of him, he was in a saloon, with his head shoved clear through his plug hat, while his whole general appearance was that of a man who is rapidly gliding into the mysterious realm of navy blue jimjams and peculiar assorted snakes.

OUR SCHOOL DAYS.

Dear reader, in the midst of the hurry and the distraction of business do you ever look far out across the purple hills, with misty vision, and think of the days, now held in the sacred silence of your memory, when you trudged through the June sunlight to the little log school house, with bare feet and happy heart?

Do the pleasant memories come thronging back to you now of those hallowed years in your history when you bowed your head above your spelling lesson, and, while filling your mind with useful knowledge, you also filled your system full of doughnuts and thought?

How sweetly come back to us to-day, like an almost forgotten fragrance of honeysuckle and wood violets, the recollections of the school-room, the busy hum of a score of industrious scholars, and, above all, the half-repressed sob of the freckled youth who thoughtlessly hovered o'er the bent pin for a brief, transitory moment. Oh! who can give us back the hallowed joys of childhood, when we ostensibly sought out the whereabouts of Timbuctoo in our geography while we slid a vigorous wasp into the pants pocket of our seat mate.

Our common schools are the foundations of America's free institutions. They are the bulwarks of our liberty and the glory and pride of a great republic. It is there that the youth of our land learn the rudiments of greatness and how to throw a paper wad with unerring precision.

Do you remember when you had no dreams of statesmanship and when the holy ambition to be a paragrapher had never fired your young blood? Do you remember when you had no ambition except to be the boy who could tell the most plausible lie? Do you still remember with what wonderful discretion you sought out and imposed upon the boy you thought you could lick? and do you still call to mind the thrill of glad surprise that came over you when you made a slight error and the meek-eyed victim arose in his wrath and left you a lonesome ruin?

Do you ever stop to think of those glorious holidays you took without the teacher's consent? How you rambled in the wildwood all day and gathered nuts, and crab apples, and wood ticks, and watermelons and mosquito bites? Have you returned tired and hungry at night and felt that your parents wouldn't be so tickled to see you as they might be?

Do you know of the day when you rashly resolved to lick your father, and he persuaded you to change your mind and let him lick you?

Who would rob us of these green memories of other days? Who would snatch from us the joy we still experience in bringing up those pictures of careless childhood when we bathed in the clear, calm waters of the smooth flowing river, or pelted each other with mud or dead frogs while the town people drove by and wondered why the authorities didn't take some measures to prevent boys from bathing in public places.

People come into *The Boomerang* office every day and see us writing out checks and raking in the scads and think that we must be happy, but we'd give all these gaudy trappings of wealth and luxuriant ease for one week of those schooldays, when we had less wealth but more appetite.

It might not look dignified for a man upon whom the eye of the nation rests, to descend to the sports of youth, but every little while an almost irresistible spell comes o'er us to lay aside our white vests and costly gems, while we·don a gingham shirt, a pair of top boots and some other finery, and make a raid on the watermelon trees of Wyoming.

UTE STATESMANSHIP.

There will be a big pow wow at the White River agency on the 25th, at which the Utes will decide whether they will go away to their new lands peaceably or not.

We are permitted to. publish in advance the written statement of Chief Colorow, which he will submit to the meeting on that occasion, and give it below:

GENTLEMEN OF THE CONFERENCE, WARRIORS AND PALE-FACED SNOOZERS FROM THE LAND OF THE RISING SUN:

My people are to-day cordially invited by the white father to pack up their furniture and go west to grow up with the country.

We are asked to leave our lands and take up some claims in another locality under the desert land act.

The white father tells his children to scoot. He says he needs these lands in his business, and asks the red man to gather his pappooses and take a little excursion into a strange land.

The white father knows that when he speaks we must obey his voice. He has the regular army and another man to enforce his commands.

HEAP SWEAT.

We accept the situation. The bones of our ancestors are here. Here are our homes. Here are the spirits of our dead. We have handed in our remonstrance, but it don't count.

In a few moons we must turn our backs upon these hills and valleys, and go to our new reservation.

White men with their pale squaws and spindle-shanked pappooses will build their wigwams here. The prospector will come here and dig holes in the earth, and the farmer will plant his crook-neck squash above the ashes of my people.

When the white father starts the music, we waltz to it.

We have been asked to irrigate the country here, and hoe corn like the white man. Our hearts are heavy, and we cannot promote the string bean. We will do what is right, but we cannot work. The Indian cannot hunt the potato bug when the deer and antelope are ripe. He cannot dig post-holes in the hot sun when the chase calls upon him to go forth into the forest.

Here, where we have roamed through the tall grass, and hunted the deer and buffalo, the pale face asks us to dig irrigation ditches, and plow the green earth with a rebellious mule.

Here, where our war cry has been answered back by the giant hills, we are told to whack bulls and and join the church.

They come to us and tell us to go to school, and wear pants. They ask us to learn the language of the pale face and go to congress. They send men to us who want us to learn how to spell and wear suspenders.

We cannot do this. We are used to the ways of our people. Our customs are old as the universe. We scratch our backs against the mountain pine as my people did a thousand years ago. We cannot change. We can leave our land, but we cannot change our socks every spring and do as the white man does.

We can go away from our homes and live in a strange land, but we cannot wear open-back shirts and lead in prayer.

Warriors, we will go to the land our white father has given us. We will take our squaws and our yaller dogs, our wigwams and our fleas.

We will go to our new home beyond the river now, and when the autumn comes we will take a bridal tour back to this country.

We will construct a holocaust, whatever that is, and spatter the intellectual faculties of the ranchers all over the country.

That is all. I am done. I have made my remarks. I have twittered my twit.

ABOUT THE MORMON.

Yesterday's train No. 7 was loaded with some more Mormons, who had been proselyted by the bunko steerers of the church of Jesus Christ of Latterday Saints from the various poorhouses and lunatic asylums of creation.

Most every one who don't know much about Mormonism thinks that the church is simply ignorant, with a morbid desire among its communicants to get married.

The plain, stub-toed truth, however, is that the average Mormon not only wants to get married at every available opportunity, but he is a man who glories in the clothes he wore ten years ago, and who brings with him the dust and dirt of foreign climes.

He comes among us from every benighted land under the sun, bringing with him the flavor of his native hog pen, and the choice fragrance of the steerage passenger. He lands upon our shores unable to speak our language or to adopt our style of soap. The first words he learns are those necessary to ask some cross-eyed old hag with a wen on her nose to marry him, and he goes on inducing the old condemned hens of Zion to be sealed to him till a merciful providence cuts him down and he leaves a herd of snorting widows with feet like a sack of flour and complexions like an old hair trunk. ·

Mormonism is not alone reprehensible because it induces a chronic and insatiable desire to marry the whole broad universe and a portion of York State, but because when a man dies it takes so much gloom to go around among the members of his family.

Think of the regular amount of surging grief over the death of the husband and father, divided up among twenty purple-nosed women and one hundred children with old gold hair and skim-milk eyes.

It is said that the Mormon church is rapidly gaining a foothold in Wyoming, and we believe it to be true. Anyhow, the air seems awful close here this spring. Something must be done.

We thought that the sanitary condition of the territory was getting bad, and that the dead cattle on

the plains had something to do with it; but it seems
that it is the growth of Mormonism.

If the church of the Mormon prophet extends its
domain over this side of the range, people will have
to go about their work day after day with an elastic
band or a patent clothespin on their snoots.

In saying that Mormonism is in bad odor with our
people, we feel that we are borne out by the facts.

If Mormonism, and a wild and frenzied longing
to marry every wappyjawed woman in Christen-
dom, be a stench in the nostrils of the president,
what must it be here within a hundred miles of
polygamy, bigamy, trigamy and pigamy.

A RELIC

The editor of this paper, who has made the study
of the Indian character a life work, has in his possession a letter written by the well known Pocahon-
tas˙ to her father, and publishes it below for the
benefit of his readers. Although we have, as we
said, made the subject of the Indian character a life
study, it has, of course, been at a distance. When
it was necessary to take some risk in visiting them
personally, at a time when they were feeling a little
wild and skittish, we have taken the risk vicariously
in order to know the truth.

WEROWOCOMOCO, Sunday, 1607.

DEAR PAW: You ask me to come to you before
another moon. I will try to do so. When Pow-
.hatan speaks his daughter tumbles to the racket.

You say I am too solid on the pale face Smith. I
hope not. He is a great man. I see that in the future my people must yield to the white man.

Our people now are pretty plenty, and the pale face seldom, but the day will come when the red man will be scattered like the leaves of the forest, and the Smiths will run the entire ranch.

Our medicine man tells me that after a time the tribe of Powhatan will disappear from the face of the earth, while the Smiths will extend their business all over the country till you can't throw a club at a yaller dog without hitting one of the Smith family.

My policy, therefore, is to become solid with the majority. A Smith may some day be chief cook and bottle-washer of this country. We may want to get some measure through the council. See?

Then I will go in all my wild beauty and tell the high muck-a-muck that years ago under the umbrageous shadow of a big elm I plead with my hardhearted parent to prevent him from mashing the cocoanut of the original Smith, and everything will be O. K.

You probably catch my meaning.

As to loving the gander-shanked pale face, I hope you will give yourself no unnecessary loss of sleep over that. He is as homely anyhow as a cow shed struck with a club, and has two wives in Europe and three pairs of twins.

Fear not, noble dad. Your little Pocahontas has the necessary intellect to paddle her own canoe, and don't you ever forget it.

Remember me to Brindle Dog, and his squaw, the Sore-Eyed Sage Hen, and send me two plugs of tobacco and a new dolman with beads down the back. At present I am ashamed to come home, as my

wardrobe consists of a pair of clam shell bracelets
and an old parasol.   Ta, Ta,

POCAHANTAS.

Some men are born bilious, some achieve biliousness, and others have biliousness thrust upon them.

> With tender, dreamy eyes she stands,
>   And looks out o'er the velvet plain,
> Guiding with white and shapely hands
>   The garden hose with gentle rain.
>
> I lift my hat to thee, my queen,
>   With gingham apron 'round thee girt,—
> Great Scott! you've fancied me so green,
>   You've drowned me with the garden squirt.

THE FLY.

Much has been said of the fly of the period, but
few write about him who are bald-headed.

Hence we say a word.   It is of no use any more to
deny the horrible truth.   Although beautiful as a
peri in other ways, our tresses on top have succumbed to the inclemency of the weather, and our
massive brow is slowly creeping over toward the
back of our neck.   Nature makes all things even.
If a man be possessed of such ravishing beauty and
such winning ways that his power might become
dangerous, she makes him bald-headed.

That is our fix.

When we have our hat on and go chasseing down
the street with that camel glide of ours, everyone
asks who that noble-looking Apollo with the deep
and melancholy eye is; but when we are at the office
with our hat hung up on the French walnut side-

board, and the sun shines softly in through the rose-
wood shutters, and lights up the shellac polish on
our intellectual dome, we are not so pretty.

Then it is that the fly, with gentle tread and
seductive song, comes and prospects around on our
bump of self-esteem, and tickles us and makes us
mad.

When we get where forbearance ceases to be a
virtue, we haul off and slap the place where he was,
while he goes over to the inkstand and snickers at
us. After he has waded around in the carmine ink
awhile, he goes back to the bump of spirituality,
and makes some red marks over it.

Having laid off his claim under the new mining
law, he proceeds to sink on it.

If we write anything bitter these days; if we say
aught of our fellow man that is disagreeable or un-
just, and for which we afterward get licked, it is
because at times we get exasperated, and are not
responsible.

If the fly were large and weighed 200 pounds and
came in here and told us that if we didn't take back
what we had said about him, he would knock out
the window with our remains, and let us fall a hundred feet into the busy street, it wouldn't worry us
so much, because then we could strangle him with
one hand, while we wrote a column editorial on
Conkling with the other. We do that frequently;
but a little fragile insect, with no home and no
parents, and only four or five million brothers and
sisters, gains our confidence, and then tickles our
scalp, till we have to write with a sheet of tar roof
ing over our head.

Then he comes in and helps us read our proof. We don't want him to help, but he insists on making corrections and putting punctuations in the wrong place, and putting full stops where they knock the sense all out of the paragraph.

If the fly could be removed from our pathway, we would march along in our journey to the tomb in a way that would be the envy and admiration of the civilized world. As it is, we feel that we are not making a very handsome record.

BUCK BRAMEL'S BLONDE BRONCO.

"Did you ever see them buckskin broncos of mine that I used to drive, named Yeller and Yaller?" asked Buck Bramel the other day of General Worth, while he looked out across the green billowy divide toward the eternal whiteness of the snowy range.

The General lit the refractory stump of a Havana filler for the twenty-seventh time, and then said:

"Why, no, Bub. Blank it all to blank. Never heard of 'em."

"Well," said Buck, as a tender light came in his blue eye and a three-cornered nugget of tin tag tobacco was stowed away in his cheek, "both of them same cayuse plugs could scoot over more mountain road between sun and sun, than anything in the line of hoss I ever see.

"Yeller was pretty midlin' rapid, but Yaller was an imported terror. You ought to see him gather up his limbs in a wad and vanish. One day I was out on board of Yaller, tryin' to round up an American cow that had strayed away from the corral, and

over west of the divide I woke up a long-legged
buck antelope.

"I made a little shassay over toward the antelope
to see him light out, but he first pranced along kind
of careless like, as much as to say, 'I guess I won't
give you no 2:13 gait this morning. Life is too brief.
I can't run that way just to amaze every snoozer
that comes this way on a blonde plug like that.'

"So I touched up old Yaller with the quirt and
sailed over toward the antelope, thinkin' I'd stir him
up a little.

"The antelope trotted along a few rods and then
looked back over his shoulder and smiled a sardonic
smile that made old Yaller mad as a wet hen.

"Then he got up an got. Jewhillikins, how he
pawed the gravel! Occasionally the antelope would
look around and snort and jump stiff-legged and
laugh. Then old Yaller would consume some more
space.

"The antelope turned himself loose, and for
awhile all I could see was a little cloud of dust and
the white spot that is always behind this amusin'
little animal.

After awhile, however, I could see that the white
patch got bigger. Yaller was gainin'. I jabbed the
Mexican spurs into him to encourage him. In less
than an hour I was alongside of him. His tongue
hung out so that he stepped on it every little while.

"He didn't laugh any more then. It was a horrible reality. He was the saddest antelope I ever see.
He seemed to think that we had imposed on him
somehow. Every little while he'd look at old Yal-

ler kind of reproachful, as if we'd taken advantage of him.

"Bye'n bye I reached over and took him by the ears and laid him across the saddle ahead of me, and took him home. I kept him for years, but he never rallied.

"He seemed to lose all hope, and would walk around the corral like an old Billy goat that had been betrayed some time. Life for him seemed to be nothing but a wide, shoreless waste of bitter disappointment and regret.

"I tell you, General, it takes the hope and joy and pride all out of an antelope to be scooped by a $15 buckskin bronco."

"Yes," said the General, musingly. " I should think it would. If I was a broken-legged antelope with one foot done up in a gum overshoe, and had to go on crutches, and couldn't outrun any buckskin hoss I ever saw, I'd go away to some lonely spot and stick my head into a prairie dog's hole and die in remorse."

A letter written from the east and addressed to this office, asks if we can give any information as to the whereabouts of Big Nose George. We cannot give any definite information, but the last seen of him he was standing on a flour barrel near a telegraph pole, and a man with a stop-watch was standing near him and preparing to kick the flour barrel out from under him. It is thought that the man with the abnormal nasal protuberance has gone some where by telegraph.

ODE TO THE CUCUMBER.

O, a cucumber grew by the deep rolling sea,
And it tumbled about in reckless glee
Till the summer waned and the grass turned brown,
And the farmer plucked it and took it to town.

Wrinkled and warty and bilious and blue,
It lay in the market the autumn through;
Till a woman with freckles on her cheek
Led in her husband, so mild and meek.

He purchased the fruit, at her request,
And hid it forever under his vest;
For it doubled him up like a kangaroo,
And now he sleeps 'neath the violets blue.

HEAP GONE.

Thursday evening the Rodgers started out to look for the Jeannette up among the icebergs. In about a year from now another boat load of brave men will be sent up there to look for the Rodgers.

Blamed if we haven't got more of a navy yard clustered around the north pole than we have here at home, to say nothing of the shin bones and pants buttons that America has contributed to science.

Let the good work go on. The open polar sea is getting to be quite a watering place. A man can go up there and spend the summer, and fill his system up full of pemmican and blubber and star candles, and be entirely safe from the prying eyes of his political enemies and creditors.

Think of going over there where it's nine months late in the evening and three months before breakfast. Think of a land where there are no mosquitoes,

no bumble bees, no Fourth of July, no sunstroke
and no taxes.

Nothing but a wide shoreless waste of shrinking
starless night and polar bear. Nothing but Esqui-
maux dog on toast and the eternal stillness of a twilight which extends from July to eternity and sticks
out into space like a sore thumb.

Think of going out and catching a whale for
breakfast, and eating a polar bear and a walrus for
luncheon. Imagine yourself living in an ice house
through dog days, and rubbing your chilblains
through the Fourth of July.

Ah, it's singular why people prefer to die that way
so long as there are so many brick buildings standing around handy where a man can bang his brains
out whenever he gets sick of life.

THE TRUE TALE OF WILLIAM TELL.

William Tell ran a hay ranch near Bergelen,
about 580 years ago. Tell had lived in the mountains all his life, and shot chamois and chipmunks
with a cross-gun, till he was a bad man to stir up.

At that time Switzerland was run principally by a
lot of carpet baggers from Austria, and Tell got
down on them about the year 1307. It seems that
Tell wanted the government contract to furnish hay
at $45 a ton, for the year 1306, and Gessler, who
was controlling the patronage of Switzerland, let
the contract to an Austrian who had a big lot of
condemned hay, farther up the gulch.

One day Gessler put his plug hat up on a telegraph pole, and issued order 236, regular series, to

the effect that every snoozer who passed down the
toll road should bow to it.

Gessler happened to be in behind the brush when
Tell went by, and he noticed that Bill said "Shoot
the hat," and didn't salute it; so he told his men to
gather Mr. Tell in, and put him in the refrigerator.

Gessler told him that if he would shoot a crabapple from the head of his only son, at 200 yards,
with a cross-gun, he would give him his liberty.

Tell consented, and knocked the apple higher
than Gilroy's kite. Old Gessler, however, noticed
another arrow sticking in William's girdle, and he
asked what kind of a flowery break that was.

Tell told him that if he had killed the kid instead
of busting the apple, he intended to drill a hole
through the stomach of Mr. Gessler. This made
Gessler mad again, and he took Tell on a picnic up
the river in irons.

Tell jumped off when he got a good chance, and
cut across a bend in the river, and when the
picnic party came down, he shot Gessler deader than
a mackerel.

This opened the ball for freedom, and weakened
the Austrian government so much, that in the following November they elected Tell to fill the long
term, and a half-breed for the short term.

After that Tell was recognized by the ruling
power, and he could get most any contract that he
wanted to. He got the service on the stage line up
into the Alps increased to a daily, and had the con-
tracts in the name of his son Albert.

The appropriation was increased $150,000 per year,
and he had a good thing.

Tell lived many years after this, and was loved by
the Swiss people because he had freed their land.

Whenever he felt lonesome, he would take his
cross-gun and go out and kill a tyrant. He had
tyrant on toast most every day till Switzerland was
free, and the peasants blessed him as their deliverer.

When Tell got to be an old man he would go out
into the mountains and apostrophize them in these
memorable words:

"Ye crags and peaks, I'm with you once again. I
hold to you the hands I held to you on previous occasions, to show you they are free. The tyrant's
crust is busted, so to speak. His race is run, and he
himself hath scooted up the flume. Sic semper
McGinnis, terra firma nux vomica Schweitzer kase,
Timbuctoo erysipelas, epluribus unum sciataca, mul-
tum in parvo, vox populi vox snockemonthegob."

SLIDING DOWN A MOUNTAIN IN A GOLD PAN.

Dear reader, did you ever slide down a mountain
in a gold pan? Did you ever experience the exhila-
ration of scooting down the range while the panorama of the great west flew past you like a dream?

Early in the spring a North Park miner, who had
been prospecting for gold on the headwaters of the
Platte, got up on the continental divide, about 12,000
feet above high water mark, to view the beauties of
nature, and as he had heard of the wild, glad intoxication of sliding down hill in a gold pan, he concluded to experience the delightful thrill.

There was really too much thrill to the superficial
foot, as he found to his sorrow.

COASTING IN A GOLD PAN.

He had, of course, climbed far above snow line, and had a chance to start on an incipient glacier. This gave him a velocity which filled him full of eager surprise.

The speed, as it became more accelerated, took his breath away. There was a good deal of pure mountain air all about him, but he hadn't time to select any. He seemed in a hurry to get there.

On and still on he flew like a wild-eyed meteor, and still he clung convulsively to the gold pan in which he sat.

Anon he got below the snow line and began to scoot over the boulders on the mountain side. This heated the pan to a white heat, and the occupant felt as though someone had knocked him over on a red-hot stove.

＊　＊　＊　＊　＊　＊　＊　＊　＊

Days passed, and weeks were swallowed up in the filmy night of the irredeemable previously. Weeks grew into months, and still the miner came not to his cabin.

He had been almost forgotten by his companions, when, on the green banks of a mountain stream, the boys, one day, a short time ago, stumbled over a gold pan.

It only contained the copper rivets of a pair of canvas overalls, and a few charred fragments of a fried prospector.

That was all. Silently, and with bowed, uncovered heads, in the midst of the solemn mountain hush, by the banks of the bubbling stream, where the melancholy coyote howls his sad refrain, and where the greasewood and the sagebrush are weeping o'er his final resting place, they planted his remains, and on the candle-box cover, o'er his lonely grave, they wrote with red chalk:

> Over the river on the golden street,
> Slim-nosed William we all shall meet,
> Over the river, on the other side,
> Somewhat disfigured and muchly fried,
> Slim-nosed William has crossed the tide.

A Laramie man who used to own a water-melon patch and a bull-dog, in Iowa, is having constructed for the world's fair, a log-cabin bed-quilt, containing 2,135 pieces. The blocks are relics of boys' pants, pried out of the jaws of the bull-dog during the years that the owner was general manager of the melon patch.

THE ECCENTRIC SQUIRT.

Yesterday, an uptown lad, whose pants were hanging by one button, and whose nose had evidently recently been used to plow corn, decided to drink out of the nozzle of a hose that was placidly coiled up in front of a store on Second street.

He had just wrapped his features around the nozzle, and closed his eyes, to take a long, invigorating pull at the dripping fountain, when a clerk inside the store, who had been watching the thing a little, turned on the full pressure of 110 feet to the square inch.

There was a smothered gurgle and the sound of hissing waters for a moment, then all was still.

The clerk came out with a door-mat, and wiped the water from the calm features of the boy as he lay there, then turned him over and opened his mouth so that the water could run out of him; tenderly spanked him with a pine board to restore animation, and sent him home.

We never bet except on a dead sure thing, but we will bet a week's salary, or $1,500, that this same lad will hereafter submit to the irksome customs of our modern civilization, and drink out of a tin cup.

TABLE ETIQUETTE.

There are a great many people who behave well otherwise, but at table do things that if not absolutely *outre* and *ensemble*, are at least *pianissimo* and *sine die*.

It is with a view to elevating the popular taste and etherializing, so to speak, the manners and customs of our readers, that we give below a few hints upon table etiquette.

If by writing an article of this kind we can induce one man who now wipes his hands on the table cloth to come up and take higher ground and wipe them on his pants, we shall feel amply repaid.

If you cannot accept an invitation to dinner do not write your regrets on the back of a pool check with a blue pencil. This is now regarded as *ricochet.*

A simple note to your host informing him that your washerwoman refuses to relent is sufficient.

On seating yourself at the table draw off your gloves and put them in your lap under your napkin. Do not put them in the gravy, as it would ruin the gloves and cast a gloom over the gravy. If you have just cleaned your gloves with benzine, you might leave them out in the front yard.

If you happen to drop gravy on your knife blade, back near the handle, do not run the blade down your throat to remove the gravy, as it might injure your epiglottis, and it is not considered *embonpoint*, anyway.   ·

When you are at dinner do not take up a raw oyster on your fork and playfully ask your host if it is dead. Remarks about death at dinner are in very poor taste.

Pears should be held by the stems and peeled gently but firmly, not as though you were skinning a dead horse. It is not *bon ton.*

Oranges are held on a fork while being pulled, and the facetious style of squirting the juice into the eye of your hostess is now *au revoir.*

Stones in cherries or other fruit should not be placed upon the tablecloth, but slid quietly and unostentatiously into the pocket of your neighbor or noiselessly tossed under the table.

If you strike a worm in your fruit do not call attention to it by mashing it with a nut-cracker. This is not only uncouth, but it is regarded in the best society as *blase* and exceedingly *vice versa.*

Macaroni should be cut into short pieces and eaten with an even graceful motion, not absorbed by the yard.

In drinking wine, when you get to the bottom of your glass do not throw your head back and draw in your breath like the exhaust of a bath tub in order to get the last drop, as it engenders a feeling of the most depressing melancholy among the guests.

After eating a considerable amount do not rise and unbuckle your vest strap in order to get more room, as it is exceedingly *au fait* and *dishabille.*

If by mistake you drink out of your finger bowl, laugh heartily and make some facetious remark which will change the course of conversation and renew the friendly feeling among the members of the party.

Ladies should take but one glass of wine at dinner. Otherwise there might be difficulty in steering the male portion of the procession home.

Do not make remarks about the amount your companion has eaten. If the lady who is your company at table, whether she be your wife or the wife of some one else, should eat quite heartily, do not offer to pay your host for his loss or say to her "Great Scott! I hope you will not kill yourself because you have the opportunity," but be polite and gentlemanly, even though the food supply be cut off for a week.

If one of the gentlemen should drop a raw oyster into his bosom and he should have trouble in fishing it out, do not make facetious remarks about it, but assist him to find it, laughing heartily all the time.

A CHILD'S FAITH.

During a big thunder shower awhile ago little Willie, who slept up stairs alone, got scared and called his mother, who came up and asked him what he was frightened about. Willie frankly admitted that the thunder was a little too much for a little boy who slept alone.

"Well, if you are afraid," said his mother, pushing back the curls from his forehead, "you should pray for courage."

"Well, all right," said Willie, an idea coming into his head; "suppose you stay up here and pray while I go down stairs and sleep with paw."

THE FOURTH AMONG THE UTES.

The Utes on White River will celebrate the glorious natal day of the republic, and they ask us to publish the programme, which we cheerfully do:

The oration of Pop-Eyed Caterpillar we will give as soon as the manuscript is received.

PROGRAMME.

Sunrise—Salute of thirteen guns (to be pointed at the agent and loaded with buckshot).

9 o'clock a. m.—Parade of the ancient order of Squint-Eyed Squaws.

10 o'clock—Forming of procession in following order:

1.—White River Elastic Band.

2.—Ute warriors, mounted on cayuse plugs, marching Indian file.

3.—Chaplains, marching four abreast.

4.—Reader of Declaration of Independence borne on a shutter.

5.—Orator of the day, wearing paper collar and pair of summer spurs.

6.—Chairman of committee, pensive and drunk.

7.—Beautiful Indian maidens, clothed in flour sacks.

8.—Other beautiful Indian maidens of English descent.

9.—Indian girls representing the different States —mainly, however, representing a state of beastly intoxication.

10.—The Anti-Fine Comb league, carrying entomological specimens of the tribe.

11.—Other citizens on foot.

12.—Indian dogs.

On arriving at the grounds, the following will be
the order of exercises:

1.—Song by the White River Glee Club, "Whoop
'Em Up, 'Liza Jane."

2.—Oration by Pop-Eyed Caterpillar.

3.—Passing around the hat.

4.—Foot race of cross-eyed Indians under two
years old.

5.—Shooting match to be entered into indiscrimi-
nately by all present, in a social interchange of
friendly feeling, with double-barreled shot-guns.
Prize to be awarded to the survivor.

Evening—Fireworks, firewater, scalp dance, and
general flow of soul.

THE COMET.

Yesterday morning, between 3 and 4 o'clock we
were called from our bed by the presence of a sorrel
cow, with an inadequate tail, in the grounds of our
winter palace.

She had eaten a row of tube roses and some
mignonette, to sweeten her breath, and was just
smelling of the statue of Eli Perkins, which stands
on the west side of our boulevard, when we came up
behind her with a bed slat, and smote her on the
snoot.

While merrily romping with her over the velvety
lawn, our attention was suddenly called to a large
$250 comet, northwest by nor', and about three feet

above the horizon, with its tail over the dashboard.

When first seen it was in perihelion with the dome of the court house, but, while we watched it, either the court house changed its position, or we did, and the space became more clearly defined.

Some are of the opinion that this comet is the one that appeared about twenty-five years ago, but our own idea is that it is a new one that has never been used.

It is something the style of Roscoe Conkling, with a more subdued and pensive air, however, and is making good time.

It has a nucleus that shines with a nebulous light. It also carries with it a hyperbola and a parabola, in a common valise.

A well known astronomer claims that this is a comet, which, according to the books, was not due yet for 1,500 years. There must be some mistake, however, unless it lost some thing when it was here 500 years ago, and has returned to see if it cannot find it. Still, its running time may have been changed in order to stir up competition with other comets.

We had no time to fully investigate the wonderful celestial phenomenon, as people began to pass where we were taking observations and noticing our simple costume called the attention of other people to us, and in a short time a large and demonstrative audience had gathered near us, which disturbed our scientific researches and concluded the early morning session.

A LITTLE INCIDENT.

Many years ago, in the early days of Dodge City, Kansas, when society was in a crude state, and when the wheels of justice moved with a good deal of deliberation, there dwelt a justice of the peace and ex-officio coroner named McIntosh.

This advance agent of square-toed justice didn't know much about law, but he had made the subject of fees a life study. He was therefore called "McIntosh on Fees."

McIntosh was generally wrapped in the dignity of his important official position and fully impressed with the magnitude and majesty of the law. Sometimes, however, mercy tempered justice to that extent that McIntosh would remit the fine with the understanding that the fees were to be paid.

He never remitted the fees.

The fines were never excessive, but the fees were generally pretty stout. He almost always mentioned the fact that in each case there had been a good deal of "folio writin'," and therefore the costs would be pretty heavy. What "folio writin'" consists of we are not able to state, but McIntosh on Fees was the man who knew how to dish up this sort of trimmings.

One day McIntosh on Fees presided over a case wherein there was a jury, and after deliberating on the case for a day the jury rendered a verdict against the defendant, who hadn't a cent on earth.

Then the majesty of the law raised up on its hind legs and made itself felt. McIntosh on Fees discharged the jury, and, with a few preliminary remarks, vetoed the verdict and reversed the effect of the entire proceedings by rendering a judgment against the plaintiff, thus securing the costs.

The plaintiff appealed the case, but was killed one morning before breakfast prior to the session of the circuit court which was to dispose of the case.

McIntosh on Fees didn't know the difference between a *quo warranto* and the erysipelas, but he had more dignity than the chief justice of the supreme court of the United States.

Once, however, his dignity was seriously ruffled. He didn't know what to say. It was about the close of his official career.

An old snoozer, whom we will call Spangler, because that was not his name, lived with his partner out on a hay ranch, about nine miles from Dodge City. We call him Spangler partly because he is still alive, and he is said to be a bad man with a double-barrel shotgun.

It is not our intention to be personal where a man is concerned who is trying to live a different life and who is at all reckless with firearms. Of course a man's official record is the property of the public; still it has never been our policy to attack the official acts of a man who would, in an unguarded moment, be careless of human life.

Well, Spangler and his partner had in their employ a negro named Emancipation Higgins. One evening Emancipation Higgins, who was the cook, in wiping the dishes, forgot himself and polished the majolica butter plate on his overalls. This so irritated Spangler's partner that he took a Smith and Wesson revolver of the old pattern and shot a hole into the intellect of Emancipation Higgins, through which his immortal soul leaked out and winged its way to a brighter land.

Although both Spangler and his partner regretted the unfortunate direction that affairs had taken, they decided that it would be better, considering the highly excited state of affairs in Kansas, to keep the matter from the public. So they buried Emancipation in a very unostentatious manner at one corner of the corral. The exercises were very brief, and, no doubt, nothing would have been said of the affair had it not been that Spangler and his partner had a misunderstanding after a while, and the former got the worst of it. While he was getting the swelling out of his eye and recovering from the desolating effects of his encounter, Spangler resolved that he would atone for his past life in a measure by going to the authorities and confessing that his partner was a murderer.

As soon as he had made this resolve his heart seemed lighter and his conscience more clear than it had been for years. He determined to make a full and free confession relative to his partner, no matter how much the effort might cost him.

About half past 11 one summer evening McIntosh on Fees was wakened and called to his door by Spangler, who told him that he had a confession to make. He told McIntosh that his partner was the most bloodthirsty unhung cut-throat in Kansas, and asked the acting coroner to investigate the recent murder of Emancipation Higgins.

"To save time," said Spangler, "I have exhumed the remains and brought them with me, or enough of them, at least, to hold an inquest on."

He then took a gunnysack from his saddle, where it had been tied, and deliberately untying it extracted from its sombre depths the head of Emancipation Higgins.

It was something that McIntosh on Fees was not prepared for.

The negro was not a handsome man even in life and when fixed up in his good clothes, but now in the chastened moonlight, with a large aperture in the side of his head, there was something about the gory fragments of the late lamented that seemed to cast a gloom over the whole face of nature.

All the rest of the night McIntosh on Fees lay awake. Whenever he would try to go to sleep, the hollow sightless eyes of Emancipation Higgins would seem to look down into his face, as if inquiring dumbly the result of the inquest.

The next morning McIntosh on Fees resigned his office, and with the archives turned over to his successor in office there was a gunnysack containing the material for a phrenological post mortem examination.

A TEARFUL APPEAL.

There is a good deal of interest manifested these days on the part of the American people relative to the matter of separate sleeping cars for the two sexes. It is a move in the right direction, and we hope it will win. As it is now, no gentleman traveling alone is safe.

Several months ago, entirely alone, we traveled from Laramie to Chicago and back, making the round trip with no escort whatever. Our wife was detained at home, and that entire journey was made with no one to whom we could look for protection.

When we returned our hair had turned perfectly white with the horror of those dreadful nights.

There was one woman from Philadelphia, whose name we will not mention, and who rode all the way between Omaha and Chicago in our car. Almost the first thing when we started out of Omaha, she began to make advances toward us by asking us if we would not hold her lunch basket while she went after a drink.

She also asked us for our knife to peel an orange.

These things look small and insignificant, but in the light of later developments they are of vital importance.

That evening we saw with horror that the woman's section was adjoining our own!

We asked the conductor if this could not be changed, but he laughed coldly, and told us to soak our head, or some such unfeeling remark.

That is one bad feature of the present system. A man traveling alone gets no sympathy or assistance from the conductor.

It would be impossible to describe the horror and apprehension of that awful night. All through its vigils we suffered on till near morning, when tired nature yielded, and we fell into a troubled sleep.

There we lay, fair and beautiful, in the soft gray · of approaching day, thousands of miles from our home, and, less than ten feet away, a great, horrid woman from Pennsylvania, to whom we had not even been introduced.

How we could sleep so soundly, under the circumstances, we are yet unable to tell, but after perhaps

twenty minutes of slumber, we saw, above the foot
board of our berth and peering over at us, the face
of that woman. With a wild bound we were on our
feet in the aisle of the car. The other berths had all
disappeared but ours.

The other passengers were sitting quietly in their
seats, and it was half-past 9 o'clock. The woman
from Pennsylvania was in the day coach.

It was only a horrid dream.

But supposing that it had been a reality! Any
man who travels alone is liable to be insulted at any
time. We do not care for luxury in traveling. All
we want is the assurance that we are safe.

The experience which we have narrated above is
only one of a thousand. Did you ever note the care-
worn look of the man who is traveling alone? The
wild, hunted expression on the countenance and the
horrible apprehension that is depicted there?

You may talk about the various causes that are
leading men downward to early graves, but the nervous strain induced by the fear that while they are
taking out their false teeth or buttoning their suspenders, prying eyes are looking over the footboard
of their berths, is constructing more new-made
graves than consumption or the Ute war.

THE CZAR.

"Yes," says the *Boomerang* correspondent, writing from St. Petersburg under date of April 3d,
"the Czar leads a very simple and unostentatious life
indeed. In the morning he has family prayers in
the cast-iron chapel in the backyard, after which he

retires to his own fire and burglar proof bank vault, and is locked in by a domestic.

"At noon his head cook squirts a quart of oxtail soup through the key-hole into the midst of the imperial presence.

"Then the Czar assays it, and if there be anything except the essence of ox, he squirts it back into the head cook's ear, and orders by telephone that the head cook be worked up into a pie.

"Yes, the Czar courts retirement more than any monarch known to history, giving all his orders through the keyhole of a fire and burglar proof door.

PIE.

A young man whom we will call Dudley Ashton went out to the North Park a few weeks ago to write up the mines, and otherwise to whoop up the country and make it blossom as the rose.

After he had been there some time, he thought that the miners didn't live high enough. He had been accustomed to luxury and pie, so he said he would show the boys how to make a pie.

Everyone was glad that a professional pie-promoter had struck the camp, and there was general good feeling all around.

So Dudley took off his coat and took a chew of tobacco, and laid the foundations for six fire-proof pies. He made some plaster-of-paris dough with amalgam filling, and proceeded to put in the "works." He got some canned blackberries that were on Jack Creek when the Indians invaded the camp years ago, and that were so hard even then that the Utes would not touch them.

12

These he kiln-dried and laid in the pie, holding them in place with ten-penny nails, and trimmed with overskirt of the same. After that, he was ready to put on the sheet-iron roof. This he did, fastening it down with wrought-iron rivets. Then he got an engraver to put his monogram on the top, and put the whole six pies in the retort of the assayer's furnace.

The following week the pies were taken out, still at a white heat. They were gradually cooled, and after the midday meal of bacon and coffee every man put his napkin under his chin and smacked his lips while Dudley took a pie out to the blacksmith shop to divide it up for dessert.

Only one man ate any pie that day. He was the man above whose lowly tomb the blue-eyed poison weed is waving, and where, in the quiet midnight, the soft-voiced coyote coos a mellow requiem.

The boys in the park feared that they would have to kill a man in order to start a cemetery, but when that pie penetrated the system of its victim, death entered the new metropolis, and on the plain white slab erected over the new made grave they simply wrote:

> Turn, sinners, turn; why will ye die
> From eating cold cast-iron pie.

ENTOMOLOGICAL.

Dear children, did you ever study the structure of the bumble bee, and notice how wisely nature has provided him with delicate anatomical arrangements, by which he is enabled to propel himself through the air, and protect himself from the changes of climate.

Did you ever stop to think how wisely he has been constructed, and, although small in size, yet perfect in mechanical operation.

First, let us notice the buffalo overcoat which he wears. This enables him to withstand any change of temperature from hot to cold, without catching pneumonia. Then he has a buff vest which he can wear to picnics, and a dark, seal-brown style of pants.

See also the soft, velvety covering to his foot. This enables him to meander softly up the pants leg of the young man who puts up the picnic swing.

Then, again, if you look closely at the bumble bee and tickle him with a straw, you will see a protuberance on him which he uses as a glad surprise. When the exercises lag a little, and he desires to throw a little variety into the proceedings, he takes his mirth-provoking little instrument out of his pocket and sharpens it on his boot. Then he steals up to the young man with the striped pants and clocked socks, and waits for the regular order of business, so that he can introduce his bill.

Then when the young man looks far out across the waving green of the fragrant meadows, and says to the blonde girl with the Swiss muslin dress: "O, Peri of North America, fairer than all the grand aggregation of living wonders, queen of my heart and acting assistant general manager of my glorious ultimately, did you ever ponder on the great wide rolling sea of life's tempestuous hitherto, or cast your longing eyes upon the bright-hued promise in the all pregnant contiguously, and then consider how adown life's inveterate perspicuity, unflecked by storm cloud, we two shall glide athwart the woof of efflorescent consanguinity—"

Then the bumble bee gets the speaker's eye, and introduces his bill. The young man rises to a point of privilege, and he does it so earnestly, and looks so wild and agitated, that most every one thinks he is going mad.

When a bumble bee has vaccinated a man, the best thing to do is to put the hot place on ice.

Bumble bees like to roll up their pants legs and wade around in the syrup, and then come out and walk over an oil painting.

In picking up one of these birds, the best thing to do it with is a pair of red-hot tongs or a pair of sheet iron mittens.

HOW A CHINAMAN RIDES A BRONCO.

When a Chinaman does anything in his own peculiar Oriental style, it is pretty apt to attract attention; but when he gets on a bucking bronco with the cheerful assurance of a man who understands his business, and has been conversant with the ways of the bronco for over 2,000 years, the great surging mass of humanity ceases to surge, and stands with bated breath and watches the exhibition with unflagging interest.

A Chinaman does not grab the bit of the bronco and yank it around till the noble steed can see thirteen new and peculiar kinds of fireworks, or kick him in the stomach and knock his ribs loose, or swear at him till the firmament gets loose and begins to roll together like a scroll, but he does his hair up

in an oriental wad behind and jabs a big hairpin into it, and smiles and says something like what a
Guinea hen would say if she got excited and tried
to report one of Bjoernstjerne Bjoernson's poems
backwards in his native tongue.

Then he gets on the wrong side and slides into the
saddle, making a remark as though something inside of ˏhim had broken loose, and the grand difficulty begins.

At first the bronco seems· surprised and temporarily rattled intellectually, and he stands idly in
the glad sunlight and allows his mental equilibrium
to wobble back into place, while the Chinaman
makes some observations that sound like the distant
melody of a Hancock club going home at 2 o'clock
A. M., and all talking at one and the same time.

By-and-by the bronco shoots athwart the sunny
sky like a thing of life, and comes down with all his
legs in a cluster like a bunch of asparagus, and with
a great deal of force and expression.

This movement throws the Chinaman's liver into
the northwest corner of the thorax, and his upper
left-hand deuodessimo into the middle of the subsequent week, but he does not complain. He opens
his mouth and breathes in all the atmosphere that
the rest of the universe can spare, and readjusting
his shirt tail so that it will have the correct inclina-
tion toward the horizon, he gently tickles the
bronco on the starboard quarter with the cork sole
of his corpulent shoe. This mirth-provoking movement throws the bronco into the wildest hysterics,
and for twenty minutes the spectators don't see anything very distinctly. The autumn sunlight seems
to be mixed up with blonde bronco, and the softened

haze of October seems fraught with pale blue shirt
tail and disturbed Chinaman, moving in an irregular orbit, and occasionally throwing off meteoric
articles of apparel and prehistoric chunks of igneous
profanity of the vintage of Confucius marked B.
C. 1860.

When the sky clears up a little the Chinaman's
hair has come down and hangs in wild confusion
about his olive features. The hem of his shirt flap
is seen to be very much frayed, like an American
flag that has snapped in the breeze for thirteen
weeks. He finds also that he has telescoped his
spinal column and jammed two extra ribs through
the right superior duplex, and he has two or three
vertebrae floating about through his system that he
don't know what to do with. The casual observer
can see that the Chinaman is a robust ruin, while
the bronco is still in a good state of preservation.

But the closing scene is still to come. The bronco
summons all his latent energy, and humping his
back up into the exhilarating atmosphere, he shoots
forward and upward with great earnestness and the
most reckless abandon, and when he once more
bisects the earth's orbit and jabs his feet into the
trembling earth, a shapeless mass of brocaded silk
and coarse black hair, and taper nails, and Celestial
shirt tail, and Oolong profanity, and disorganized
Chinese remains, and shattered Oriental shirt destroyer, comes down apparently from the ninth-
story window of the New Jerusalem, and the coroner goes out on the street to get six good men and a
chemist, and they analyze the collection.

They report that deceased came to his death by
reason of concussion, supposed to have been induced

by his fall from the outer battlements of the Sweet
Bye and Bye.

FOOD FOR THOUGHT.

The *Sunny Clime*, published at Terrell, Texas, is
a mighty good paper, and said the following about
The Boomerang the other day: •
" Just fancy 'Jolly Old,' the wicked editor of the
Sunny Clime (as Kit Adams, the dear, good soul of
the *Modern Argo*, dubs us), running his eyes eagerly
and with their pupils dilated, over the well-filled
columns of the *Weekly Boomerang*, breathing, as it
were, the life of Bill Nye, a man who is known to be
a big, tall, awkward-looking person, with a heart of
the largest size, and to have given the people fits of
laughter until they reddened in the face. We are
glad to read in *The Boomerang* one of the brightest,
freshest and most original humorists of America;
and hope for longevity under the vitalizing influence
of Nye's jokes unapproached and unapproachable."
The editor also asked us in a pleasant, gentlemanly way to exchange. So we wrote a nice, cheerful letter, as near as we can remember, something
like the following:

Editor Sunny Clime, Terrell, Texas:

DEAR SIR:—So you want to exchange with *The
Boomerang,* do you? You want to trade a gentle,
subdued wad of literature for a priceless treasure, a
casket of rich and radiant gems of purest ray serene?

You want to get $11 worth of fragrant mirth every
week, that you can work over into your paper and
palm off on your subscribers as your own. That's

the kind of an old, bald-headed snipe of the alkali swamps that you are, is it?

I never saw you, but I can picture you in my mind's eye sitting there in your three-legged chair, with your feet up on the hat rack and your coat tails in the cuspidore.

You're a healthy old snoozer from Bitter Creek, very evidently. Perhaps you'd like to trade your old rattle-trap semi-annual for a library of 50,000 volumes.

We haven't seen your old tract, and we don't want to. Now, put that in your pipe and smoke it, you cross-eyed old bow-legged rooster from the rural districts.

Life is too brief to be frittered away on every little, one-horse editor who ought to be hoeing corn or mashing squash bugs, instead of ekeing out a miserable existence as a literary curiosity.

Hoping you will accept the above in a friendly spirit, you old bald-headed, glass-eyed relic of antiquity, I remain,

Yours, gently but firmly,

BILL NYE.

Last night we got a copy of the *Sunny Clime*. It is edited by two brown-haired, dimpled girls, with great liquid pleading eyes, and voices that thrill the heart like a blessed memory.

We feel that perhaps we would have written differently had we known all this before. Somehow our letter seems rough and uncouth now that we know more about the circumstances. There are passages in it that grate harshly upon the ear when we come to read them over again in the chastened light of more mature reflection.

Still, we were annoyed a good deal the day we wrote that letter. A man had asked us to die and endow an institution for the encouragement of young men who parted their hair in the middle, and a subscriber in Delaware had written us to print more Delaware local news or he would stop the paper, and we were feeling bitter toward all mankind.

This, however, was no excuse. It has been a valuable lesson to us, and shown us that we must govern our fiendish temper, or some day we will overdo this thing and get licked till our system won't hold our political opinions.

A $2,000 TUNNEL.

Some people who don't know the honest miner very well think that he don't know much about things in general, but there is where they make a fatal mistake. The honest miner has his eyes open most all the time, and those who think he don't read the papers and fill himself up with valuable information are very much in error.

A company of eastern capitalists, who had a claim over near Georgetown, notified its agents to run a tunnel into the mountain for 200 feet, to strike the vein and see what it looked like. The agent closed a trade with a hard-handed miner named Thompson to run the tunnel for $2,000.

The fall of snow in the canyon was very great that winter, and in places it was twenty and thirty feet deep. Mr. Thompson, having surveyed the ground before snow fell, discovered that by changing the

direction of the tunnel slightly, he could strike a
level plateau, and by digging along the surface of
this plateau through the snow and timbering it up
in good shape, he could get along pretty fast. At
$10 a foot a man can make pretty good wages dig-
ging through snow and timbering it up. It does not
necessitate the expense of giant powder and fuse,
and sharpening drills, and all that business.

So Thompson got along first-rate. He didn't have
to hire at all, and he completed the job some time in
February all right; got the agent up to his cabin;
played " draw " all the evening and smoked, and in
the morning both started out for the tunnel. It
looked good at the mouth, was well timbered, with
a pile of dirt and boulders, and had a good scatter-
ing of ore on the dump. Two thousand feet into the
mountain apparently stretched the black, cold tunnel.

It looked mighty forbidding in there, and the agent
had his new seal skin cap on, and Thompson found
that he had no matches. They had used them up
the evening before in lighting their pipes while they
played draw.

So Thompson said it would be all the same for
him to take one end of a line and the agent hold the
other, and Thompson could go in with a sledge hammer and hit the face of the tunnel a lick when he
got to it, and then they could measure the line and
it would save the agent going in and spoiling his
clothes.

Thompson always was considerate that way. If
he could save any one an unpleasant task by taking
it upon himself, he would do it, and the agent said
to himself that Thompson was a rough, ignorant

MEASURING THE TUNNEL.

man, but that he had a great, noble heart in him,
anyhow. So Thompson took one end of the line and
went into that cold, damp tunnel, entirely forgetful
of his own discomfort, and when he got in 200 feet
he banged a big boulder with the sledge hammer,
and the agent marked the line, and when Thompson came out they measured the string and found it
was all right.

Then the agent took some of the ore from the
dump to get it assayed, and he and Thompson went
down to the cabin.

The agent gave Thompson a $2,000 check on Den-
ver, and after drinking some dark red whisky that
tasted like eternal punishment, they separated.

Thompson got his check cashed and went away
somewhere on a kind of excursion by himself.

He said that he had exposed himself too much,
and had got to take better care of his health.

So, when the soft-eyed spring, with balmy breath
and the gentle, seductive odor of wood violets, came,
Mr. Thompson seemed to melt into the great hungry
maw of the irredeemable past.

So did the 200 foot tunnel which he left behind.

Late in June the Philadelphia capitalists came to
Colorado to see the mine. They brought some more
capitalists with them to show them the rich ore,
and get them to help bear the honor and the assess-
ments of the Esmeralda mine.

The agent went with them to show them the
property.

When he got there he seemed to be dumbfounded
with the grandeur of nature, and the might and
magnificence of the giant mountain peaks, lifting
their heads to heaven.

Most everyone seemed awed into silence by the glory of the thrilling landscape.

Finally, one fat old snoozer from Vermont asked the agent what in thunder they had built that covered bridge, 200 feet long, on the side of the mountain for.

But the agent was wrapped in thought, and a harsh, matter-of-fact question like that made him mad, and he did not answer it.

Then the party went home, and left the tunnel there on the bald brow of the eternal hills.

It is there yet, and it looks like a sheep corral that has wandered into the lonely mountains to think over its past life, and then forgotten the way home.

CIRCULAR FROM COLOROW.

OFFICE OF CHIEF MUTILATOR, May 1, 1881.

To all to whom these presents may come, greeting:

It is my desire and aim, this summer, to make the Ute picnic season for 1881 the most successful ever known in history. Arrangements have been made by which comfort and convenience will be added to the opportunity to see some of the most delightful scenery in Colorado.

I desire, therefore, the entire co-operation of all our people, and will spare no pains necessary to make the excursion one long to be remembered by those who survive.

I wish to secure as large a campaign fund as possible, and therefore ask those who read this circular to contribute $50 each to assist in defraying the expenses of the grand farewell tour of Colorado.

This sum is very small when we consider the amount of unadulterated hilarity we will have

Among the attractive features of the approaching season will be a supply of canned fruit, Boston baked beans, picnic crackers and lemons.

We shall also carry a better grade of whisky than on former trips of this kind.

There will, of course, be dull days when we cannot well go out of camp, and when, of course, we cannot kill anybody. To do away with the *ennui* of such days, we will have with us a well selected stock of agricultural reports, and patent office reports, which some one of the party will read aloud to the rest.

Some new styles of torture for prisoners taken on the trip, will also be introduced this season, which will not only prolong the exercises, but give a much higher grade of entertaiment to everyone than heretofore.

In addition to the mirth-provoking farce of roasting Colorado people over a sage-brush fire, we will introduce the side-splitting comedy entitled "Starvation made easy, or Dr. Tanner in the Rocky mountains."

The victims will be picked up on the various ranches of Colorado.

Children will not be wasted as formerly, but those not worked up into pot pie along the road will be canned for winter use.

In looking over and assorting game after the day's sport, bald-headed men will be fed to the coyotes, after their pockets have been assayed.

A prize for the largest number of scalps obtained during the excursion will be awarded, consisting of a gold-headed cane; second highest number, one year's paid up subscription to the *Daily Boomerang;* third highest number, handsome portrait of Anna Dickinson as "Hamlet."

In the above award no bald-headed scalps will be counted. Scalps must be in a good state of preservation, and properly tanned, with the fur on.

To the member of the excursion stealing the largest number of horses and ponies, a fashionable suit of clothes, consisting of a gold collar-button, will be given.

At the scalp dances, this season, there will be but little change in party dresses. A swallow-tail coat of red paint, with trimming of ranch butter, will be the *recherche* thing for the cooler months, and during July and August the paint will be omitted.

The new racquet scalp dance will be very popular this season, and will be just too sweet.

The Ute German will be abolished; also all other Germans found along the route.

The utmost harmony and unity of purpose is urged by the Chief Mutilator, as we desire that the coming summer shall give the New Jerusalem a bigger boom in immortalized ranchmen than the history of the world has ever known.

WILLIAM H. COLOROW.

Chief Mutilator.

O. SNOCKEMONTHEGOB,

Acting Custodian of Valley Tan.

AN EXPLANATION.

Our exchanges are very much annoyed because the grave of Brigham Young is not kept green. They seem to think that, with the family he left to mourn his loss, there ought to be enterprise enough to make old Brigham's ton b one vast wilderness of green lawn.

The plain, oil-finished truth is, that when the multitudinous widow and shoreless waste of orphan gather above the silent dust of the late lamented, and give way to a wild burst of anguish, it tears up the ground so that a bilious cactus in one corner of the prophet's corral has all it can do to drag out a miserable existence.

You ought to see the family phalanx when it begins to shed the scalding tear, and tear up the dirt and howl. A Buffalo stampede on the plains is a very tame and docile affair compared to the domestic snort of Brigham's mourning family.

At first there is a low sob by the assembled widow that shakes the earth and tears off the pickets from the graveyard fence. Then the innumerable caravan of orphan swells the mighty refrain, and a high priced wail, like the unanimous chorus of universal and innumerable gongs, arises to heaven, which cracks the cerulean dome and scatters the tombstones for miles around.

Oh, it isn't a matter of serious wonder to us that the grave of Brigham Young is not kept green. If there had been any grass there in the first place, the sexton would have had to go out there every morning and nail it down with nine-inch spikes to hold it in place.

You can go to the grave of the dead and defunct prophet of the bogus Church of Jesus Christ of Latter Day Saints most any time after the heirs and assigns of the busted prophet have held a semi-weekly sob, and you can gather up enough grief and tearful agony, and hairpins and polygamous weep, to supply the United St .tes for two years.

It is true that the grave of Brigham Young is not kept green ; but if convulsive emotion and great big wads of upheaving sob are what he wants, he is probably the tickledest immortal soul that look~ down over the battlements of the skies.

THE DEATH OF BIG-NOSE GEORGE.

Last year a little surprise party met at Rawlins, and hung one of the most notorious scoundrels of the west. Big-Nose George was not only a mur-derer, but he was essentially a coward. His last act, viz: the attempt on the life of his jailor, after the ostensible contrition which he had hitherto man-ifested, and his grief over his past life, shows con-clusively the kind of a man he was.

Much as we deplore lynch law, we still recognize the fact that Big-Nose George precipitated this little incident upon himself. It was not a new sensation to him in some respects, as he had been hung sev-eral times previous to last night. They never hung him so that life was extinct, but they hung him enough so that he could look over into the sweet ultimately. Then they would cut him down, and after he got his breath they would let him confess.

Rawlins people had fully decided to let the law take its course, and would have done so had not the now defunct Road Agent attempted to place Jailor Rankin on file.

They then arose as one man, and put the kibosh on him.

We are in favor of law and order, and always have been, but this summary death of the man with the abnormal nasal protuberance will have a good effect on the scattered remnant of the most danger-ous band of highwaymen that ever infested our territory.

We shall mark this article, and send the paper to them out of respect for their feelings.

ENTOMOLOGIST.

THE DOG WITH THE BALDHEADED TAIL.

Come, little boys and girls, and hear me tell about a dog I once owned.

Some dogs are prized for their faithfulness, others for their sagacity, and still others for their beauty. My dog was not noticeable for his faithfulness, be-cause he only clung to me when I did not want him, and when I felt lonely and needed sympathy and deep devotion, he was always away from home.

. He was not very sagacious, either. He was always doing things which, in the light of a chastened ex-perience and cooler, calmer afterthought, he bitterly regretted.

Thus his life was a wide waste of shattered ambi-tions and the ghastly ruins of what he might have been.

Neither did I prize him for his beauty; for he was brindle where there was any hair on him and red

where there was none, and he had, at one time,
dropped his tail into a camp-kettle of boiling water.
So that when he took it out and looked at it sadly,
he was surprised to see that it looked like a new
sausage.

When visitors came to my camp on the Boomerang
Consolidated, and I gave them a lunch, my dog
would sit near them and look yearningly at them,
and pound the floor with his baldheaded tail, and
lick his chops, and follow each mouthful of the lunch
with such a hungry, hopeless look, that the visitors
wished that they were dead.

When I first went out to the mining camp I did
not have any dog. I was not poor enough. After a
while, however, by judicious inactivity and my
æsthetic love for physical calm, I got poor enough.
So that I knew I ought to procure a dog, and thus
herald my poverty to the world.

I also desired a constant companion who would
share my humble lot and never forsake me.

I secured a dog, which I named Entomologist. Do
you know what an entomologist is? He is one who
makes large collections of antique bugs and peculiar
insects and studies their characteristics and peculiarities.

Entomologist seemed to be entirely wrapped up in
his collection of insects, and they were very much
attached to him.

.He had a good many more insects on hand than
he really needed, especially fleas. Entomologist introduced into Slippery Elm Gulch a large, early,
purple-top, Swedish flea that had an immense run in
camp. Most everybody got some of them.

He was very proud of his collection of singular and peculiar fleas. It was about all that he had to be proud of except his appetite.

Entomologist had a wild, ungovernable desire for food that made him a good deal of trouble. He would keep this unnatural appetite under control for days and weeks together, and then he would yield to it and become its willing slave again.

He would eat too much during the day, and at night he would creep into my tent and fill the air with his vain regrets.

I used to try every way to make him overcome his corroding grief, and at last I got to throwing pick-handles and drills, and pack-saddles, and large chunks of specimen quartz and carboniferous profanity at him in the night, to see if I couldn't convince him that it was better to suffer on in silence and smother his woe than to give way to such wild and robust grief.

One night he did not come home, and I feared that he had fallen down the shaft into the lower level of the Boomerang. I found him, however, down at Dobe Abraham's trying to eat a twenty-five foot rawhide lariat.

It seems that he had swallowed fifteen feet of it before he discovered that the other end was tied in a hard knot to an iron picket-pin. When he discovered this, he had moved to reconsider, but the motion was defeated. I untied the lariat, however, and let Entomologist swallow it and go home. Then I went to the owner and purchased the lariat. I had one at home just like it, but I thought that it would be as well for Entomologist to have one of his own. I would do anything for my dog. I did not wish to neglect him while he was alive, for I knew I would regret it some day, if he were to be taken from me.

One day in the mellow autumn I went over to town to purchase grub for winter, and took Entomologist with me. He ran around a good deal, and tasted of almost everything; but he knew his weakness, and did not yield to it at first. Finally he found some soft plaster of Paris that had just been mixed near a new house, He had eaten a good many things, but he had never tasted plaster before, so he ate what there was.

It was the effect of a blind impulse, and not the result of Entomologist's more mature judgment. Ah, how rashly the best of us sometimes fly into the face of Providence, and in later years we struggle in tears and agony of spirit to overcome the foolish action of an unguarded moment!

That's the way it was with Entomologist. Five minutes after he ate that plaster he felt as though years of integrity and self-denial could not overcome this rash act.

He lost his old vivacity, and never came up to me any more to lick my face with his warm, damp tongue, or put his cold, wet nose in my ear and sneeze, as he was wont to do when he was well. He gradually lost all interest in his fleas, and allowed them to shift for themselves.

Although he did not moan or complain, I could see that little Entomologist was climbing the golden stair.

One day, just as the sun was lighting up the west and glorifying the horizon with its royal coloring,

Entomologist rolled himself up into a small globular wad and died.

* * * * * *

He died without a struggle, but I always knew that he would die easy. If it hadn't been easy he wouldn't have done it. He never would do anything that was difficult, or that required a struggle.

As I write these lines, memory takes me back to those days of the long ago; and while the scalding tear wells up anon to my eyelids and falls upon the page before me, a large paper-weight, white and symmetrical, is lying by my side, and on it is written :

Plaster cast of Entomologist, taken by himself, (interior view.) "He bit off more than he could chew."

THE MAN WHO LICKS THE EDITOR.

Throughout the great newspaper reading world, scattered promiscuously around, you will find at regular distances apart, the man who makes a business of whipping editors. He is generally a man who is suffering for a puff and don't get it. He searches the columns of his family paper, hoping that each issue will announce that he is the most intelligent, far-seeing, illustrious cuss in the Republic. He hankers after the taffy paragraph, and if it don't appear at certain intervals, he stops his paper and thinks that in consequence of the withdrawal of his support, the paper will be crushed out of existence.

After a while he borrows a paper and finds in it that the editor has touched upon some little weak-

ness of his, and then he proceeds to whip the editor.
When he puts on his hat and his brass knuckles,
and starts down town, his wife thinks that he means
to kill the editor, and jam his lifeless corpse down
through the sidewalk. But something else draws
his attention aside, and the next morning the editor
sits in his office smoking some fragrant cigars contributed by the man who minds his own business,
and pays so much per line for his puffs. No ghastly
wounds or tin ears are erected on the classic outlines; no broken bones grind together as he writes;
he is all there, and his anatomical arrangement is
the same that it was the day before, and he smiles
cheerfully as his pencil moves rapidly over the vir-
gin page. What does he care how many men
threaten to lick him? He knows that they never
will. He knows that they can't lick a piece of court
plaster. He has been there before.

Men who go around thrashing editors (in their
minds), and neglecting their families, always come
to some bad end; while the editor goes on doing
good, and conscious that he is the heir-apparent to
an immortal crown.

When we were young we used to go down town
filled with a horrid fear that we would get 'killed
and thrown into an alley before night; but now we
are older and homelier, but we know more. We
find that insurance companies are still willing to
take risks on us; and the man who has been
advertising for three years to lick us, has failed to
perform the smallest portion of the programme.

PUFF.

The newspaper puff is something which makes you feel bad if you don't get it. The groundwork for a newspaper puff consists of a good, moral character, and a good bank account. Writing newspaper puffs is like mixing sherry cobblers and mint juleps all through the summer months, for customers, and quenching your own thirst with rain water.

Sometimes a man is looking for a puff and don't get it; then he says that the paper is going down hill, and that it is in the hands of a monopoly, and he would stop the paper if he didn't have to pay his bill first.

Writing a newspaper puff is like taking a photograph of a homely baby. If the photograph doesn't represent the child as resembling a beautiful cherub with wings, and halos, and harps, and things, it shows that the artist does not understand his business. So it is with a newspaper puff—if the puffee don't stand out like the bold and fearless exponent of truth and morality, it shows that the puffer doesn't understand human nature.

It is more fun to watch a man read a puff of himself than it is to see a fat man slip up on an orange peel. The narrow-minded man reads it over seven or eight times, and then goes around to the different places in town where the paper is taken, and steals what copies he can. The kind-hearted family man goes home and reads it to his wife, and then pays up his bill on the paper. The successful business man, who advertises and makes money, starts immediately to find the newspaper man and speak a word of grateful acknowledgment and encouragement. Then two men start out of the sanctum and walk thoughtfully down the street together, and the successful business man takes sugar in his, and the newspaper man doesn't put anything in his, and then they both eat a clove or two, and life is pleasanter and sweeter, and peace settles down like a turtle dove in their hearts, and after awhile lamp-posts get more plenty, and everybody seems to be more or less intoxicated, but the hearts of these two men are filled with a nameless joy, because they know just where to stop, and not make themselves ridiculous.

WYOMING FARMS, ETC., ETC.

LARAMIE CITY, June 10, 1880.

It has snowed a good deal during the week, and it is discouraging to the planters of cotton and tobacco very much. I am positive that a much smaller area of both these staples will be planted in Wyoming this year than ever before. Unless the yield this fall of moss agates and prickly pears should be unusually large, the agricultural export will be very far below preceding years, and there may be actual suffering.

I do not wish to discourage those who might wish to come to this place for the purpose of engaging in agriculture, but frankly I will state that it has its drawbacks.

In the first place, the soil is quite coarse, and the agriculturist, before he can even begin with any prospect of success, must run his farm through a stamp-mill in order to make it sufficiently mellow.

This, as the reader will see, involves a large expense at the very outset. Hauling the farm to a custom mill would require a large outlay for teams, and would delay the farmer two or three hundred years in getting his crops in, thus giving the agriculturist who had a pulverized farm in Nebraska, Colorado, or Utah, a great advantage over his own, which had not yet been to the reduction works.

We have, it is true, a large area of farming lands now lying on the dump, but they must first be crushed and then treated for alkali, in which mineral our Wyoming farms are very rich.

Then, again, the climate is erratic, eccentric and peculiar. The altitude is between 7,000 and 8,000 feet above high water mark, so that during the winter it does not snow much, we being above snow line, but in the summer the snow clouds rise above us, and thus the surprised and indignant agriculturist is caught in the middle of a July day with a terrific fall of snow, so that he is virtually compelled to wear his snow shoes all through his haying season.

This is annoying and fatiguing. The snow-shoes tread down the grass ahead of him, and make his progress laborious; besides, he tangles his feet up in the winrows, and falls on his nose nine times out of a possible ten.

Again the early frosts make close connections with the late spring blizzards, so that there is only time for a hurried lunch between.

Aside from these little draw backs and the fact that nothing grows without irrigation, except white oak clothes-pins, and promissory notes drawing two per cent interest, the prospect for the agricultural future of Wyoming is indeed gratifying in the extreme.

I am glad to announce that I have been called upon recently, in my official capacity as United States Commissioner, to dish out some even-handed justice, and grosgrain equity.

I have held this office now for nearly two years, and during that time it has been the most magnificent sinecure that I ever knew.

During that time I have taken the acknowledgment of a deed, and drawn a copy of the Revised Statutes of the United States. I charged fifty cents for the acknowledgment. This makes fifty cents for the two years, or twenty-five cents per year. I am glad I do not occupy any more official positions under the government. I would then have to take in plain sewing in order to get along.

Still the duties are not irksome as United States Commissioner. I get a good deal of leisure time to go about town sawing wood at $1 per cord. This gives a pleasing variety to my labors and keeps me cheerful and happy, though at times my meals may not be as rectangular as I would like.

I presume that this fall under the strict regime adhered to by the administration relative to civil service reform, I shall be assessed $11.35 as my proportion of campaign expenses. This looks unjust to me in some respects; still I will not complain; I am, perhaps, better able to stand the expense than the government is.

Last week, however, I was called upon to issue papers in my official capacity, and I am cheered very much. The future looks bright, and I am hopeful.

Before closing this letter I want to mention a little incident, which goes far to show some of the peculiarities with which we are daily brought in contact.

The Thornburgh House, at this place, named for the dead hero of Mill Creek, is the leading hotel, and is managed in a style far ahead of the surrounding institutions. The Eastern capitalist, tourist, mining speculator, man of ease, and the wealthy invalid, alike stop there, and are gratified and pleased.

A short time ago a western character, who has been accustomed to grapple with his grub on the prairie and pick various entomological specimens out of his food, was casting about him for a new boarding place here. His old quarters had gone into new hands, or into bankruptcy, or something of that kind, so that the change was necessary. For weeks he searched the town over with indifferent success, till at last some one said: "Joe, why don't you go to the Thornburgh? It is not such a very high priced house, and there is no question about its being the supreme boss of the hotel gang in this country."

"Yes," said Joe, "that's all right. Perhaps I know what kind of a house I want, and perhaps I don't. Probably you have never chucked up at the Thornburgh, and don't know what you are talking about. Mebbe I can be played for a Chinaman, and mebbe I can't."

"You just keep still while I tell you something. Just uncoil your ear and absorb about two and one-half gallons of my bazzoo.

"I thought about the Thornburgh. Thought, about it seriously. Price is all right. Rooms all right. Grub all right. Landlord all right. Waiters all right, but I went along the piazza one day while the gang was in the dining coral standing off the bill of fare and I looked in. I hope I may be everlastingly, tetotally dodd buttered if there wasn't a —— bald headed snipe of the desert in there with a white towel under his chin, eating pie with a fork."

After this remark, Joe took out a plug of tobacco about the size of Sherrod's addition to Laramie City, and while he was spreading his upper lip over it, the surrounding congregation was wrapped in a solemn and substantial chunk of dark blue silence.

MILLIONS IN IT.

"Some days ago, in company with several other eminent men of this place, I paid a visit to the soda lakes of Wyoming, and will give a short, truthful and concise description of their general appearance.

The lake or soda beds are situated about twelve miles southwest of Laramie, in a direct line according to official survey, but the road makes a slight variation from a direct line and therefore makes the distance about fourteen miles.

In a kind of basin toward Sheep Mountain, the finest of a series of hills intervening between the broad Laramie Plains and the Snowy Range, lie these lakes, four in number, with no outlet whatever.

Just as you get plumb discouraged and have ceased to look for the lakes, they all at once lie at your feet in all their glistening, dazzling, snowy whiteness.

One of these lakes, to all appearances, is the source of water supply for the balance, and from the exterior the water is constantly crystallizing in the sun and forming a thick crust of sulphate of soda.

When we went out, it was one of those dry, clear bracing days in the month of July, in Wyoming, when the crisp air fans your cheek and fills every vein, artery and capillary and pore with a glad exhilerating sense that you are freezing to death.

Well, the day we went out to the lakes it was that way only not so much so.

It was not therefore difficult to imagine the broad white crust over those lakes to be ice and snow. They are of the purest snowy white, and when cut into the crust has that deep sea blue of ice when cut in like manner.

This crust of sulphate of soda is nearly three feet in depth and is perfectly firm, so that the heaviest loads drive over it with safety.

The water which oozes up through the crust at intervals is quite warm, being at the surface on a cool day about blood temperature, and of course at a considerable depth much higher.

In 1876,—the year which the gentle reader will call to mind as the centennial,—a slight fragment of this lode, weighing over three tons, was cut in the form of a cube and sent to the Centennial, where it attracted very much attention.

Six weeks afterward the unsightly hole in the ꝺeposit at the lake was entirely filled up with a new formation.

This goes to show how inexhaustible is the mighty reservoir, and the gentle reader may give it his earnest thought as a mathematical question, what amount of this formation might be secured to the enterprising manufacturer who might see fit to purchase and develop it.

Suppose there are sixty-four tons to every 400 superficial feet, and suppose there are four lakes averaging forty acres, which is a low estimate, then we have at present on hand 17,424 tons, with the capacity to reproduce itself every two months, we will say, or at the rate of 104,544 tons per annum.

Suppose, then, we take a ten years' working test of the lakes, and we have 1,062,864 tons of soda.

This soda is not adulterated with alum or other injurious substances, and would therefore sell very rapidly.

It might be put in half pound and pound cans which would sell at, we will say, twenty-five and fifty cents per can.

Taking the very low estimate made above, as a basis we have the neat little income of $1,062,864,000.

This is more than I am now clearing, I find, over and above expenses, and I am thinking seriously of opening up this vast avenue to wealth myself.

I would have done so long ere this, were it not that I am now developing the Boomerang mine.

This mine is named after my favorite mule, and I am very anxious that it should succeed.

I have already sunk $10 in this mine, and I cannot therefore abandon it, as the casual observer will notice, without great loss to me.

THE VACANT CHAIR OF A LITTLE CHILD.

As the twilight gathers and the pale beams of the moon are streaming in through the window, the un‑ certain light of the young night is falling upon the little vacant rocker of the sunny-haired child who once sat in it by the hour, and while rocking her dolly sang with bird-like voice her mellow lullaby.

As I watch the silent reminder of my child, the little rocker fades into the mist, for my eyes are blind with unshed tears. A great grief is tugging at my heartstrings, and a wild torrent of ill-con- cealed anguish is convulsing my soul.

The dainty little rocker stands where she left it, and I seem to see her still, as with baby voice she tells her doll the nursery rhymes she loves herself so well, and as I look into the quiet night, the mighty pain and heart-sickness grow more irresistible and wild, and I ask, in stifled, broken, agonizing tones, for the blue-eyed child, but she comes not out of the darkness and the silence. She is softly sleeping.

In her little cot she is slumbering sweetly on, and dreaming of the golden sunlight of eternal fairy-land, while twenty feet away in the mocking moonlight, her gentle, ethereal father, clad in the pale robe of night, is filling the silent air with broken sobs and smothered agony, and red-hot exclamatory sentences, and navy blue profanity, as he holds on to his superior toe and rocks it gently to and fro, and madly calls for his child, and howls till the watch-dogs for nine flocks catch the sad refrain, and the calm, unruffled night, and the man in the unruffled robe of night, become a mad, melodious medley of hoarse watch-dog, and large rectangular cussedness.

Ah! how a child's little vacant chair, or even a meek little two-wheeled cart, standing alone and silent in the quiet, all-pervading embrace of night, will bring back old memories and half-forgotten styles of long-waisted vituperation and Queen Anne profanity.

THE "HOLD-UP" BUSINESS.

To-day Judge Peck sentenced Big Nosed George to be hanged by the neck until he is dead. He has been hung by the neck before, but not till he was dead. That, therefore, will be the great distinguishing characteristic of the hanging. Big Nosed George is what is known and respected as a road agent. A road agent is one who takes up an involuntary contribution from the tourist occasionally. It may be well enough to describe the fall and winter style of a road agent in Wyoming, for the benefit of those of your readers who have never experienced the wild, exhilarating sensation of being robbed.

The prevailing style of disguise among the *elite* of Wyoming road agents is the lower half of a brown canvass overall leg. Taking the fragment alluded to, the artist rips it up both sides a few inches, so that when pulled down over the head a flap of the goods cut decolette hangs down below the face in front and down the back behind. The top is then gathered into a Pompadore wad and tied with a string of old gold or gros grain burlaps. Holes are then cut for the eyes and one for the mouth, and the robber is thoroughly disguised. Proceeding to a

good point in the stage roads between towns of some
importance, the captain places his men in such a position that the coach or other outfit will meet the
cold, repulsive gun barrels of the gang before there
is time to make any preparation. This the road
agent does for his own protection, and not for the
pleasure of witnessing the glad surprise of the pilgrim. The captain then tells the tourist to throw up
his hands. This suggestion is generally obeyed, the
victim laughing heartily all the time. The driver
and passengers are then required to get down and
form in a line, still holding their hands as high as
they can without standing on something. The gang
still stand so that the squad of pilgrims may be raked
fore and aft and the captain proceeds to rummage
the pockets of the squad. In many instances these
travelers have things in their pockets that they
would like to keep, but they hardly ever mention it
at the time. I knew one man who had only about
enough fine-cut to last him one day, and the hold-up
band took the last crumb that he had, so he had to
go on without it. He was the crossest man I ever
saw for the next two days. He lost at the same time
$1,500 in cash, but he didn't mind that. He spoke of
the loss of his shining dross cheerfully and even hila-
riously, but tobacco was something he needed right ·
along all the time.

Big Nosed George, however, got excited easily and
killed people because he was afraid that while he
was turning their pockets inside out and reading
their letters they might get irritated and kill him.
This got people down on George, and when they
caught him one night they tied him up to a telegraph pole and asked him a lot of impudent ques-

tions about his past life. They asked him if he killed so and so, and who helped him, and a lot more such questions that he had to answer while his eyes hung out on his cheek like a loose overcoat button, and his tongue was swollen so he couldn't talk very fluently. Then he asked them to take him down where he could get his breath and maybe he could think of some more things to say. He said he never spoke in public before and it seemed to confuse him.

So they took him down and he told them a whole lot of things that they wanted to know, and then they took him away to jail. When he came to trial he didn't seem to think he had a good case, and the lawyers didn't seem to want to defend him because there was a good deal of popular feeling agaist Big Nosed George, and lawyer who were not prepared to climb the golden stair—and most of them are not—concluded not to take the case. So George plead guilty, and unless something happens he will pass up the flume.

HIGH ART ON VINEGAR HILL.

The art of taxidermy out on Vinegar Hill is yet in its infancy. The leading taxidermist of that booming gold camp is, as yet, nothing but an amateur.

The art critic of this paper is in receipt of a stuffed weasel which was the first handiwork of the Vinegar Hill taxidermist. Evidently he had not tried to taxiderm before.

The weasel is naturally a delicate, graceful little animal, with long, slender body and fragile proportions.

That is the reason he looks lumpy and unhappy when his remains are stuffed with baled hay.

The dado editor who writes these hints on decorative art doesn't set himself up as authority, of course, but simply desires to suggest little points of improvement.

This paralyzed weasel is too flat, for one thing. In preserving weasels, to avoid destroying the outline they should not be pressed like an autumn leaf, but stuffed like a bologna sausage.

The casual observer will also notice that the tail of this weasel is erect, which gives him a self-reliant, Roscoe Conkling air, which ill becomes the shy and timid little weasel.

This is not true to nature. It jars harshly on the æsthetic taste to see a weasel with his tail over the dash-board that way.

The weasel does not jab his tail into the middle of the horizon like a jack rabbit, unless he feels pretty hiliarious. It is not his nature. We should study the habits of these animals, and when they are preserved, try so far as possible to still retain the natural symmetry which they evinced in life.

One more suggestion. This weasel was evidently too dead before they tried to embalm him. The weasel should not be too excessively dead when he is placed in th hands of the taxidermist. After the remains have laid in state for two or three weeks, it is fair to suppose that life is extinct and the artist may then get his sawdust and poison ready to go to work.

The practice of embalming weasels who died the previous autumn is now obsolete.

One more suggestion and we are done. In this specimen the eyes are omitted. This g·ves to the subject a vacant and preoccupied air.

In the absence of artificial eye., the artist should have inserted a pair of over·· ·a.. buttons, because the delicate taste of the bric-a-bracker is shocked when he gazes down into the lustrous depths once so full of life and soul, but now so full of bran and other inexpensive stuffing.

If the weasel were not so emaciated where he ought to be plump, and so bunchy where he ought to be attenuated, he would be more true to nature, and the cast-iron lithograph which we herewith present would not look so much like a club-footed hat-rack as it does.

THE MORBIDLY MATRIMONIAL MORMON.

Now in those days, over against Jordan and in the land which is called the land of the Danites and the land of the Polygs, and the land of the numerous wife, and where dwelleth the Mormon whose family is like unto the sands of the sea for multitude, there arose a man whose previous name was George and whose subsequent name was Cannon, and the letter which stood in the midst of his name was Q.

And behold, George was a man of many wives and his family was like unto a torch-light procession for multitude.

And behold, the time drew near in which the people were wont to vote, for to select him who should go up into the council of the nation for to deliberate and for to draw every man his salary, and for to lift

up his voice and spout with an exceeding great
spout.

And George, whose surname was Cannon, smote
himself upon the thigh with the palm of his hand
and said unto himself:

"Go to, I will run even for this office."

"For behold, I am solid even with my own people, and I will run. Yea, I will run even as a steer
in the corn."

And it was so.

Now, when the voters with their votes went up
unto the place where they were wont for to cast
their votes, them that did vote for this man were as
five to one, for in that country the Gentile is exceeding seldom, insomuch that he is lonesome, but
the excessively and extremely married man doth
abound.

So that George, whose surname was Cannon, did
win the race, and one Campbell, who did strive with
him for to gain the office, did get left; for, behold,
he gat not to himself the requisite number of votes
which is after the fashion of that people.

And the Danites, and the Taylorites, and the
Smiths, which prevail even unto the ends of the
earth, and the Cannonites, and the Brighamites re-
joiced and blew upon th ram's horn and the cornet
and the mouth-organ, d hey played upon the cym-
bals and the bass-drum nd the horse-fiddle.

And, behold, they cried with a loud voice and said
one to another: "We are the chosen people of the
Lord, and don't you forget it;" and they wagged
their heads, and talked with one another, and said:
"Verily, we have the bulge even over the Gentile,
and we will wipe him out, and our people shall rise

up and sit down on him, and we will snuff him out like an unpopular czar.

And they went up unto the feast, and they did fill themselves full of sour mash and valley tan and aquafortis, which is after the fashion of that people.

And they were full even as a goose.

And they went every man to his house, and as they went they did fall over one another, and they sang with a loud voice that they would not go home till morning.

Now, Cannon, whose previous name was George, was an alien, but his people wot not that it was so.

Therefore, when he came up unto Eli, the governor, and said unto him, "Give me even my documents wherewith I shall take my seat with the law-givers and the brigadiers, and wherewith I shall draw my salary and have a high old time."

The governor said: "Nay. Ye know not what ye ask. Thou knowest that it is written in the law, except ye be a citizen of that country where ye dwell, ye shall in no wise catch on."

And the Gentiles that stood about did wink each man unto his fellow, and the wink with which he wunk waxed great, and they said unto Eli, the governor: "Behold, thou art the boss, for thou hast even the requisite spinal column for this thy people."

And they gave him a great feast and a gold-headed cane.

Now, George, whose surname was Cannon, was very wroth, and behold he was red hot, for he was cast out of the councils of the people, and he could not be the high muck-a-muck of his people, neither could he draw his mileage which he had drawn aforetime.

And he went into his harem, and he called a mass-meeting of his wives and concubines, and they murmured one to another, and they cried aloud against Eli, the governor, and said among themselves: "We will rise up even as one man, and we will slay the governor. We will send him across the divide. We will rise up in our wrath, and, behold, we will lay him out colder than a mackerel."

And Eli, the governor, wot not that it was so, neither did he care a continental.

And he abode long in the land, and was solid with the people, and likewise with the administration.

SOME EARNEST THOUGHTS.

Young man, what are you living for? Have you an object dear to you as life, and without the attainment of which you feel that your life will have been a wide, shoreless waste of shadow, peopled by the spectres of dead ambitions? Is it your consuming ambition to paddle quietly but firmly up the stream of time with manly strokes, against the current of public opinion, or to linger along the seductive banks, going in swimming; or, careless of the future, gathering shells and tadpoles along the shore?

Have you a distinct idea of a certain position in life which you wish to attain? Have you decided whether you will be a great man, and die in the poor house, and have a nice comfortable monument after you are dead, for your destitute family to look at; or will you content yourself to plug along through life as a bank president ?

These, young men, are questions of moment. They are questions of two moments. They come home to our hearts to-day with terrible earnestness.

You can take your choice in the great battle of life, whether you will bristle up and win a deathless name, and owe almost everybody, or be satisfied with scads and mediocrity.

Why do you linger and fritter away the heyday of life, when you might skirmish around and win some laurels ? Many of those who now stand at the head of the nation as statesmen and logicians, were once unknown, unhonored and unsung. Now they saw the air in the halls of congress, and their names are plastered on the temple of fame.

They were not born great. Some of them only weighed six pounds to start with. But they have rustled. They have peeled their coats and made Rome howl.

You can do the same. You can win some laurels, too, if you will brace up and secure them when they are ripe.

Daniel Webster and President Garfield and Dr. Tanner and George Eliot were all, at one time, poor boys. They had to start at the foot of the ladder and toil upward.

They struggled against poverty and public opinion bravely on till they won a name in the annals of history, and secured to their loved ones palatial homes, with lightning rods and mortgages on them.

So may you, if you will make the effort. All these things are within your reach. Live temperately on $9 per month. That's the way we got our start.

Burn the midnight oil if necessary. Get some true,
noble-minded young lady of your acquaintance to
assist you. Tell her of your troubles and she wil
tell you what to do. She will gladly advise you.

Then you can marry her, and she will advise you
some more. After that she will lay aside her work
any time to advise you. You needn't be out of advice at all unless you want to. She, too, will tell
you when you have made a mistake. She will come
to you frankly and acknowledge that you have made
a jackass of yourself.

As she gets more and more acquainted with you,
she will be more and more candid with you, and, in
her unstudied, girlish way, she will point out your
errors, and gradually convince you, with an old
chair-leg and other arguments, that you were wrong,
and after she has choked you a little while, your
past life will come up before you like a panorama,
and you will tell her so, and she will let you up
again.

Life is indeed a mighty struggle. It is business.
We can't all be editors, and lounge around all the
time, and wear good clothes, and have our names in
the papers, and draw a princely salary. Some one
must do the work and drudgery of life, or it won't
be done.   .

A NEW FRAUD.

A recent order written by the pope has resulted in
a circular from the cardinal, addressed to the Cath-
olic administrators of the world, warning them
against spurious relics.

The pope intimates that no bodies have been exhumed from the catacombs within the past thirty
years, and naturally draws the inference that the
supposed remains of early Christian martyrs that
have been placed upon the market recently are
bogus.

It is a sad commentary upon our modern civilization and progress, when the Christian martyrs are
counterfeited and adulturated.

We boast of the mighty strides we have made in
our onward march toward perfection in the arts and
sciences, literature and statesmanship, but are we
justified in so doing when fraud is creeping into the
relic trade, and sapping the life blood of a great and
growing industry.

For years our Indian relics have been made in Con-
necticut, our Aztec jugs and prehistoric cuspidores
in Oshkosh, and now the trade mark on the early
Christian martyrs has been infringed. Consumers
may well be alarmed when the country is flooded
with defunct Indian organ grinders of the past decade, who are palming themselves off upon an over-
credulous public as relics of a remote period when
religious persecution was abroad in the land.

We naturally ask ourselves, where is this thing to
end? How is the trade to be protected? How are
we to know whether these relics were originally
Christians who died rather than yield one jot of their
religious belief, or simply the shattered remnants of
Italian road agents who died of delirium-tremens?
How do we know that Stewart's body hasn't been
palmed off upon us as the relic of early Christian
persecution? How are we to be assured that Big

Nose George will not be played on us some day as an early Christian martyr?

These are serious questions. They involve the trust and confidence of the civilized world, and the stability of our faith in mankind. It is not simply a question of whether a specimen saint may or may not be what he purports to be. It is a question of whether mistrust and incredulity shall give place to assurance and confidence in our fellow man.

Can a nation prosper when it allows deceptions of this kind to be practiced? One hundred years from this Colonel Ingersoll may be played upon the people as a Christian martyr who died at the stake centuries ago. This is not right, and severe measures should be used.

It has been suggested that bodies brought to this country should be examined by a coroner's jury duly empaneled to inquire into the cause of their death. This might or might not be successful, but it is worthy of a thought, at least.

Then again, it might be well to select some person who remembers the early Christian martyrs, say Susan B. Anthony, and let her see if she recognizes them. If so, well and good. If not, let the shipper be made to suffer.

All these may be impracticable, but we offer them simply as suggestions.

THE PLUG HAT IN WYOMING.

Perhaps no evidence of an advanced stage of mental culture and social superiority has been received in Wyoming with more marked coolness and disfavor than the plug hat. This intolerance is not easily accounted for; but there are several causes which may indirectly touch upon the subject under discussion.

In the first place, the climate of Wyoming is not congenial to the plug hat. You may wear one at 1 o'clock with impunity, if you can dodge the vigilance committee, and at three minutes past 1 a little cat's paw of wind will come sighing down from the Snowy range, that makes the cellars and drive-wells tremble, and the hat looks like a frightened picket fence.

It is not pleasant for a stranger to wear a plug hat in Wyoming, because the police and other officers of the law look upon him with suspicion; but he can wear out this feeling if he leads an upright life. The climate, however, is something that he cannot wear out. You can wear a hole in your pantaloons if you wish, or you can dress up in chapparejos and a yellow necktie, without attracting much attention; but when you put on a plug hat, the hoodlum and the elements are against you.

We wore a plug hat here one whole day once. It was not a very large or heavy hat, but before night it seemed to weigh a ton, and it felt as large as a bass drum.

The air of Wyoming, when it is feeling pretty well, will wear out a plug hat in about two hours, and leave it looking like a joint of iron stovepipe. When the atmosphere is full of geological specimens, and blossom rock, and deceased tom cats, it is not a good time to wear the plug hat. At the first sigh of the wind the hat gets fuzzy, like the corset of a bumble bee. Then some more little whispering zephyrs come along from the same bed of violets on Vinegar Hill, and after that man has followed his hat for fifteen or twenty miles as the crow flies, he picks it out of a bunch of sagebrush, and it is as bald-headed as a door-knob.

In former years they used to hang a man who wore a plug hat west of the Missouri, but after awhile they found that it was a more cruel and horrible punishment to let him wear it, and chase it over the foot-hills when the frolicsome breeze caught it up and toyed with it, and lammed it against the broad brow of Laramie Peak.

An old hunter was out among the Black Hills, east of town, last summer, hunting for cotton-tails and sage-hens, and he ran across a little gulch where the abrupt rocks closed together and formed a little atmospheric eddy, so to speak. There in that lonely reservoir he found what he at first considered a petrified hat store. It was a genuine deposit of escaped straw hats and plug hats that the frolicsome zephyrs had caught up and carried for ten miles, until this natural hat-rack had secured them. Of course there were other articles of apparel, and some debilitated umbrellas, but the deposit seemed to assay mostly hats.

Time may overcome at last the public disfavor, but until the Rocky Mountain wind is lulled to repose, so that a plug hat will not have to be tied on with a wrought iron stair-rod, the soft hat will be the prevailing style of roof.

SNORING IN A FOREIGN TONGUE.

"It's funny how careless they get about joint powder after they get used to it," said Woodtick Williams, the other day. "It's mighty harmless looking
stuff, and you wouldn't think, if you didn't know
what it was, that it would blow a man up any
quicker than a ball of Nebraska butter. I know
when I was sinking on the Feverish Hornet mine,
and had a cabin up in Slippery Ellum Gulch, at first
we was powerful careful about our joint powder,
and kept it in a hole in the side of the hill; but after
we got more familiar with it, we got to keeping it
in the cabin, and in about two weeks we used to sit
on the box when we played Black Mariar and Pedro.
After that we found that this kind of groceries
worked better if it was kept kind of warm, and we
used to put the little cakes of joint powder under the
mattress nights, so they'd be kind of warm in the
morning to blast with. We had a Polander on the
night shift of the Feverish Hornet and the boys called
Neuralgia Phlaskowhiski. He was the worst man
to swear nights and snore days that I ever saw.
When he used to go down in the shaft and swear a
few times in the dialect of his fatherland, the other
men had to come to the surface for fresh air. He
generally swore till he got excited, and his jaw got
cramped on an important bit of profanity, and then
he would quit awhile.

We called his style of swear the Anglo-Kosciusko
swear. It generally jarred the foot-wall, and shattered the vein matter so that we had to timber up a
little after he got through. His snore was about as
blood-curdling as his unique style of swear. He

used to snore in his own native tongue. Of course, the force of habit is strongest on a man when he is asleep. That's why he never tried to snore in English. When he seemed to be getting the most comfort out of his slumbers, and had his mouth open so you could throw a ham down his throat, and snored so as to get in all the double f's and q's and z's and Polish diphthongs, and other funny business, it made the floor of the cabin creak, and the cook-stove would fall down, and the clock used to stop, and stock in the Feverish Hornet would go down to ten cents a share.

Well, Neuralgia Phlaskowhiski, working on the night-shift, as he did, had to do his heavy sleeping during the day, while the rest of us was to work in the shaft. The day-shift consisted of myself and a man named Marco Bozzaris Smith, and the night-shift was composed of a picked crew, consisting of Neuralgia Phlaskowhiski and a man from Zion that we called Anonymous, because we never knew what his name was.

Anonymous slept in a tent, because he said he was a little nervous and fidgety like, and couldn't sleep in a boiler factory. So he pitched his tent about a mile down the gulch, where the sound of Neuralgia's snore was partially deadened.

About 2 o'clock P. M., one pleasant July day, there was a loud crash in Slippery Ellum Gulch that agitated the country for four miles around, and filled the air with fragments of bed-clothes and cooking utensils. We went down to the cabin, but it wasn't there. The concussion of Neuralgia Phlaskowhiski's snore had set off the joint powder concealed about his bed, and distributed the whole dog-gone rauch over the surrounding scene.

We postponed the funeral for two weeks, and asked the prospectors of the State to bring in such fragments of deceased as might be found. At the nour appointed, the mourners gathered around a baking-powder can, containing all that was mortal of Neuralgia. Death had worked a wondrous change in the expression of the features of the remains. Very few could recognize the deceased. Mr. Phlaskowhiski had always been cursed with a fear that he would be buried alive, and Marco Bozzaris Smith suggested that the remains should lie in state fcr a week or two ; but the rest of us felt so positive about his death that the ceremonies were allowed to go on.

This little episode seemed to us like a solemn warning, and after that we kept our joint powder under the mattress of a man who didn't snore in a foreign language. The Anglo-Saxon snore is good enough for the every-day hum-drum of life. When the language of this country isn't good enough to snore with in a mining-camp, it's time to adjourn."

FICTION.

One of the very noticeable improvements of the age in the literary line is the remarkable bracing up of the mental faculties of those who write fiction. From the Sabbath school book to the more elaborate novel, there has been in the last few years a pronounced effort on the part of those who erect this class of literature to introduce so far as possible characters who resemble live people.

Not many years ago the boss heroine of the prevailing novel could not catch the popular eye without being so artistically scrumptuous that she could
walk over a bed of violets and not scrunch a single
one. Now it is not unusual to ring in a leading lady
who weighs 125 pounds, and who can eat a dozen
fried oysters at the expense of the hero of the story.
We can remember back to the time when, according
to the average novel, a young lady could cross the
plains in a Swiss muslin dress with short sleeves, and
with satin slippers and silk clocked hose.

It was not an uncommon occurrence for a frail girl
who had been the pampered child of luxury all her
life to be kidnapped by hostile Indians about four
miles from Chicago and carried away into the wigwam of the red man in a ball dress.

The all-wool facts in the case generally show that
when a Caucasian woman from Chicago is captured
by the Indians, she has to sit astride on a lame bronco
and ride all day clothed in the uniform of a private
soldier.

Pictures of beautiful white girls sitting on the
back of an ambling palfry and looking like Rowena
riding to the castle of Front de Beuf, will hardly go
down. Captive maidens in the hands of the Indians
are in luck if they can ride at all. A picture representing the pale prairie flower walking over the
velvety cactus in her stocking feet, and holding on
to the tail of the chief's pony, would be more life-like,
although it might mar the stage effect of the book.

In later years, however, people are introduced into
books who wear overcoats and ulsterettes when it
is cold, and who eat, and get vaccinated, and quar-

rel, and lie abed in the morning, and act like the balance of mankind.

Stories about languid young gentlemen who do not have to work, and who, although showing up no visible means of support, don't seem to feel called upon to do anything but stroll at set of sun or stretch themselves at the foot of some venerable oak and let the 1,000 legged worms crawl up their trowsers legs, are apparently losing their grip.

Formerly it was not the thing for a young man in a book to get mad. If he he did so it was in such an unnatural style, and his remarks sounded so much like reading from manuscript, that the reader couldn't help pitying him. The high-salaried hero of those days either allowed the leading villain to get up and walk over him and grind him into the sod without resenting it, or he got on his ear at nothing and made a post mortem examination of the villain with a Spanish hay knife because he said the heroine had a freckle on her nose.

Another noticeable and highly praiseworthy change is the falling off in the horrible mortality in recent fiction. It was not an uncommon thing at one time in the history of literary prevarication for a brave young Apollo, bearded like a buffalo robe, to roll up his pants legs about four feet and wade through a torrent of gore every Monday and Wednesday evening, with sanguinary matinee on Saturday afternoons.

Now the style is changing. When the author wants to introduce some carnage he don't butcher a tribe of Sioux and spread their busted remains all over Dakota in fifteen minutes. He just throws in a railroad collision or the burning of a theater and lets it go at that.

The plot of modern stories is a little more human than it used to be and a little more diversified. Nowadays you can't tell for an absolute certainty whether Reginald will marry the girl in the thirty-first chapter or not. He may be dead or divorced from another woman before he gets to the third chapter.

You cannot gamble on it any more. Modern fiction has reached that pass where the twentieth chapter may wind up with a funeral of twins. Death or dyspepsia may befall the hero at any moment, and the old-time schedule has been abandoned. It is as delightfully surprising as prospecting for a quartz lead. You may discover a bonanza or sit down on a tarantula at any moment. You may tumble out of an ore bucket and reach the foot of the shaft with your shoulder blade in your pistol pocket, or you may sit down on an ostensibly extinct blast to think over your past life and the next moment go crashing through the milky way without clothes enough to keep off the night air.

RAILROAD SOCIABILITY.

"Speaking about the sociability of railroad travelers," said the man with the crutches and a watch pocket over his eye, "I never got so well acquainted with the passengers on a train as I did the other day on the Milwaukee & St. Paul Railroad. We were going at the rate of about thirty miles an hour, and another train from the other direction telescoped us. We were all thrown into each other's society, and brought into immediate social contact, so to speak.

I went over and sat in the lap of a corpulant lady from Manitoba, and a girl from Chicago jumped over nine seats and sat down on the plug hat of a preacher from La Crosse, with so much timid, girlish enthusiasm that it shoved his hat clear down over his shoulders.

Everybody seemed to lay aside the usual cool reserve of strangers, and we made ourselves entirely at home.

A shy young man with an emaciated oil cloth valise left his seat and went over and sat down in a lunch basket where a bridal couple seemed to be wrestling with their first picnic. Do you suppose that reticent young man would have done such a thing on ordinary occasions? Do you think if he had been at a celebration at home, that he would have risen impetuously and gone where those people were eating by themselves and sat down in the cranberry jelly of a total stranger?

I should rather think not.

Why, one old man who, probably at home led the class-meeting, and who was as dignified as Roscoe Conkling's father, was eating a piece of custard pie, when we met the other train, and' he left his own seat, and went over to the front end of the car and stabbed that piece of custard pie into the ear of a beautiful widow from Iowa.

People traveling somehow forget the austerity of their home lives, and form acquaintances that sometimes last through life.

A RELIC.

Running our hands into the pockets of an old spike-tail coat the other day, preparatory to turning over the venerable garment to a poor man who needed a spike-tail coat to herd sheep in, we found a relic of bygone days that took us back over the rugged path on which we had journeyed for tho past ten years; back through sun-painted valleys and through the sloughs of despond till we stood again where we did before the past decade with is burden of sorrows, and its seldom joys had made its impress on our brow.

It was only a soiled and worn ball programme.

Looking upon it, the mist of gathering years lifted from the still features of the past like the pall that hides the calm lineaments of the dead, and out from the silent tomb of buried memories came back that regal night we spent in the heart of the forest, with the wealth and beauty of nature's children gathered about the camp-fire, while the seductive strains of the Strauss Waltz, played on a camp-kettle and a Ute bass-drum filled the air.

The programme reads on the outside as follows :

Grand Dress Ball, Select War Dance, and Raw Dog Supper. July 15, 1872.

Opening the programme, we find, in addition to several hand-painted grease-spots and the odor of smoked bacon, the following list of dances, with our partners :

Grand march around the Firewater barrel ; maiden with the Tin Ear.

Scalp Waltz; Cleopatra Colorow.

Flying Trapeze Quadrille; Veni Vidi Vici Colorow.
Hoopla Schottisch; Tay-To-Ba Smith (one half
breed belle).
Lanciers (free for all); Honi-Soit-Qui-Mal-y-Pense-
Shavano.
Tomahawk Waltz · Daughter-of-the-Cooing-Bliz-
zard.

SUPPER.

(Guests are requested not to throw discarded bones
at the musicians, or change their clothing in the
ball-room.   They might take cold.)
Quadrille de Mexicana; Ma-wah-tan-ni-han-ska-con-
tinued-on-fourth-page.
Maniac Polka; Daughter-of-Anonymous-pale-face.
Firewater Reel; Daughter-in-law-of-the-full-Moon.
Waltz (half mile dash); (Omitted on account of
fatigue.)
Scalp Quadrille (scalp to be furnished by visiting
pale face).   Omitted on account of unavoidable
absence.
Grand Knock-Down-and-Drag-Out-Waltz-Quadrille
with Butcher Knives. (Omitted. Didn't have any
Butcher Knife.)

ABOUT SLEEPING-CARS.

There is some talk of discarding the Pullman cars
on the Union Pacific road, and we do not regret it.
If the company wll construct a car with a series of
wood boxes arranged in tiers, and fitted out with a
blanket with hinges to it, so that it will adapt itself
to the form, it would be an improvement.   Now, if
you get an upper berth, the motion of the train, and

the friction on the roof of the car wears the end of
your nose off, and the blanket is about as malleable
as a marble slab.

One of these days they will invent a sleeper with
a quart of pure air for each person, instead of only
a mouthful. If there could be more pure air, and
less mahogany corners on which to bump the system, and the porter received a regular salary instead
of mobbing the train with a whisk broom, and gar-
roting the passengers for $1 each, life would be
more desirable.

When we get our own special car we shall build
a berth in it long enough so that we shall not have to
lie all night with our feet stuck out over the curtain
rod, and our nose against the cold, frosty roof of the
car. We shall also have the head and foot of the
berth padded, so that when the train stops at a water
tank, in the middle of the night, it will not knock all '
our teeth loose, and mix up our brains.

A PECULIAR PEOPLE.

Last September, a minister who stopped at a hotel
in La Crosse, Wisconsin, lost his pocket-book, which
he had placed under his pillow at night. A few days
ago the pocket-book was found on the floor under
the bed where he had slept.

When a pocket-book lies under a hotel bed five
months, without being found, it shows how long a
bed in La Crosse can stand without being swept
under.

We stopped at a La Crosse hotel one night in 1870,
and the chambermaid tried three times to force an

entrance into the room before 7 o'clock, and fix it, before breakfast.

All that we ever saw a chambermaid do, except to cuff the bell boys of the house, was to stand with a broom in one hand, and a slop-bucket in the other, and kick the door where she knew the occupant was not up. When the occupant gets up and goes away, the idea of sweeping the room and making the bed does not occur to her again.

Once, in Salt Lake, we had forgotten to lock the door, and a white-eyed maiden, 49 years old walked in with her inevitable etruscan slop-jar, while we were *en dishabille*, trying to jab a diamond stud into the bosom of a clean shirt.

We did all that any man could do under the circumstances. We yelled a couple of times and crawled behind a valise.

When you are cleaning your teeth, and have your mouth full of toothbrush and soap, and cannot hold a conversation, the chambermaid comes and opens the door, and asks you if you want your room overhauled.

APOSTROPHE ADDRESSED TO THE BUSTED STATUE OF A GLADIATOR.

Cold, pulseless fragment of the long ago, who sittest calm and passionless through scooting years. Thy busted snoot, awry amort, bemoiled with dust of passing feet, thy fractured bugle looming 'neath the twinkling stars, a gloomy wreck of former grandeur tells not of what hath thee betid.

Across thy scarred cold breast no trouble rolls and o'er thy brow yet frozen in dumb agony bestraught,

the swift and sable clouds of night do struggle like
an aged dying joke cast in the dust of ancient. amphitheatre.

Little thou reckest, in thy broken state, that thou
art clothed with nothing but the wailing wynd. Thy
cold, hard cheek is still unclothed with shame, tho'
in the chilly air anight, thy marble fragments are
exposed.

Who, gazing at thy busted brow and panic stricken
features, now would ere surmise thy prowess in the
days agone! Who, looking o'er thy mansard intellect and cast-iron frame, knocked galley west by
time's effacing fingers, ere would give a passing
thought to what thou'st been in previous years !

I trow, not one of all mankind would pick thee up
to be the once proud snoozer of the Roman ring.

Misguided relic of an era past, when men were
muscled like an aged hen, and brave men fought
with cheese knives long and well, or gouged the lion's
liver out and mixed it with the sand, while beauteous ladies smiled and munched the Roman caramel,
he who would grudge thee pity now in this thy hour
of need, would rob a pauper's grave to get the gold
with which his teeth were filled.

Proud fragment of heroic days, in dreams no doubt
thou livest on, and in the amphitheatre with quivering blade thou fightest still.

Methinks I see thee in the dusty ring, straddling
about and slashing right and left, filling the air with
toe nails and fresh gore. Again I hear thy new-laid
joke as up against the galleries the fragments of thy
foe are hurled.

Dream on, thou fractured warrior of ye olden

time, and reck not one cold, careless clam that all thy limbs are knocked into a shapeless mass.

Forget the present in thy glorious past. Live over still the days when in thy wondrous strength thou wast more deadly than the modern pie. Remember still the days of long ago, when he who banged thee midst the face and eyes got scattered o'er the dry and thirsty ground, and dusted off the quivering earth with his remains. Lose not thy grip, bold warrior of the fly-blown past. Brace up with memories of forgotten years, thou busted warrior of ye Roman time, for he who thus apostrophizes thee is busted too.

A MILD CRITIC

One of our exchanges comes to us illuminated with an allegorical lithograph, showing the [career of man through life, and the different deals he is liable to get. In the upper right hand corner is a very graphic and truthful representation of heaven. The place looks more like Salt Lake City, however, than we thought it did, and the Lombardy poplar shade trees are not exactly what our fancy had painted; still the artist, no doubt, knew what he was about.

The streets are broad, and macadamized in good shape, although the residents do not seem to use them much—most every one, apparently, floating through the air from one place to another. That is why a street car on the main thoroughfare looks out of place and lonesome.

The Court House and City Hall of the New Jerusalem, as shown by the artist, are a credit to any city, and the electric light system is apparently an excellent one.

Over the whole city there seems to be a dense cloud, lit up with golden splendor; at least we presume it is intended for golden splendor, although it looks more like a big conflagration.

The angels as shown in this illustration are not exactly what we had been led to believe an angel looked like, their faces being too red, and their feet too large. Some of them are coming out, apparently to meet a new soul. As shown by the artist, it is the custom to meet a stranger at the depot with a band. Several of the host are swallowing clarionettes, in the picture; but we are glad that in this representation the bass drum and tuba are omitted.

The angelic host coming out to meet an immortal soul, and playing the large horn and bass drum, would be in violation of taste, and cast a gloom over the lithograph.

We are glad that the artist thought of this and avoided it.

In the lower right-hand corner, and about forty rods from heaven—as nearly as we are able to judge distances in a picture—hell is situated. It is about due west from heaven, and apparently just outside the city limits

Perdition, as depicted by the artist, is extremely tropical. The exact area is hard to determine from the picture; but to all appearances it covers about twenty acres, and, judging from the multitudes flocking in that direction, most every one will have to stand up.

The artist, in depicting the infernal regions, has given us a pretty fair representation of Omaha. The place is situated in a deep gulch, with poor ventilation, and very inadequate precautions against — fire.

There may be little inaccuracies in this portion of the picture; but we hate to criticise the representation of a portion of country with which we are not familiar.

There are other little minor details in the picture which may be all right, but they clash harshly with our own narrow and preconceived notions of these things. For instance, two pilgrims are shown in the background, traveling toward heaven on horseback, and, farther on, there is an excursion party in a barouche. All this may be correct, but it is not as we had been led to believe.

One more suggestion, and we will close.

Harsh criticism, of course, is not beneficial in any case; but it seems to us that in the faces of those apparently aiming for perdition, there is an unseemly and unnatural haste, an unbecoming eagerness and enthusiasm, so to speak, while the artist has painted upon the faces of those who are on the straight and narrow path a look of extreme unhappiness, and the idea is conveyed that they ar 'lone some and miserable. It would seem that a better impression would have been created had these people been depicted as more cheerful, instead of looking as though they were doing right because they were compelled to.

Relative to the fact that the artist has placed heaven in a very unhealthy place, where the fumes from Brimstone Gulch must be extremely annoying when the wind is from that direction, we will say nothing. We will also pass over the fact that a convict is shown breaking rock away out on the prairie, where it will do no one any good, and without an officer anywhere near to collar him if he should take a notion to light out.

Neither will we comment on the costumes shown in the picture. If the artist desires to dress a man in red flannel, with a green hat and purple umbrella, on his way to glory, it is none of our business ; and if it is consistent with the painter's ideas that an old lady who weighs 225 should wear a sealskin sack and a pink parasol to perdition, it would be an usurpation of prerogative on our part to cruelly criticise it.

[The more we scan that last sentence, the more we are tickled with its rythmic flow.]

A BIT OF BIOGRAPHY.

WHY BILL NYE IS NOT A BRIGADIER.

There are a good many people who don't know how close the writer of this little sketch once came to being a great military leader. The wild and fearless contempt for death, which constitutes the most prominent feature of the true soldier's character, is still mine. I can stand more carnage and death scattered around than most anybody. 1 love the clash of arms and the tocsin of war. It stirs up my nature, and I "rare" and plunge around in a manner that convinces people of my wonderful courage and love of slaughter.

Some years ago there was a vacancy at West Point from our Congressional District, the original appointee having been clubbed to death by the cadets, I believe, for refusing to join in some festive game peculiar to that hot-bed of intellect.

Anyhow, there was a vacancy, and I applied to the Examining Board for an opportunity to fill it. The Examining Board consisted of a select gang of venerable frauds, who pumped us dry intellectually and then turned us over to a surgeon for physical examination.   The latter examination is still a pleasant memory, fraught with little flecks of sunshine, as it were.   The surgeon required the applicant to disrobe, so that he could make a thorough diagnosis.   I can remember now how timid I was as I pulled off my shoes, keeping in the background all the while a large and attractive hole in my sock.

Then I piled my raimant up in a corner and stood before the bald-headed surgeon in all my dazzling beauty.   I was only a lad then, and a little slab-sided and eccentric, perhaps, but from what the surgeon said, I knew that he was struck.

He said : "My son, you are as fine a specimen of Gothic architecture, I think, as I ever saw.   You have the most intense and pronounced backbone I ever saw.   You also have a wide, bold waste of shoulder-blade, that looks like the subdued yet plastic sweep of the dorsal fin of a codfish.

"Apollo did not have the economical physical make-up you possess, because as a hat-rack he was a failure.   You would be a great addition to the military department of our country, because you could stand up in the arsenal and let the boys lean their muskets against your frame.   Your proud bearing,

too, is very noticeable. You have the stately martial tread of an absent-minded hen on the trail of
an eccentric and evasive bug.

"It is full of quaint originality and peculiar
beauty. There is a wild, wobbly freedom about it
that few have been able to attain.

"Then, too, you are dignified. There is a cold, re-
pellant expression to your feet, and a self-possessed
reserve about your elbows that would indicate that
you were born to command.   ·

"A uniform that could be made to fit the right of
way to a railroad track, would set you out in good
shape.

"There is a noble poise to your knee-joints, and a
stately reserve about the calves of your legs that impress me almost painfully."

Then he asked me to jump about twenty feet, and
to do other mirth-provoking tricks, in order that he
might see if I had been foundered.

After that he wrote silently in a little book, while
I pensively put my clothes on again.

There were eighteen young Napoleons among us
who applied for a chance to fight our country's bat-
tles, and lead her through the dark night of disaster
and carnage up to the glorious sunlight of peace and
prosperity; but seventeen of us went home and
hoed corn, or clerked in drug stores, while the
eighteenth went to West Point. He, it seemed,
stood a better examination than we did, and was a
better waltzer, too. His father, also, assisted in
electing the Congressman for our district. I do not
say that this had any bearing, but I throw out the
remark casually.

16

One of the committee who took an interest in me, and who spoke to me afterward, said that some of my answers to the written questions were a little eccentric. He said that in stating that Timbuctoo was in Michigan, I had furnished to science a matter of information which would be useful mainly as a curiosity.

He also said that in charging Kosciusko with the murder of Julius Cæsar, I differed materially from many of our most respected historians. I told him that as these historians were dead, and as it would be cowardly to controvert the statements of men who had gone down to their graves believing all this sort of slush, I would not discuss the matter any farther.

There were also other little matters of difference between myself and the leading scientists of those days, and just because I dared to stand up in the face of these antiquated snoozers and say something original and spicy about Kosciusko and Timbuctoo, the military history of the country has been deprived of a ferocious and blood-thirsty warrior.

Still, the old martial feeling is strong in my breast. The mellow whoop of a hostile Indian to this day arouses me to deeds of heroic valor, and I hurry away to some quiet glen where I can control my devilish hunger for warm, fresh blood.

NEW YEAR'S AMONG THE UTES.

New Year's Day was pretty generally observed among the children of the forest at the Fort Thornburgh reservation, as well as at the old White River headquarters.

Mrs. Veni-Vidi Vici Colorow, with her three charming daughters, received at the parental tepee from 1 P. M. until further orders. Mrs. Colorow was dressed in plain ashes of sage brush, gunny sack cut a la robe de sleeping car, with ear ornaments of copper rivets and bracelets of mother of clamshell, strung on strips of brocaded buckskin.

Miss Cleopatra-Union-Forever-One-and-Inseparable Colorow wore a gros grain army tent, with brass overcoat buttons and hand-painted with the device

```
•  •  •  •  •  •  •  •  •  •
•                        •
•      U. S.             •
•                        •
•  •  •  •  •  •  •  •  •  •
```

in Roman characters on the back. Her hair was frescoed with antelope tallow and bangles of grizzly bear toe-nails, held in place with tarred rope.

Miss Walk-Around-the-Block Colorow wore a husk door mat, cut decollette, with embroidery across the shoulder blade, forming the letters

```
•  •  •  •  •  •  •  •  •  •  •
•                          •
•      WELCOME.            •
•                          •
•  •  •  •  •  •  •  •  •  •  •
```

Miss Knock-Down-and-Drag-Out Colorow wore a pair of agency suspenders and a hectic flush. She was the only lady at the Colorow tepee in full evening dress. Refreshments were served here, consisting of cottonwood sandwiches and Mumm's Extra Dry Rat and Roach Destroyer.

Mrs. Shavano and several others received at the magnificent Shavano dugout, on Fine Cut avenue.

Mrs. Shavano wore a cavalry blouse and ear orna-ments.

Mrs. Sighing-Mountain-Pine wore a plug hat and Queen Elizabeth bed quilt, held in place with Roman safety pin, rescued from the ruins of White River agency.

Refreshments were served here, consisting of prairie dog pie with variations, and a symphony in sage hen salad, with dressing a la Chinaman. No liquor was served here, the ladies in an unguarded moment having surrounded the supply.

At the palatial buffalo wallow of Chief Antelope the ladies were not receiving, but gentlemen callers were cordially invited to stop at the front door and kick the large and hospitable aggregation of yaller dogs in honor of the day.

Colorow, in a spike-tail coat and a pair of high-cut gum boots, led the list of callers.

- The Son-in-law-of-the-Nebraska-blizzard was with him, and wore a cotton umbrella and a headache. He was very sociable, being on the borders of deli-rium tremens, so that his odd fancies and facetious attempts to scalp his hostess several times made him a welcome guest wherever he went.

Toward evening the gentlemen callers became very frolicsome and mirth-provoking, pulling over several royal edifices where the ladies were receiv-ing calls, and in one instance tipping over a bed-room in which The-Daughter-of-the-Wailing-Wind was paring a favorite corn.

Everything passed off pleasantly until a young chief, who had become excited by contact with the flowing bowl, attacked an old Ute on Fine Cut ave-nue with a three-year-old club and killed him be-

cause he was making calls in a state of beastly so-
briety.

Of course the young man saw on the following
day that he had perhaps been too hasty, and said
that if he had it to do over again he thought he
would do quite differently, but in the hurry and confusion he did not have time to consider what the result might be.

The most attractive street costume was that worn
by a son of Colorow, who was dressed in a gray
army shirt held in place by a broad band of Wam-
sutta muslin. He wore beaded moccasins without
socks, and hair ornaments of tar roofing and selec-
tions from a feather bed. He also wore a necklace
made of the back teeth of friendly whites, strung
on the E string of a violin.

The most gorgeous costume noticed among the
ladies was that of Mrs. Brazos DeSoto-Nom-de-
Plume, a half-breed squaw, whose pedigree runs
back into some of the best Spanish and Ute families.
She had disguised herself by washing her face un-
beknown to even her most intimate friends. Still a
few recognized her, she being the only Ute lady receiving calls who weighed over 350 pounds.

She wore two soldier overcoats, one buttoned in
front and one laced down the back with a clothes
line. She wore her hair negligently in the form of
a rat's nest, the deception being perfect and the effect very much heightened by the use of maple
syrup as a bandoline.

The following day was characterized by the usual
amount of unavailing remorse and several post
mortem examinations.

GROWING OLD.

What can be sadder than to feel the chill autumn of life coming on when the shady side of the valley has been reached and the eye is turned backward toward the green and sunlit fields which exist in memory alone. How sadly settles down upon the human heart the sorrowful truth that the brightest and best of existence has fled. The tear will unbidden start as we think of those years replete with gladness now gone forever. Those dear, delightful years before we trod the rough and rugged road of experience and bit off more than we could masticate. One by one we count the priceless bits of knowledge we have gained and look over the store as the miser reckons his treasure.

We call to mind how the cold, clammy truth was revealed to us at one time that, in gathering the full-blown roses of life, too oft we gather also the feverish and irritable bumble bee nestling in its petals.

How freshly now comes back to us the memory of that bright autumnal day when the sky was one vast sea of golden billows and the spicy aroma of decaying vegetation pervaded everything; that day when we made some scientific experiments with what is called three card monte and went home without our overcoat.

This was a long time ago, but how fresh it is in our memory, and how fresh it seemed to our parents when we unfolded the account of our scientific experiments.

Yes, we are not so frolicsome now as we were forty or fifty years ago, but we know more. It is true we cannot go in swimming all day with impunity or walk around a billiard table all day and then glide through the Blue Danube waltz all night as we once could, but we have acquired some high-priced experience and put it where we can get at it.

We were making an estimate last evening of the value of a few items of experience which we now have on hand, and among the more valuable ones we will name the following:

Cost of experiments with mixed drinks, $2,000.

Expense of calling a large, healthy man a liar, $50.

Experiments in going without underclothes, $5,750.

Experiments with ostensibly disabled hornets, $375.

Cost of winning the love and confidence of an orphan mule, $500.

Little lessons in investigating different games of chance, with a view to making them a business, $2,500.

Experiments with watermelons, guarded by irritable bulldogs, $525.

Cost of unavailing efforts to prevent baldness, $783.20.

Expense of personal investigation of lotteries, $935.26.

Actual cost of obtaining $13 worth of fame, which is now for sale at the above price and still in good working order, though slightly tarnished, $17,380.

There are other expensive little nuggets and gobs of ripe experience that we have on hand, and we cannot look on them without a pardonable pride,

'Tis true that what we have learned is not very valuable to others, but it is a good thing to have, and we can use it right along in our business. We will try to work it off on our oldest son when he gets here, but he will not use it.

He would rather go and buy it the way we did. Information that don't cost $2,000 a hunk is no good. It comes high, but we must have it.

THE COMING LEGISLATURE.

It is generally conceded that there is an all winter's job for the Wyoming legislature to work over our territorial laws already passed and published, without attempting to make any more—but we must have some more laws also. We want some nice, new ones that have never been used. Never mind the old and injurious ones. What we are suffering for is something novel and attractive in this line.

It is now two years since we have had any new statutes. The fee bill, for instance, hasn't been timbered up or tampered with since '79. The law in relation to the protection of Lop-Eared Pole Cats has not been remodeled for two long years, and the election law has been running now for the same length of time and there is a wearisome sameness about it that we do not like.

The county officers throughout the territory are nicely mixed up now, some working under the fee bill and others living on their friends. Now let the legislature pass a law, for instance, establishing a poor house in some central portion of the territory, and then compel the county officers to live there in place of drawing a salary, and this thing could be harmoniously adjusted.

Another good scheme for amusement would be to declare all divorces granted under the present law null and void. This might not be a good or valid law, but it would be about as good and about as valid as those we have now. It would also introduce a pleasing variety into our social system and make life more enjoyable. It would inaugurate a long and productive period of litigation which would build up the legal fraternity throughout the territory and make our lawyers glad that they were born.

By changing the marriage and divorce laws about every two years we fill the territory with a multitude of grass widows and partial orphans, to say nothing of the brevet bachelors and confused mother-in-laws. It mixes up the social relations in such a way that there is a delightful uncertainty and a vague feeling of apprehension all the time. A man may retire at night in the bosom of his family, as it were, and the legislature, holding an evening session, may abrogate an old divorce of his, and when he awakes in the morning he will be occupying apartments with another man's family. This may be amusing to the law makers, but it's annoying to those who desire to lead a moral, upright life. It is also a cause for vain regret sometimes on the part of the rising generation.

When in future years the young man of Wyoming shall rise before a mass meeting of his fellow citizens as a candidate for justice of the peace, or some other fat office, and shall jam his hand into the breast of his Prince Albert coat, and begin to call the attention of the intelligent voter to his good points, it will be annoying if some old-timer on the other side divulges the horrible truth that in consequence of an act entitled an act, etc., passed in 1881, the candidate is left with a pedigree that don't run back into the dreamy past more than two feet, and that the act aforesaid has ruthlessly left him in the cold, cruel world an orphan *nunc pro tunc*—it will be annoying and no doubt productive of ill feeling.

Among the new laws we need, and to which we call the attention of the legislature, are the following:

1.—A law for the prevention of cruelty to indigent bedbugs.

2.—A law for the more successful propagation of the doughnut plant in Wyoming.

3.—A law for the prevention of large air-holes in baker's bread.

4.—An act in aid of an institution for bald-headed orphans.

5.—A law in aid of a home for victims to the fine-cut habit.

6.—An amendment to the act incorporating the town of Laramie City, forbidding the use of barbed wire fences within the city limits, and for other purposes.

7.—An act appropriating a certain amount as a contingent fund, to be used in aid of disabled Justices of the Peace.

8.—An act regulating the size of chunks of ice sold to consumers during the summer in Wyoming territory, and for other purposes.

9.—An act whereby Judge Peck shall be compelled to reside in his own district until released by executive clemency.

There are some other laws which we really need, and which we will suggest more fully in the future, but the above will do for the legislative mind to tackle first.

A SORROWFUL CIRCUMSTANCE.

A very sad thing occurred in California the other day. A young bride and groom living on the coast were compelled to elope, as their parents absolutely refused to sanction the marriage. The happy couple went down to Los Angeles, where the bride became ill with cholera infantum and died, while the groom was attacked with membraneous croup and worms at about the same time, and nearly lost his life also. Thus, far away from home, and with no parent near to soothe her last moments, the young bride breathed her last, while her husband, in another room, was so ill that he could not go near her to soothe her last moments on earth.

A few weeks later the widower went back to the broken-hearted parents, lonely and desolate. He was so changed by the sorrow that he had passed through, that, though only nine years old, his hair was white as the driven snow. He never smiled again, but shut himself up in a primary school, and always seemed wrapped in his own gloomy thoughts.

When his seat-mate put a bent pin under the teacher, and the teacher tried to jump out through the belfry, and all the rest of the school laughed, the lonely little widower did not smile. His heart was too sore.

At the Sabbath school, or at the circus, it made
no difference. The stricken husband was wrapped
in gloom, and no joy could apparently churn him
up. His soul seemed to stagnate, and to sour on all
humanity. Though young in years, his mind
seemed to have matured suddenly, through sorrow
and death,

Finally, just as he was about to be promoted to
the third reading, and the future seemed brighten-
ing for him, he came in contact with a bunch of
watermelon colic that was more vigorous than he
was, and before morning he had rolled himself up
in a spherical wad and died.

Thus within one short year this bride and groom
passed from earth. Just as they began to lisp each
other's names, and as their minds were opening out
and unfolding like a head of cauliflower. Just as
they were beginning to acquire information, when
the bride had reached the happy age when she could
count up to 100, and the happy young husband had
as a result of scientific research learned that the
verb to be, to act, or to be acted upon, and just as he
had learned also to whistle through his teeth and to
wear suspenders, death came and busted a happy
little play house.

It is such occurrences as these that cast a gloom
over matrimony and drive many of our fairest and
brightest children from wedded life. Either these
young bridal couples must provide themselves with
a nurse when they make their wedding tour, or the
whole land will be filled with new-made graves.

THE JURY SYSTEM.

There seems to be a kind of one-horse effort now being made by the enemies of the jury system to do away with it, and thus leave us with the national fabric tottering to its very foundation. There can be nothing in the whole mechanism of a free republic more important and necessary to the success of national security than the jury system, a system which not only gives every American citizen the right to submit his grievances to a panel of twelve enlightened peers, but which insures to each juror $2 a day and board, with a period of mental calm and intellectual rest which is priceless as a soother and tranquilizer to the invalid who generally sits on a jury by advice of his physician instead of filling his system full of opiates. Sea air and a change of scene of course are good, but give us the sweet, unruffled sleep of the juryman as a health-promoter by all means in place of the expensive sea voyage and the high priced foreign hotel.

William H. Root was giving us his experience this morning on a Chicago jury, showing how the free, unfettered love of even-handed justice is ever burning in the breast of the true American juror, even in Chicago.

"I was empaneled," said William, sadly, "in a damage case there one time. I most always fixed it so as to be drawn on a jury when other avenues to employment seemed closed, and sometimes I would make $30 or $40 a day, according to the nature of the case. People have widely different notions about the market value of substantial justice. Some are willing to pay a fair commission to the poor juror, and others are timid and reserved about putting up.

" This was a case where a little kid had stuck his foot through a defective sidewalk, and injured the sciatic nerve so that the leg was paralyzed, and the boy a sure enough cripple for life.

"Suit was brought for $18,000, and it was proved up all right and a good case, but we had the blankety blankedest cosmopolitan jury you ever saw.

" We had a Polander that couldn't speak a word of English, a deaf man from Oshkosh, and a half-witted cuss from Blue Island. Then there was a one-eyed man from the Rhubarbs, who had to be waked up with a chair for meals. There was also a Norwegian on the jury who hadn't been in this country very long, and didn't know a verdict from a porous plaster.

"The whole mob was about the most ornery and trifling aggregation of unprejudiced intellect you ever saw. The first thing that we did was to disagree.

"It was the afternoon before Christmas that they locked us in with two overworked spittoons, a volume of Greenleaf on Evidence, and a work on medical jurisprudence. We looked at the pictures in the medical work, read aloud a few pages on the rule regulating the verdict in cases of manslaughter and malicious tape-worm, and then took a ballot.

' "It stood all the way from $50 to $10,000. We voted till about 3 o'clock Christmas morning, and then I got mad. We had exhausted all the stories we knew, and argued and cussed and swore, but the vote stood just the same every pop. Finally, I took the 'Colonel' to one side and made a proposition to him. The 'Colonel' was the only man on the jury (except me) that seemed to know what the jury was for. Most of the outfit seemed to think a jury was empaneled mostly to disagree, and draw their per diem.

The 'Colonel' nodded, and said that was all right when I conferred with him, and I rose to address the free, enlightened, unprejudiced and illiterate jury of my country.

"I said: 'Now, gentlemen, you are aware that we seem to be divided considerably on this question. We are now beginning on the Christmas holidays with about $9,000 between the two extremities of this jury. I see no way of arriving at a conclusion until after the usual Christmas festivities are over. In a few hours the court will be raking hot stuffing out of the open countenance of a baked turkey, and asking the various guests whether they will take some of the light or some of the dark meat, while we are here eating Bologna sausage and Rip Van Winkle cheese. Before night the counsel on both sides will be so drunk that they can't get home without a directory and a posse comitatus, while we are drinking cistern water and ruining our health. I propose we put on our ballots the amount of damage we are individually in favor of, and then we will add the whole gosh blasted thing up and divide it by twelve. That will be the measure of damages and the verdict.'

"They greeted my proposition with applause.

"When the votes were examined, they found that the Polander had voted as usual, and so had everybody but the 'Colonel' and me. We voted $40,000

apiece That brought the average up to $9,000 for
the cripple.

"We made out a verdict, signed her, called in the
bailiff, submitted our decision, wished each other a
merry Christmas and went home.

"O, I tell you, you can't abolish the jury system.
It's one of the abutments upon which rests the
structure of freedom and equity, and all those
things. If you bust the jury system you'll have to
abolish also three-card monte and other games of
chance. I tell you Americans will not be denied
this kind of mental relaxation. It's about all the
fun we have.

THE MODERN STORY OF CAIN.

Now in process of time it came to pass that Cain
brought of the fruit of the ground an offering unto
the Lord.

And Abel he also brought of the firstlings of his
flock and of the fat thereof. And the Lord had respect unto Abel and to his offering.

But unto Cain and to his offering he had not respect. And Cain was very wroth and his countenance
fell and he swore a great swear and he elevated his
spine and kicked like a bay steer.

And behold he went forth unto Abel, his brother,
and talked with him, and it came to pass that when
they came in the field together that Cain rose up and
slew Abel with a stick of stovewood.

And the Lord said unto Cain, where is Abel, thy
brother, and he said I know not. Am I my brother's
keeper ?

And he said, what hast thou done? The voice of
thy brother's blood crieth unto thee from the ground.
And Cain said, Lord thou doest me injustice. Behold I was insane when I smote Abel and "removed"
him, and I have always been insane and off my ker-
base, insomuch that I wot not what was right and
what was wrong, and moreover the belt with which
I did belt Abel over the eye was not necessarily fatal,
and behold he hath died because of malpractice, for
behold a man may have his head caved in by a stick
of cordwood and yet live, and moreover, Lord, I am
a partner with Thee, and in the business are we not
known as Cain & Co.? and when I shall see fit to
remove my brother it ill becometh Thee to find fault
with Thy partner.

And behold Abel was also a half-breed, therefore
I slew him.   For, lo! the country was not safe with
a half-breed at large among the people, and behold
I removed him; and, finally, Lord, I am innocent
until I am proved guilty, and if Thou hast a reason-
able doubt Thou shouldst give me the benefit of the
doubt.

Behold he might have killed himself, or it might
even be a case of mistaken identity and I may be able
to prove an alibi, and too much weight should not be
given to circumstantial evidence.

Therefore withhold thy judgment, O Lord, or I
shall be compelled to file an affidavit and motion for
change of venue.

And the Lord saith unto him, Now art thou cursed
from the earth which hath opened her mouth to re-
ceive thy brother's blood.

17

When thou tillest the ground, it shall not henceforth yield unto thee her strength, and the grass-
hopper and the army worm shall be a burden to
thee, and thy swine shall die with the cholera, and
thy steeds shall perish from the glanders and the
pink-eye, and thy watermelon vines shall perish
with the squash bug, and the pip shall bring low
thy fowls, and a fugitive and vagabond shalt thou
be in the earth.

And Cain answered and said, My punishment is
greater than I can bear, for behold I am driven out
of the land, and every one that findeth me shall
slay me.

And the Lord said unto him, Therefore, whoso-
ever slayeth Cain, vengeance shall be taken on him
seven fold.

And a mark was set upon Cain, and he was ban-
ished to New Jersey.

THEY LET HIM STAY.

In the early history of Cummins City, when Calamity and Lengthy Johnson and Tapeworm Charlie were the bon ton of the new gold camp, there
was a man whom we will call Doctor Farrar, who
went there partially to assay for the camp, and partially to wear out his young life. Doctor Farrar had
a pretty up-hill job of it from the start, for the mines
hadn't boomed very fast at first, and a good many
of the boys sent their samples of ore to Salt Lake or
Denver for assay, and the rest of them used to salt
his flax and get a big showing, and then stand him
up for his pay. One honest miner gilded his pestle
one night in the assay office, and sold his gopher-

hole on Vinegar Hill the next day on an assay of
$1,528 to the ton.

After awhile Doctor Farrar found that he had to
lock up his mortar and flax in his trunk and sleep
with his crucibles, or his reputation as an assayist
would become a by-word and a stench in the nostrils
of the pilgrim with the plug hat, and the tenderfoot
would say, "fie upon him," and spit upon him, and
smite him on the bugle.

On top of all this an injurious report got out over
the camp reflecting upon the morality of Doctor
Farrar. Society was in a crude state, and most every stove-pipe in town had been bored so full of bul-
let holes tnat it wouldn't draw, and there was a general feeling of insecurity.

Most every one said that unless steps were taken
to quiet things a little before long, there would be
music by the entire band.

It was generally decided that the vigilanters
would have to begin on Doctor Farrar. The town
was getting a bad reputation outside, and something
must be done. The committee, however, was not in
working order, as a part of the number had gone
over toward Last Chance on a placer stampede, and
half a dozen more were in Laramie on district court
business. However, it was decided that two members of the committee, whom we will call Trustworthy Kersikes and "The Annihilator" were dele-
gated to arm themselves and drive Dr. Farrar out of
town or inform him they would shoot him on sight.

Great care was used to prevent Dr. Farrar from
getting any premature notice of this arrangement,
because those who knew his very shrinking and
gentle disposition were sure that if he were to drop

on the programme he would skip the camp, and the amusement would have to be postponed.

It was therefore decided that Trustworthy Kersikes and "The Annihilator" should go down to the assay office armed and prepared to either scare the assayer to death or spatter his quivering flesh all over Pole Cat avenue.

About opposite the palatial dugout occupied by Calamity the avengers met Dr. Farrar.

He had just been down to Sam Wood's and hoisted in about six fingers of what was known at that time as Vinegar Hill Sheep Dip. It was way billed over the Union Pacific as "Liquid Crime."

The avengers stood back a moment to give the fugitive a chance to escape if he wanted to, but he didn't avail himself of it.

He seemed to court death.

He simply walked up to Trustworthy Kersikes and Twisted the double-barrel shotgun out of his hands like a flash. Then he pulled in on "The Annihilator" and told him to throw up his hands. Calmly as though he were making an assay on Gilt Edge blossom rock, Dr. Farrar went through the garments of the avengers. The six-shooters he stowed away in the bust of his pantaloons, and the double-barrel shotgun he broke over a pine log and threw it up on the woodshed.

Then he told the avengers that he would spare their unprofitable lives this trip, but if they ever tried to kill him again there would be a good deal of hilarity on the main street. He said he was not of a revengeful or antagonistic disposition, but that if this thing was repeated every evening with a matinee for ladies and children every Saturday af-

~ernoon, he would get a repeating hoe handle and clean out the entire vigilance committee.

Doctor Farrar said he had never been looked upon as a quarrelsome or deadly man at all ; he was just a plain, every-day style of citizen, without any consuming ambition to fill the world with funerals, and hang a sable pall of mourning over the land ; but if the vigilance committee wanted to make an example of him, and would give him notice enough so that he could arm himself with an old salt-bag full of convalescent eggs, and an old pick handle, he would be willing to abide the result.

The committee turned in silent scorn and left him, and the disagreeable subject was never broached afterward.

WILTING A LION.

Many years ago, when the country was new and infested with the grizzly bear and the prairie dog, there used to be a couple of mountain lions at the Green River eating house. They were kept in a big iron cage at the east end of the platform, and the average tourist was regaled each day by their ferocious antics.

After awhile Cap Lang, who kept the house, got tired of the mountain lions, and traded them to a traveling circus for an old and highly respected African lion with false teeth. He was thoroughly under subjection, and had got so docile that he didn't draw any more as a man-eater for the circus, and they had to feed him Cayenne pepper and turpentine to make him scare the women and children on the front seats, in the greatest living aggregation on earth, and only boss double-hump dromedary and ten-elephant show in the known world.

Still, he was obedient, and when the lion-tamer would pound on the floor of the cage with his foot, the venerable old fraud would open his mouth till you could throw a cook-stove into it, and he would gnash his store teeth and roar till the center-pole would tremble, and pink lemonade would go up to ten cents a glass.

Well, Cap Lang established the king of beasts in his new quarters, and by feeding him hotel soup and chopped feed, with a sprinkling of Cayenne pepper and ground mustard, continued to make him lively enough to give the overland passengers fifty cents' worth of roar after each meal.

Ira Carrington, who used to brake on the passenger between Laramie and Green River, was also a western curiosity. He didn't work for the company so much on account of the salary as he did for the fun he had lying to the tenderfoot. If the pay-car didn't catch him regularly he didn't care much, but if he failed to pick up a victim every trip and fill him full of the wild and gory west, he went home hurt and despondent.

One day he ran across a passenger in the day-coach who was a professional lion-tamer from away back. He admitted that he could paralyze an African lion with the cold and cruel glare of his baleful eye. He had met the king of beasts in his tropical home, and wilted him hundreds of times with his double-barrel glitter.

Mr. Carrington then said that when the train got to Green River there would be an opportunity for him to turn loose on a ferocious brute at the hotel.

The news rapidly spread among the passengers that a lion-tamer from Timbuctoo was on board who would, on reaching Green River, give a free performance, in which he would enter the cage and pull the lion's tail out by the roots and throw the bob-tail king of beasts over the eating house.

When the train arrived at Green River the lion-tamer, with his coat off and a blue cotton handkerchief tied around his head, walked up to the cage with his cruel eye fixed on the lion in a reproachful way calculated to fill the ferocious monster with remorse.

The entire load of passengers stood near with bated breath, wondering whether the brave man would cow the haughty king of the forest or get himself chewed up into Vienna sausages.

At this moment Mr. Carrington, who knew the characteristics of the feeble old circus lion of the present day, pounded on the platform with his foot in a loud and boisterous manner, and the king of beasts responded in a way that did great credit to himself and scared the passengers half to death. He opened his mouth so that you could see the basement of his liver, and lashing the cage with his tail, let off a bass solo that pretty near shattered the blue vault of heaven. The hot, fiery breath of the monster came thick and steaming against the cheek of the bold lion-tamer. The red gums and fiery eyes of the mad brute gleamed close to the bars of his cage. The lion-tamer forgot about casting a withering glitter on the lion. In the hurry and excitement it escaped his mind.

Backing slowly away from the cage in order that the king of the forest might recover from his fright,

The lion-tamer fell off into a bunch of sage brush.
The crowd then greeted him with round after round
of applause.   Mr. Carrington took him by the suspenders and rescued him.

The lion-tamer then went into the car. He had no
business particularly in the car, but he went in there
so that he could be away from the prying eyes of
the passengers.

This shows how a truly brave man shuns the ap·
probation and applause of the multitude, and also
how a bass-wood lion stuffed with baled hay and
fitted out with plaster of paris teeth and a heavy
baritone voice can out-glare an able-bodied lion-
tamer from Kalamazoo.

THE READY LETTER WRITER.

Thoroughly appreciating the popular hunger for
information, and more especially in the line of in-
struction and example relative to the subject of cor-
respondence, we have consented at enormous expense to give our readers a few sample letters which
will greatly aid those who are not fluent and graceful correspondents.   The whole number will ultimately be bound in elegant style and sold in book
form.

Our first letter will be the form that should be
used in addressing a soulless corporation relative to
a pass:

OFFICE OF FREEDOM'S BUGLE HORN, *Wahoo, Neb.*,
    February 22, 1882.

*To Hon. J. Q. A. Gall, General Passenger and
    Ticket Agent J. I. M. C. R. O. W. Railway, Chi-
    cago, Ill.:*

DEAR SIR:—Unfortunately you have never experienced the glad thrill and holy joy of my acquaintance.

You have groped through the long and dreary heretofore without that solemn gladness that you might have enjoyed had Providence thrown you in the golden sunlight of my smile.

I have addressed you at this moment for the purpose of ascertaining your mental convictions relative to an annual pass over your voluptuous line. The Bugle Horn being only a semi-annual, you will probably have some little reservation about issuing an annual on the strength of it.

This, however, is a fatal error on your part.

It is true that this literary blood-searcher and kidney-polisher, if I may be allowed that chaste and eccentric expression, does not occur very often, but when it does shoot athwart the journalistic horizon, error and cock-eyed ignorance begin to yearn for tall grass.

You will readily see how it is in my power to throw your road into the hands of a receiver in a few days. It will occur to you instantly that, with the enormous power in my hands, something should be done at once to muzzle and subsidize me. The Bugle Horn stands upon the principle of pure and untarnished independence. Her clarion notes are ever heard above the din of war and in favor of the poor, the down-trodden and the oppressed. Still it is my solemn duty to foster and encourage a few poor and deserving monopolies.

I have already taken your road and so to speak, placed it upon its feet. Time and again I have closed my eyes to unpleasant facts, relative to your

line, because I did not wish to crush a young and
growing industry. I cannot point to many instances
where hot boxes and other outrages upon the traveling public have been ignored by me and allowed to
pass by.

Last fall you had a washout at Jim-town which
was criminally inexcusable in its character, but I
passed silently over the occurrence in order that you
might redeem yourself. One of your conductors,
an overgrown bald-headed pelican from Laramie,
a man of no literary ability and who could not write
a poem to save his measly polluted soul from perdition, once started the train out of Wahoo when I
was within one half of a mile of the depot and left
me gazing thoughtfully down the track with a 150
pound hand trunk to carry back home with me.

What did I do? Did I go to the telegraph office
and wire you to stop the train and kill the conductor with a coal pick? Did I cut short his unprofitable life and run the road with my cruel pen?

No, sir.

I hushed the matter up. I kept it out of the
papers so far as possible in order that your soulless
corporation might have a new lease of life.

Another time when my pass and pocket money
had expired at about the same moment and I undertook to travel upon my voluptuous shape, a red
headed conductor whose soul has never walked
upon the sunlit hills of potent genius, caught me by
the bosom of my pants and forcibly ejected me from
the train while it was in motion, and with such
vigor and enthusiasm that I rolled down an embankment 100 feet with frightful rapidity and loss
of life.

A large bottle of tanzy and sweet spirit hear my
prayer, which I had concealed about my person to
keep off malaria and rattlesnakes, was frightfully
crushed and segregated. Beside all this my feelings were hurt and outraged, and so was the portico
of my pantaloons.

Others would have burned down a water tank, or
dusted off a crossing with the mangled corpse of the
general passenger agent, but I did not. I bound up
my bleeding heart, and walked home beneath the
cold unblinking stars and forgave the cruel wrong.

I now ask you whether in view of all this you
will or will not, stand in the pathway of your company's success? Will you refuse a pass and call
down upon yourself the avalanche of my burning
wrath, or will you grant me an annual, and open up
such an era of prosperity for the J. I. M. C. R. O. W.
railway as it never before knew?

Do you want the aid and encouragement of the
Bugle Horn and success, or do you want its opposi-
tion and a pauper's grave beneath the blue-eyed
Johnny jump-ups in the valley?

Ostensibly I am independent and fearless, but if
you are looking around for a journal to subsidize,
do not forget the number of my post-office box. I
have made and unmade several railroads already,
and it makes me shudder to think of the horrible
fate which awaits you if you hold your nose too
high and stiffen your official neck.

Should you enclose the pass, I would be very
grateful to you for any little suggestion during the
year, as to what my fearless and outspoken opinion
should be relative to your company.

Hoping to hear from you favorably in the contiguous ultimately, I beg leave to wish you a very pleasant *bon vivant*. Very sincerely yours,

EPHRAIM BATES,

Moulder of Public Sentiment.

The next sample letter in the series is one of condolence to a polygamist who has lost a wife. It should be in the following style, as nearly as possible, changed, of course, to suit the circumstances.

No. 123 CHESTNUT STREET, BOSTON, Mass., February 29, 1882.

William Variloid Smith, Esq.; Apostle of Zion, and Chief Defaulter of the Tithing Rink, Salt Lake City, Utah.

REVEREND SIR:—It is with the most profound sense of grief that I address your Apostolic Nibbs on this sorrowful occasion.

I learned by yesterday's mail of your great affliction in the loss of No. 19, Class D, in your affectionate harem. The death angel has swooped down upon your little household aggregation, and partially bereft you of your wife. Where her merry song was once heard throughout the sunny hours, now the house is fractionally quiet and measurably still. The wheel is broken at the cistern, and the water pitcher is frozen up, and busted on the second floor.

The glad smile that welcomed you on your return at evening's hallowed hour has been reduced twenty per cent., and the grocery bill is a hollow mockery.

I do not know what it is to be a partial widower. The King of Terrors has never fractionally afflicted me, but I can enter into your heart and see the howling ruin that has been made in your warm affections.

The grave has swallowed up in its impenetrable darkness the only wife you had who was a strawberry blonde with eyes like a moss agate and a full set of natural teeth. She was the only peri of your home circle who could get through the winter without ground feed. She was the only one of your vast wealth of wife who could milk the brindle cow with the stumpy tail.

Death, however, is the lot of all mankind. It is also the lot of womankind. We cannot live always, under the present regulations.

We are born into the world without our knowledge or consent, and we go hence like a man who fondles the wrong end of a mule.

Death is as certain as a poll tax, and it generally claims us as its own, just as we get our debts paid and yearn for existence.

Do not be cast down, however. Cling to hope through the storm of affliction, and all will be well.

Remember that the wind is tempered to the Texas steer that is just off the trail. The violence of your fragmentary bereavement will soon be past and the keen edge of your sorrow will soon wear away.

When the grave of No. 19 is green in the valley and your great grief has measurably abated, you can rope in another tenderfoot and be sealed to her for all eternity.

Now, to be sure, you are stricken, and you feel as one who don't care whether school keeps or not, but that will soon pass away and the sun will once more light up your pathway. When the emigrant train comes in some pleasant summer day, it will bring to you from the old country a helpmeet who will far surpass and everlastingly lay over the home made daughter of Zion. Then you will rejoice that you still live, and your home will once more howl with mirth and music. You will bring her to your fireside to gladden your declining years, and the balance of the harem will make it interesting for you.

In closing, I desire to express my hope that ere this letter has reached you, the mighty torrent of your first sorrow has abated, and that you are beginning to take your meals at regular intervals.

Give my love to your mourning household when you have leisure, and believe me always your solid pard and comforter in any event of this kind which may occur in your establishment.

Should small pox or any other fatal disease get into your little aggregation of household curiosities and sweep off a car load or two, do not hesitate to draw on me for what genuine grief and sympathy you need to carry you through.

Yours to command,

T. DeWitt Brownbread,

Dealer in Condolenc .

THE SIAMESE TWINS.

In answer to a correspondent who writes us for information on the above subject, we have compiled the following information:

Eng and Chang were born simultaneously on the 15th day of April, 1811, and died at the age of 63 years.

They were connected together by a patent coupler which entered the body of each in the region of the vest pocket.

This connecting arrangement necessarily threw them a great deal in each others society. When they were boys, their lives were rendered more or less unhappy by their widely different tastes.

Eng was very fond of sour apples in his youth, and when at night he rolled and tossed upon his couch with a large stock of colic on hand, Chang had to lie awake and get the benefit. Later in life Chang developed a strange longing for the flowing bowl, while Eng was a Good Templar.

When Eng went to lodge, the worthy outside guard would refuse to let Chang in, because he couldn't give the pass word, and as Eng couldn't go in and leave Chang in the ante room, he had to go home and wait till another meeting.

Eng was a Mason and Chang was a Knight of Pythias, and they used to give each other away. sometimes and have lots of fun.

Eng was a half-breed and Chang was a stalwart, and that made it bad about attending caucuses.

Chang joined the Episcopal church and believed in sprinkling, while Eng was a Baptist, and he not only got immersed himself, but fixed it so that Chang had his sins washed away at the same time.

Once in a while Chang would get an invitation to a private party in a set to which Eng did not belong, and then they had to settle the question by putting Etruscan noses on each other as to whether they should go or remain at home.

Chang died first, and Eng died a few hours later as a matter of courtesy. Eng was not prepared to

die, and regretted that he was not consulted by
Chang before this important step was taken, but he
said it would save the expense of two funerals, and
he wanted to do what was right.

The lives of these two men were somewhat peculiar in many respects. There were many little
nameless annoyances to which each was compelled
to submit, and which would not at first occur to the
student. For instance, Chang had to get up and go
for the doctor in company with Eng, whenever Eng's
children had the croup, and whenever Chang's wife
thought there was a burglar in the woodshed, Eng
had to get up in his night-shirt, and go with his
brother in search of the villain

They couldn't ride the festive velocipede, and when
Chang got biling drunk, Eng had to go to the cooler
with him, and stay there till the law was satisfied.

From what we have said it will be seen that with
the opportunities each had of forming an intimate
acquaintance, the facility afforded for giving each
other away was almost boundless, and in looking
over their history we feel that we cannot be too
grateful that we were not born a twin, with a partnership existing between us in the shape of a liga-
ment eight inches in circumference.

No one who has never been a Siamese twin can
estimate the peculiar annoyances to which he would
be subjected.

Among the many blessings which cluster about
us, and are showered down upon us through life, we
are prone to lose sight of the fact that with all of
our sorrows and disappointments, we were not born
Siamese twins.

SIC SEMPER GLORIA COLOROW.

It is with becoming sorrow that we make these
sad comments upon the death of Wm. H. Colorow,
Mayor of North Park and author of Baxter's Saint's
Rest. Mr. Colorow left nothing to posterity but a
few damaged scalps in brine and his untarnished
name.

He early learned that what was worth doing at
all was worth doing well, and his private cemetery
at White River was a proof of his devotion to this
rule.

Late in life he acquired a love of strong drink,
which made him at times morose and despondent.
At these times he would go out and kill a prospector
and then return cheered and encouraged. This
morbid appetite for funerals at last grew upon him,
however, to such a degree that his personal intima-
cies were seldom and isolated. Many of his friends
learned to regard him as eccentric and perhaps un-
safe. His room mate refused to occupy the same couch
with him, partly owing to the fact that Colorow was
liable at any moment to be overcome with this mad
impulse, and partly because Colorow snored and
kicked in his slumbers like a bay mule.

Still and pulseless lie the hands of Colorow. In
his mountain grave beneath the wintry sky no more
anguish or bilious colic can ever come to him. Cold
and silent are the lips that were wont to whoop 'em
up Liza Jane. Noiseless is the bazoo of the brave
inebriate of the forest. His work is done, and his
labors have followed him. When the death angel
came he did not repine or complain. He bowed his
head to the universal decree, and humped himself

18

to the mandate of the inexorable fiat. When the Colorado zephyr sighed among the blossom rock of the mountains, Colorow gathered himself into an irregular mass, wiggled his off leg a couple of times and lit out for the evergreen shore.

We have always felt a little reserved about visiting Colorow during life, but there is no earthly power that can prevent us from going and weeping above his lonely grave.

APOSTROPHE ADDRESSED TO O. WILDE.

Soft eyed seraphic kuss
With limber legs and lily on the side,
We greet you from the raw
And uncouth West.

The cowboy yearns to yank thee
To his brawny breast and squeeze
Thy palpitating gizzard
Through thy vest.

Come to the mountain fastness,
Oscar, with thy low neck shirt
And high neck pants;
Fly to the coyote's home,
Thou son of Albion,
James Crow bard and champion aesthete
From o'er the summer sea.

Sit on the fuzzy cactus, king of poesy,
And song.
Ride the fierce broncho o'er the dusty plain,
And let the zephyr sigh among thy buttery locks.

Welcome thou genius of dyspeptic song,
Thou bilious lunatic from far-off lands.
Come to the home of genius,

By the snowy hills.
And wrestle with the alcoholic inspiration
Of our cordial home.

We yearn
To put the bloom upon thy alabaster nose,
And plant the jim jams
In thy clustering hair.
Hail, mighty snoozer from across the main!

We greet thee
With our free, untutored ways and wild,
Peculiar style of deadly beverage.
Come to the broad free West and mingle
With our high toned mob.

Come to the glorious Occident
And dally with the pack mule's whisk-broom tail;
Study his odd yet soft demeanor,
And peculiar mien.

Tickle his gambrel with a sunflower bud
And scoot across the blue horizon
To the tooness of the sweet and succulent beyond.

We'll gladly
Gather up thy shattered remnants'
With a broom and ship thee to thy beauteous home
Forget us not,
Thou bilious pelican from o'er the sea.

Thou blue-nosed clam
With pimply, bulging brow, but
Come and we will welcome thee
With ancient omelet and fragrant sausage
Of forgotten years.

TROUBLE IN A SILVER MINE.

A few nights ago, a well organized attempt was
made to jump the Centennial mine, which came

very near being a success. The parties who undertook to jump the mine were two Rocky Mountain polecats with a bad record. Almost as soon as they entered the tunnel from the east, the men in the mine began to be suspicious that somebody with a bad breath was in the lower level. The suspicion grew until it assumed about the size of a bale of hay. It was resolved to drive out the intruders.

Major Downey went down and threw a chunk of free-milling quartz at the enemy. Then the major went back to the rest of the party to hold a consultation. The rest of the party didn't seem so tickled to see him, as he thought they ought to be. They shunned and evaded him, and told him that his presence wasn't agreeable under the circumstances. Although the mine is a very valuable one, it was almost decided at one time to abandon it to the jumpers. At last, however, everybody made a grand rush for the tunnel, and demolished the enemy with long-handled shovels.

Major Downey handed the above information into the office with a long pole. He also told a friend that he would go out of town this forenoon to a quiet spot beyond the grave-yard, and change his clothes.

The Rocky Mountain polecat before it is domesticated, is not prized as a songster very much, but he has a way of making his presence felt wherever he goes, and, even in death you cannot forget him.

There was one of these docile creatures got into our cellar once, a good many years ago, and the ventilation being very poor, the air was soon vitiated to such an extent that the clock stopped.

We don't care for death in any form in which it may come; those who know us will agree that we

never weaken. We have faced the deadly watermelon when strong men were falling thick and fast,
and we have stood at the muzzle of a daily newspaper and mowed down spring poets like broad
swaths of timothy hay, and never weakened or
squealed; but the dappled quadruped with the all-
pervading presence appeals to our valor in vain.
Our victory over him has always been vicarious.

WANTS TO COME.

The following letter is in reply to an article which
appeared some weeks ago in these columns relative
to the almighty seldom condition of our female
population in the West compared with the male. It
shows that our appeal is not altogether worthless
and that the day is not far distant when this frightful preponderence of the great horrid man over
woman will be done away:

POTTSVILLE, December 1, 1881.

Editor Boomerang:

DEAR SIR:—I have saw a piece in several of our
home papers credited to your pen which states that
Wyoming is greatly overrun with men. I do not
write this because I yearn to get married, for I do
not. I have a good home with my relatives, and do
not sigh for to go away and marry a total stranger.

What I do desire is some great strong arm upon
which I could lean when the storm of life beats upon
me and the angry billows knock me galley west.

I have waited long and patiently for such an one
to come to me, but he dost not come. He is delayed by a washout, or something of that kind.

I would like to nestle down into the home of some true and noble man, who is a good provider and does not chew plug tobacco. O, I would love him so earnestly, so sincerely and so persistently. I would go and meet him at the twilight hour when he came home from the bank, and I would make it interesting for him.

I had a wonderful wealth of affection, even as a child, and I have been saving it for over thirty years. I've seen many men who would gladly have taken me to their hearts, but they did not have courage to propose the important step.

If you know in all your acquaintance a man who is athirst for sympathy and love, a man who does not object to cold feet, you may tell him you know of a coy young thing in Delaware who can be won if he will go at it right.

Impress him with the idea that I am the pampered child of luxury, and that I never had my hands in dishwater. Tell him that I am all soul, and that I would shine as the central figure in a $50,000 home.

No objection to a cattle man with leather pants on if I knew I could trust him, and he was beyond the reach of want. A good waltzer would be no object. I would rather be the dear one of a sheep man who could turn in 20,000 pounds of wool each spring and couldn't walk through a quadrille without breaking his neck, than to be linked with a good waltzer with two Texas steers and a chattel mortgage.

From the above you will gather my meaning and aid me. If you can I will name our oldest and most gifted twin after you, if it is that kind.

Respectfully yours,

CAROLINE VAN STUBB.

Early in the history of Nebraska there was a spirit of religious intolerance in the neighborhood of Fremont, that made the warfare of the pioneer christian a red hot combat at times.

The Germans of Fremont got a preacher in those days, who could round up the sinner in two different languages. He spoke equally well in English or German, and in order to evade a deadly war among the members of his fold, he used to beseech his people to flee from the wrath to come alternately in English and German.

At last, however, those who preferred the German gospel thought they were in the majority, and asked that the imported variety of salvation be used altogether.

This created a feeling on the part of those who were paying their money for a Yankee sermon bi-weekly, and for a time Zion languished.

The following Sunday the sermon, according to the schedule, was to be delivered in English; but after singing "Jesus, Lover of My Soul," and offering a short prayer, the pastor turned loose with an earnest and tearful appeal in the German language, which about one half of the congregation couldn't understand a word of.

They sat there a few moments until they saw that the preacher had declared himself in favor of the other side, and then there was music by the entire choir.

The congregation had prepared for an emergency of this kind, and every man had a cottonwood club under his coat tails. When the tocsin of war sounded, the destructive hoe-handle and concealed bed-slat came to the front.

It was about the first free-for-all fight in the west that ever opened with prayer.

An old man who lived down the track, and who was on probation, had his nose shattered by a blow from "Songs of the Sanctuary," and a school teacher who had recently experienced a change of heart, got a clip under the ear with the organ stool.

Finally the German element got the bulge on the English-speaking portion of the congregation, and peace perched upon their banner.

The vanquished Yankees went home and after the wreck had been straightened out a little, the house went into executive session, and after that the man who couldn't lead a different life in the German language, found it pretty lonesome attending divine worship in that sanctuary.

MAXWELL'S DEATH.

The people of Wisconsin are deploring the hanging of Ed. Maxwell at Durand, and saying that it is a blot upon the history of the State, etc., etc.

We also deplore lynch law, but it has broken out in some of the most sedate and steady of the States of the Union, and the indications are that people are beginning to get a little scared about allowing criminals to be tried by the courts.

Lynch law in the West may be regarded as a condition of affairs where the people begin to feel that law is not sufficiently powerful to whoop up substantial justice.

It is also safe to prognosticate that at Durand, Wisconsin, and Bloomington, Illinois, as well as several other points, for the next few weeks crime will not have its tail over the dashboard so extensively as heretofore.

So far as Maxwell himself was concerned, we do not think his death was such a hardship as many suppose.

If he had not been hung, he would have been compelled to remain in Durand for some months, and death was really a happy release. No matter where he went after death, he struck a more congenial clime, in our estimation, than Durand.

We spent a day or two at that metropolis a few years ago. It is not a pretty town, nor a very hilarious one either. We rode about a hundred miles by stage through a bed of sand to get there and the hotel was full. It seems that two traveling men from Milwaukee had entered the town during the afternoon, and Durand was therefore having a boom. The traveling men had engaged a room apiece, which filled the hotel to overflowing.

Most everyone knows with what a shy, reluctant way a commercial man walks up to the proprietor and asks for the bridal chamber to sleep in, and the front parlor as a sample room. Well, these bummers were of that style. The landlord wasn't hardened to the usages of commercial men, so if they had asked him to make a pie of his two-year-old twins no doubt he would have done it and charged it in the bill.

Therefore we were assigned an old boudoir on the eastern battlement, that had been used as a bath room years before, but had been abandoned because it was not large enough for a tall man to bathe in unless he bathed by sections.

We went into the room and tried to lock the door. It didn't have any lock on it. It had a "screw eye" and "hook" with which we fastened it, although we knew a man could stick a toothpick in and unfasten it. Then we had to step out into the hall to undress. It was too crowded in the bedroom.

At last we retired. The bed broke down twice, and we lost the pillow in our ear and had a bad time generally till about 2 o'clock a. m., when a Chippewa river driver opened the door and walked in. He told us to hitch over, and as he was large and drunk we did so. His breath was so vigorous that it peeled the plaster off the wall.

We arose early. It is not a custom, but we wanted to see a Wisconsin sunrise by candle light. Early rising never brought a better return, for while we were at breakfast our roommate stole everything on the second floor except the soap and went away. That is why we say that Maxwell's fate might have been worse. Hanging is rather an ignominious way to die, but think what might have befallen him. He might have been employed as a clerk in that hotel, or he might have been chosen to teach the school in Durand. There are things worse than death.

UNCLE TOM'S CABIN.

Thursday evening the novel and startling drama of Uncle Tom's Cabin was rendered here by the Anthony & Ellis company.

As the play is a comparatively new one, there being only forty or fifty Uncle Tom combinations now on the road, some traveling in special cars and others by handcar and special tie rates, we give a kind of synopsis of the drama.

Mr. George Harris is supposed to be a calcimined mulatto, who is perplexed with doubts about who his parents were, on his father's side, and Eliza, his wife, is situated in a similar manner. Their little boy is the only member of the family who has a pedigree that will bear investigation at all.

Mr. Harris and wife are endeavoring throughout the play to get to Canada, where they intend to go into the restaurant business and acquire scads.

Mrs. Harris, in making her escape across the river, which is filled with large chunks of cordwood painted light blue, is followed by two blood hounds with iron cake baskets over their heads, and two men with false beards made out of buffalo robes.

Uncle Tom's Cabin is an extremely fatal play, there being four killed and three wounded in three hours. Little Eva is the first to succumb to the extremely malarious and unhealthy climate. After that her father expires on a $2 bedstead, with a sheet thrown over him and his boots on. They all die easy, to pianissimo music. Thursday evening, as Eva was dying, and her little breath came thick and fast, the janitor went around and filled up the coal stoves to hide his emotion, and two gentlemen on the south side of the opera house were so carried away with conflicting emotions that they sought consolation in a four-quart job lot of peanuts and hoarhound candy.

The next untimely death is that of Uncle Tom, who is supposed to get whelted over the head with the butt end of a loaded whip. This, however, is an optical illusion, because we asked Mr. Legree on the following day if he got a fresh Uncle Tom at each and every performance, or how he fixed it, and he said he wouldn't try to conceal anything from us, but just tell us plainly how it was.

It seems that he does not kill Uncle Tom at all. He said he had nothing in particular against the old man, so he just backed him up against the scenery and hit a glancing lick that was more fatal to the scenery than it was to Uncle Tom. He said that Tom stood in with him, and when the proper moment arrived for the sickening thud, generally clapped his hands together to heighten the effect. ·

After awhile Mr. Legree is killed also. He is massacred with a large bread knife and is dragged off the stage by a hired man.

The donkey generally brought in by Lawyer Marks sometimes introduces a melodrama that is not down in the bills. Once, while showing in Utah, one of the university students, who sings falsetto, got mad at the donkey because the animal was attracting more attention and drawing a larger salary than he was, and so just before the donkey was to go on, and while he was waiting for his cue, the university student poured about a gill of turpentine into the ear of the timid little public favorite.

When he got in where the auction sale was going on, the meek little animal seemed excited about something. He scattered Mr. Marks around among the footlights and knocked Mr. Legree through the bass viol. Most of the actors excused themselves

and retired.   Then the household pet got over into
the orchestra and went through with some calis-
thenics.   Also through some of the musicians.

For awhile it looked as though not only the entire
troupe but the orchestra and most of the audience
would go up 'he golden stair with Little Eva.

"Uncle Tom's Cabin" has been on the stage twenty
years now, but it is about as reliable as a promoter
of the scalding tear as it ever was.   It is a play that
takes first rate in this dry climate and saves the expense of irrigation to a great extent.

HOW GREAT MEN DANCE.

An exchange says that: "Mr. Sartoris, now in
Washington, dances in such a horribly muscular,
awkward and dangerous manner, that Nellie almost
wishes that she had not married him." This leads us
to say that great men are not, as a rule, note for their
swan-like movements in the dreamy dance. We are
sorry to acknowledge that we are not an exception
to the rule.   In fact, the more genius a man has, the
more successful he is as a circus and ten allied show
in one when he undertakes to dance.   The truly
great man goes into a quadrille with the same zeal and
evident relish that the average editor manifests at
the funeral of a newspaper thief, or while reading the
inscription on a tombstone reared by loving hands
over the man, who, during life, stole his jokes.   He
cannot disguse his interest in the game, like old
veteran dancers.   He swings his partner with such
wonderful zeal that her feet stand out at an angle
of 45 degrees with the centrifugal force.   In the
grand right and left, he eagerly catches hold of the

first lady he comes across, and swings her around by the thumb seven or eight times in his original and beautiful style. He seems to throw his whole soul into the business, and dances like a hired man. He doesn't seem to notice that all the occupants of the ball room are neglecting their own dances and engaging reserved seats to watch his grand and lofty tumbling.

In the Lancers, when the "side four separate," he seems to labor under the impression that he ought to separate and dance a little on both sides to avoid being called partial or prejudiced, but after a while gives it up as a physiological impossibility, picks out a good trail to step on, leaps gracefully from that one to another one, and then stops to get breath.

Then he looks around the hall for some applause, but is most always disappointed. Between dances he goes off into a dressing room, ostensibly to get a drink of water, but in reality to sew on some suspender buttons and spit on his hands.

At the first of the evening his programme looms up first-rate, but in an hour or two there are left only a few brave girls who want to go into partnership and watch him play "leap frog" or "pom pom pull-away" to fast music. None but the ladies with strong nerves care to be in the same set, and run the risk of having their front teeth knocked out when he turns hand-springs and double sommersaults, under the delusion that it is a balance or a promenade or something of that nature.

If you want to see a genuine panic in a ball room, turn a great man loose, and see him waltz like the baby elephant and promenade like the Suffolk hog going to war. He prances "up and down the center" like a guinea pig that is "cursed with an inward pain," and winds up the evening performance by trying to dance a heel and toe polka. He gives his partner the advantage of the "under hold," but she throws up the sponge just as he is getting interested. She accuses him of being drunk, and he is delighted to think how he has fooled her. He is only too happy to be considered drunk, if people will forgive him for dancing like a Ute brave with low necked clothes on. He buries his secret in his breast, and chuckles inwardly over the fact that people attribute his poor dancing to drunkenness. But away down in his heart, where nobody can see, there is a blessed assurance which buoys him up in the years to come. It is a pleasure that the world cannot give nor take away, and it is this—he knows that he wasn't drunk.

SLEEPING WITH A ROCKY MOUNTAIN.

People who think that we haven't got anything romantic or sentimental in our system are not familiar with our composition. Those who imagine that we are a plodding plebian, without any divine afflatus to speak of, are unacquainted with our true inwardness.

We have always nursed in our capacious bosom the fond hope that some day in the uncertain future we should sleep with a regular Geography mountain, and snore away the stilly night with a Rocky mountain on one side, and a prancing little streamlet on the other.

To escape from the noise and confusion of the busy street, and to give our divine afflatus a chance to whoop her up to its full extent and to have a good square face·to face communion with nature. To see the prairie dog hop from bough to bough, and hear the tuneful antelope warble his vespers as he sank to rest in his lowly nest.

We are proud to state this morning that we have had that little communion with nature, and here-after we haven't got to do that any more. We shall remain in the busy haunts of men the remainder of the summer. There isn't as much rheumatism in the busy haunts of men as these is in two or three communions with nature. Naure is all right in her place, but you don't want to get too familiar with her. The everlasting snow-capped mountains, lifting their sunlit summits to the sky, are a pretty good thing, but they look better about thirty-seven and a half miles distant than they do when they are in bed with you, because they have got such cold feet. The little dancing torrent as it canters along to the ocean and bathes the feet of the mountain, is a pretty good thing—in a blue covered book—but when you come to grasp the reality and see that same little streamlet waddle along over the corns and chilblains on the foot of the mountain, and hear it murmur all night so that you can't sleep, the mur-muring gets tiresome, and you begin to murmur yourself after a while.

"Now, Mr. Nye," said Col. Brackett, as we were smoking our pipe preparatory to retiring, "the beauty of this thing is that there isn't any dew here at all, not a dew." Well, perhaps there wasn't. Maybe it was something else, for it looked like ordinary cold water.

It might have been high priced mountain nectar or something of that kind, but if so it was awful cold nectar. After we had rolled over seventeen hundred and thirteen times trying to go to sleep, then this dew became due. We began to think that Bill Nye was an old Bill that had been due about three hundred years. Our idea is that no man can sleep warm with nothing over him but a piece of old blue worn-out sky, with a hole torn in it, and his pockets full of dew. He can put two or three stars over him, but that don't help him out any. Old Nebuchadnezzar might enjoy such a thing. He could go to grass if he wanted to, and get dew in his mane, but it must have warmer dew.

The blue canopy of Heaven is a good thing to lie and look up at in the middle of the day, but when the thermometer gets down thirty-five cents below zero, the human system demands more blankets, and less canopy. After we had shivered all night, and our teeth were coming down on each other like a twenty-stamp mill, we began to lose faith in Col. Brackett, and got to watching him, as he lay there sleeping sweetly. By and by he moved uneasily in his slumber, and stretching out his hand the palm came in contact with the outside of the blanket, soaked with this mountain coolness that felt as though it had been squeezed out of an iceberg and kept in a cool place ever since, He gradually woke up, examined the moisture, took up his note book and wrote : " Remarkable phenomenon, fine heavy dew in the Rocky Mountains."

Then he turned over and went to sleep again.

After that you might have seen a tall, graceful figure of a young man, moving away from there,

19

where he could be alone and get himself toned down to a Christian spirit, so that he could calmly eat breakfast with the man who had thus wilfully deceived him.

We thought as we dried our socks by the camp-fire, in the uncertain grey light of the morning, that a man could enjoy better religion, even in the heart of a great city, with dry socks, than he could where so much nature was lying around loose, if he had cold, wet feet. Of course no man feels like being kept within the narrow confines of brick walls, where it is all hurry and bustle, but when you come to throw in soda water, dog fights, and swinging on the front gate and lily white on your coat collar the next morning, you can count us in.

The lowing herd can wind slowly o'er the lea if it wants to, and the little mountain rivulet can riv to its heart's content, and wash the soiled feet of the mountains for fourteen years and a half. Meanwhile, if anyone inquires for us, you can say that we are studying mankind in its various phases, but we are not communing with nature so long as we can get a man to do it for us at $13 per month and found.

A vicarious study of nature in the Rocky Mountains will save a man in an ordinary life time $3573. 27 in Pain Killer and Sage's Catarrh Remedy alone.

Fooling around with nature too much is what has made Spotted Tail what he is, and Spotted Horse and Crazy Tail would neither of them have been so irritable and morose if they hadn't had wet feet all their lives, and slept cold and kicked the clothes off each other. Such books as Cooper's Novels, have been very pernicious in this respect. They have made these red skins believe that a man is more graceful,

kicking up his heels in the fresh air without hardly
any clothes on, and have made these unsophisticated
sons of the forest think, that the less clothes a man
has between himself and nature, the smarter he is,
but Cooper never slept with a Rocky Mountain.

HE WANTED BLOOD.

It occurred on the western bound train last Sunday. He was a young man who had recently started
out from Boston, and who labored under the impression that the Union Pacific railroad extended along
in front of Sitting Bull's door, and that Laramie City
was settled by a lot of barbarians who dressed in the
cool and economical costume of the Greek slave;
that Boston contributions for the heathen were distributed here, and that while the train stopped for
supper he could go out near the track and shoot three
or four grizzly bears, and have them stuffed and
sent to his girl. He was a very ferocious looking
young man, with side whiskers of the hue peculiar
to the aurora borealis, and he had one of those little
caps, shaped like an inverted spittoon with a tassel
on it.

When the train was moving along at a fair rate
of speed, a loud report rang out on the still air like
the crack of doom and the young man with the skim
milk eye was a different being. It seemed that he
was ready for something of this sort. He had got it
into his head that Laramie and Fort Laramie were
one and the same place, so he had not come into this
home of the red man unarmed. He jumped over five
car seats and sat down without much preparation in
the lap of a fat old lady from Milwaukee, executed

another spasmodic tumble and made for the car door
with an old revolver that carried a ball like a homeo-
pathic pill, took a tintype of his girl out of his hip
pocket where he had carried it next his heart during
the entire trip, gave it to a passenger, saying, "If I
die you may send this to Arminta Ann Stinger, Boston, Mass.," cocked the deadly dollar and a half
weapon, and boldly stepped out on the platform to
get seven or eight scalps as curiosities. He met the
conductor, and the conductor was more cool and
prepossessed. He said, " Young man, you are evidently hankering after blood. If you wait until we
get to Laramie, we will try to buy you some. The
cylinder under the coach has burst, but no harm is
done. Calm your fears. Go in and bathe your head.
Brace up, my friend. Do you see that red-nosed
democrat sitting there on the front seat ? Go in and
tell him you want to smell of his breath and get intoxicated."

A CRUEL STAB.

"' Bill Nye' has written a book called the 'Forty
Liars.' Judging from the way he lied about this
community, he ought to be at the head of the list of
the notable forty."

The above choice morsel was written by the Endowment Rank editor of the Mormon organ of Zion.
Closer and closer the lines have been drawn by the
Church of Jesus Christ of Latter Day Saints. Only
a short time ago the polygamists passed a resolution
not to allow the gentile with a clean shirt to mingle
in the mazy at their select dances, and now the Mormon youth who writes heavy editorials for the Des-

eret News on week days and presents his plans and
specifications to God on Sunday for the management
of the universe during the following week, has given
us a cruel blow. Long ago a resolution was passed
refusing the editor of this paper the freedom of the
Endowment House, and now we are cut adrift, with
no good society to which we can flee except the
questionable society of the gentile.

The festive reader can readily see how lonely our
life will henceforth be to us. With what a wearisome sameness we now visit the homes where only
one isolated wife runs the ranch. How we miss the
prattle of a car load of miscellaneous kids as we enter the door, and how still and monotonous are our
visits where we miss the cordial welcome of nineteen
hostesses.

We have been black-balled in the tithing shebang;
frowned upon in the endowment house, and cursed
in the tabernacle.

The next period in our downward career, will be
death, perhaps, at the hands of the avenging angel.
Some sore-eyed Danite from the Michigan Penitentiary will be selected to dog our footsteps and smite
us in the stillness of the night with an iron coupling
pin, and when the glorious god of day peeps over
the Black Hills, we will be at rest, lying in the bright
glare of the early morn with our features knocked
galley west.

No one can ever know how we feel. The church of
Zion has soured on us and we are an outcast on the
face of the earth, with only one wife and the temple
closed against us.

Branded as the boss of Forty Liars, cut adrift, with
no cadence +∽ ⸴ syren fresh from the pest house on

the Jordan, we cry out in our anguish and rend our garments, and spit upon the carpet, for our punishment is greater than we can bear.

A MASCULINE KETTLE DRUM.

Last evening's entertainment at the residence of Mr. R. Marsh, was one of the most elaborate affairs both in point of amusement and the costumes displayed by the guests, that it has been our good fortune to attend.

The hours fixed for "the beer" as it was called, to distinguish it from "the coffee" in vogue among the ladies, were 7 to 9, and about 7:30 the guests began to arrive. The host was arrayed in a dark diagonal suit and brown mustache, and had made every possible arrangement for the comfort and enjoyment of his guests.

Messrs. Sprague, Ivinson, M. H. and W. A. Mills, Marshall Schnitger, Dr. Guenster, Harper Stryker, Heath and Nichols were dressed in plain black.

Mr. Otto Gramm wore a tack-hammer coat, pantaloons and vest of Michigan gunnysack, with inlaid sole leather buttons. His tie was deep red satin, and his sole ornament was a large solitaire diamond made of the bottom of a glass tumbler set in sheetiron. His plug hat was cut two sizes too large, so that it would fit him all right this morning. His hair was parted in the middle with a damp towel.

General Nock wore a spike-tail coat of gross grain gen d'arme blue, with scarlet silk facings, and buttons made of inch and a half corks with old brass settings. He also wore a white vest with same style of button and pantaloons with old gold suspenders.

As a charm, he carried with him a large irregular shaped nugget of Lorrillard's plug tobacco.

W. C. Wilson, jr., was dressed in a calico swallowtail coat a la mode, and loose Turkish trowsers, the legs of which were constructed of different styles of material. He had the appearance of a young man who had been turned loose in an attic and been allowed to dress in the dark. He also wore a pretzel as a bouquet.

Mr. Scrymser wore a buckskin colored business suit with the tails of the coat caught back with two inch brads and glue.

Mr. Gregg wore plain black, with canton flannel sunflowers and yellow scarf. His hair was carefully combed across the bridge of his nose and held in place with mucilage.

Mr. Gibbon wore a suit of almost pure white, conveying the impression that he had overslept himself and when he awoke and saw how late he was, that he had jumped out of bed, put on his plug hat and started. His hair and whiskers were parted in the middle.

Mr. Nye wore a Prince Albert coat with the tails caught back with red yarn, and home-made sunflowers. He also wore a pair of velvet knee breeches, which during the evening, in an unguarded moment, split up the side about nine feet. This, together with the fact that one of his long black stockings got caught on the top of a window cornice, tearing a small hole in it, letting out the sawdust and baled hay with which he was made up, seemed to cast a gloom over the countenance of this particular guest. With one large, voluptuous calf, and the other considerably attenuated, Mr. Nye seemed more or less embarrassed.

Mr. VanKuran was dressed as Oscar Wilde, and with his long hair and elegantly æsthetic costume, and carrying a large lily in his hand, he was unquestionably the belle of the ball.

Mr. Dysart wore white knee breeches, spiketail coat and very æsthetic costume generally.

Mr. Williston was attired mainly in a long duster with large cream-colored tissue paper cravat, colored eye glasses and canton flannel plug hat.

Mr. Bacon wore a long duster and paper sunbonnet.

Mr. Wagner wore a plaid suit corded, and striped hose, displaying the faultless proportion of his limbs.

Mr. Reger was attired in a long, all-wool three-ply dressing gown and slippers and cap de nuit.

Mr. John Guenster was dressed in plain black, with enormous bouquet of tropical flowers and hair parted in the middle.

Mr. Clark was dressed plainly in a dark suit, and decorated with a silver-plated corkscrew.

Refreshments were served at regular intervals, every fifteen minutes, by the host, assisted by Mr. Gramm and others.

One of the attractive features of the evening was the address of Mr. John Guenster over the dead body of Cæsar, Mr. Oscar Wilde VanKuran furnishing the corpse.

At 9 o'clock a party of ladies in costume, visited the scene and remained until the close of the ceremonies about 12 o'clock.

The very novel and unique idea of an entertainment of this kind, originated with Mr. Marsh himself, and those who partook of his hospitality last evening were unanimous in the opinion that it was a dazzling success.

Those who point out a large stack of empty beer bottles in the alley east of Mr. Marsh's house as in any way connected with the programme of last evening do the gentlemen present great injustice.

WOMEN WANTED.

As the result of the publication of an article in these columns some time ago under the above head, a perfect deluge of letters has been turned loose upon the office from women all over the country who evidently mistook the drift of the editorial upon Wyoming's want.

Instead of answering all these letters separately and personally, which would be utterly impossible without nine stenographers and twenty-seven coarsehand writers, we wish to say that the original statement was correct and written in deadly earnest.

Wyoming wants women, and wants them bad, but there is no very clamorous demand for sentimental fossils who want a bonanza husband and a pass from the effete east.

This paragraph probably puts the kibosh on about 75 per cent of those who have written us so far.

A young and rapidly growing territory is of course largely populated by men, but they are not as a rule millionaires with a bad cough. Most of them are healthy and still retain their mental faculties. That is the reason they do not care to import a horde of weak-minded gushers and turn them loose upon a thriving municipality.

One soft-eyed hyena who has no doubt been ignored for thirty years, writes us a poetical epistle which
ought to melt a more obdurate heart than ours. It
is written on six pages of foolscap in violet ink and
blank verse. Every word has an ornamental tail on
it and the t's are crossed with a delicate little hair
line that looks like a Saratoga wave on a ball of butter. Her soul goes out to us in thankfulness in a
way that has created a coolness in our family which
it will take years to efface.

The idea of cooking large red doughnuts in hot
lard, or wringing out heavy underclothing in soap-
suds and hanging them out in a back yard on a cold
day, does not seem to occur to her.

There are very few households here as yet that are
able to keep their own private poet. We try to keep
up with the onward march of improvement so far as
possible, but we are most of us still too gross to give
up our meals and gorge ourselves on a stanza of cold
poem on the half shell.

The day may come when we will be glad to sacri-
fice beefsteak for divine afflatus, but it will be some
little time before that period is reached.

The crisp, dry air here is such that hunger is the
chief style of yearn in Wyoming, and a good cook
can get $125 per month, where a bilious poet would
be bothered like sin to get a job at $5 per week.

That is the reason we are writing these terse and
perhaps ungallant words. We want to discourage
the immigration of a large majority of those who
have written us on this subject. They are too fresh
and too yearnful in their nature. One of them opens
a four-column letter to us with these words :

"Boomerang, thou hast spake. Thy words hast bursted upon mine ear."

Now if we have been the cause of any such funny business as that, we are sorry and ashamed of it.

We feel that we have done something that we would give $2 to undo.

We wanted to do the territory some good and to encourage a class of women to come to this region who would know enough to construct a buttonhole on an overcoat so that it wouldn't look like the optic of a cross-eyed hog. We wanted to throw out an invitation to womankind to come here and locate, but we did not know that such people as responded classed themselves as women. We do not consider woman a drudge or a slave across the nape of whose neck the overshoe of tyrant man is planted.

A thousand times nay !

We look upon woman, however, as useful in the great struggle of life. Generally she is on one side of the struggle and the tyrant man on the other .

One thing, however, is settled. There is not such a mad rush at present fo: blank verse makers as there is for women of so nd sense who can make a pie that will not taste lik a stov lid veneered with cod liver oil.

It using these cruel words w do it in order to silence this ubiquitous howl 1 the part of these modest violets who expect to get off the train here and meet a confirmed invalid at the depot with a carriage and a marriage license.

The old man with the hectic flush and a life insurance policy for $150,000 is not at present ransacking the four quarters of the globe for a little rosebud 3* years old who don't know enough to boil a teakettle.

The young lady who thinks that the men of the west don't recognize the genuine article when they see it, is laboring under a temporary delusion. Of course the men who live in Wyoming are heathen as a class, and let their hair grow long and deserve the pity and commiseration of more cultivated people, but they would need a good deal more genuine sympathy if they were linked for all time with some of the timid gazelles who have written us on this subject.

BRASS KNUCKLES AND PHRENOLOGY.

A new style of phrenological examination was introduced at a little amateur entertainment at Grover's saloon the other day. Mr. Lowe, a warrior from the post, had been storing away a good deal of cordial in his system during the afternoon, and about 8 o'clock went into the place above named to sample the exhilerating moisture on draught there. He ran across Sam Fuller, and in order to make a chart of his head, took Mr. Fuller's hat off and hung it up carefully on a spittoon. This did not suit Sam very well, and he intimated that for a total stranger Mr. Lowe was rather forward. The amateur phrenologist, however, insisted upon examining Mr. Fuller's head, and Sam said that if it didn't cost anything he might wade in.

Mr. Lowe examined the bump of reverence on Mr. Fuller's head and said that a man with a head like that was generally a liar and a horse thief. Sam said he would steal most anything if he could do it quietly and without attracting too much attention. Then the amateur bump manipulator said some more things that showed an abandoned and malignant heart and the lecture closed with a little afterpiece in which the phrenologist made a rapid examination of Sam's head with a pair of brass knuckles.

The style of introducing brass knuckles in the interest of science is a new and unique idea. It suggests a rapid advancement in the direction of thorough knowledge and marks an era in the progress of that branch of public education.

It also gives the scientist an opportunity to add several phrenological bumps to the mental economy of the patient while under examination.

Mr. Fuller while being phrenologically explored, acquired a bump of combativeness as large as a ranch egg, and a frontal area of pink court plaster, and a knob of spirituality about the size of a tin pail

The result of the seance showed that the popular feeling is rather opposed to rapid and radical move ments in the line of science. An unknown man tried to discourage the phrenologist with a tin cuspidore, and the night policeman Mr. Stirling, put an abnormally protuberant lump of ideality on the bridge of Mr. Lowe's nose. Then he took him to the conservatory on court house square to meditate.

Mr. Fuller now says that he has no faith in a science which cannot study the human dome without peeling off the skin and pulling out the hair. He also says that in the study of physiognomy, he hates to see the custom obtaining popular favor which allows the physiognomist to hold a man's nose in his teeth an hour and a half, in order to decide whether the victim would succeed best as chief justice of the supreme court, or the foreman of a hen ranch.

The Poetical and Prose Works of

ELLA WHEELER WILCOX

Mrs. Wilcox's writings have been the inspiration of many young men and women. Her hopeful, practical, masterful views of life give the reader new courage in the very reading and are a wholesome spur to flagging effort. Words of truth so vital that they live in the reader's memory and cause him to think—to his own betterment and the lasting improvement of his own work in the world, in whatever line it lies—flow from this talented woman's pen.

MAURINE

Is a love story told in exquisite verse. "An ideal poem about as true and lovable a woman as ever poet created." It has repeatedly been compared with Owen Meredith's *Lucile*. In point of human interest it excels that noted story.

"Maurine" is issued in an *edition de luxe*, where the more important incidents of the story are portrayed by means of photographic studies from life.

Presentation Edition, 12mo, olive green cloth............$1.00
De Luxe Edition, white vellum, gold top................... 1.50
New Illustrated Edition, extra cloth, gold top............. 1.50
De Luxe New Illustrated Edition, white vellum, gold top, 2.00

POEMS OF POWER.

New and revised edition. This beautiful volume contains more than *one hundred new poems*, displaying this popular poet's well-known taste, cultivation, and originality. The author says: "The final word in the title of the volume refers to the Divine power in every human being, the recognition of which is the secret of all success and happiness. It is this idea which many of the verses endeavor to inculcate and to illustrate."

"The lines of Mrs. Wilcox show both sweetness and strength."—*Chicago American.* "Ella Wheeler Wilcox has a strong grip upon the affections of thousands all over the world. Her productions are read to-day just as eagerly as they were when her fame was new, no other divinity having yet risen to take her place."—*Chicago Record-Herald.*

Presentation Edition, 12mo, dark blue cloth..............$1.00
De Luxe Edition, white vellum, gold top................... 1.50

THREE WOMEN. A STORY IN VERSE.

"THREE WOMEN is the best thing I have ever done."—*Ella Wheeler Wilcox.*

This marvelous dramatic poem will compel instant praise because it touches every note in the scale of human emotion. It is intensely interesting, and will be read with sincere relish and admiration.

Presentation Edition, 12mo, light red cloth..............$1.00
De Luxe Edition, white vellum, gold top... .... 1.50

AN ERRING WOMAN'S LOVE.

There is always a fascination in Mrs. Wilcox's verse, but in these beautiful examples of her genius she shows a wonderful knowledge of the human heart.

"Ella Wheeler Wilcox has impressed many thousands of people with the extreme beauty of her philosophy and the exceeding usefulness of her point of view."—*Boston Globe.*

"Mrs. Wilcox stands at the head of feminine writers, and her verses and essays are more widely copied and read than those of any other American literary woman."—*New York World.* "Power and pathos characterize this magnificent poem. A deep understanding of life and an intense sympathy are beautifully expressed."—*Chicago Tribune.*

Presentation Edition, 12mo, light brown cloth............$1.00
De Luxe Edition, white vellum, gold top.................. 1.50

MEN, WOMEN AND EMOTIONS.

A skilful analysis of social habits, customs and follies. A common-sense view of life from its varied standpoints. . . . full of sage advice.

"These essays tend to meet difficulties that arise in almost every life. . . . Full of sound and helpful admonition, and is sure to assist in smoothing the rough ways of life wherever it be read and heeded."—*Pittsburg Times.*

12mo, heavy enameled paper................................$0.50
Presentation Edition, dark brown cloth.................. 1.00

THE BEAUTIFUL LAND OF NOD.

A collection of poems, songs, stories, and allegories dealing with child life. The work is profusely illustrated with dainty line engravings and photographs from life.

"The delight of the nursery; the foremost baby's book in the world."—*N. O. Picayune.*

Quarto, sage green cloth..............................$1.00

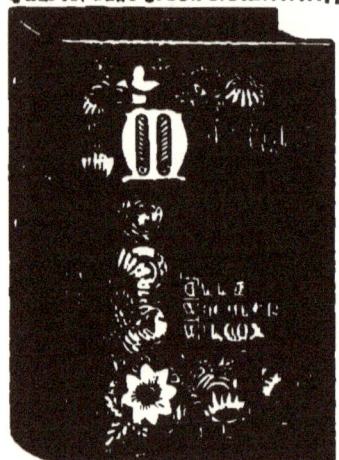 

W. B. CONKEY COMPANY.   **Hammond, Indiana**